KU-335-757

ALSO BY JOHN ROSSITER

The Murder Makers (1970)
The Deadly Green (1970)
The Victims (1971)
A Rope for General Dietz (1972)
The Manipulators (1973)
The Villains (1974)
The Golden Virgin (1975)
The Man Who Came Back (1978)

DARK FLIGHT

DARK FLIGHT

John Rossiter

EYRE METHUEN

First published in Great Britain 1981 by
Eyre Methuen Ltd
11 New Fetter Lane, London EC4P 4EE

Printed and bound in the
United States of America

British Library Cataloguing in Publication Data

Rossiter, John
Dark flight.
I. Title
823'.914[F]   PR6068.0835D/

ISBN 0-413-47420-8

Prologue

Flying Officer Philip Graham corrected fractionally his course as Nuremburg began to slide beneath the nose of his Lancaster, its black mass a winking of exploding bombs. It was bitterly cold in the high night air and his breath had frozen on the windscreen. The aircraft shivered from the shock waves of flak that searched for the stream of bombers in the upper darkness, the thin air split with flying metal and the deafening roar of engines. The dim shapes of Lancasters and Halifaxes reached out to each side and in front as they dropped their loads of high explosives and turned away on maximum boost to escape the flak and the sweeping bars of brilliance from the searchlights seeking them. They were the survivors of the many which, their dangerous passage illuminated by flare-markers, had been shot down over Germany in an unparalleled savaging by night fighters. Some had been blown up in mid-air by their own bombs, others had fallen like meteors in the flames of the highly volatile petrol and oxygen they carried. A few had died in collisions in the crowded sky. With their bombs gone, the survivors still had to fight their way back.

Prone in the nose blister beneath the pilot's feet, the bomb aimer called through the intercom his corrections of course and drift, ready to release destruction and death through the opened bomb doors. The Browning machine-guns of the dorsal and tail turrets quartered the sky, the gunners squinting into the darkness for the night fighters that were waiting like sharks on the periphery of the barrage of flak to pick off the emerging bombers. Davies, the flight engineer, was seated on Philip's right, watching his control panel. He showed nothing from behind his oxygen mask, ignoring the danger, his only reality the calibrated dials.

Philip had put the fear of mutilating death to the back of his mind, concentrating on keeping a steady run-in to the target, but conscious that he was about to kill and injure men, women and children who, for the most part, had nothing to do with the waging of the Nazis' war. He had expected to fly fighters, to kill men who were seeking to kill him, his posting to a bomber squadron being none of his choosing. This was saturation bombing, intended to demoralize the civilian population into shortening the war; something against which his conscience rebelled, but which he had never dared reveal to his fellow pilots.

When the brilliant bluish-white light hit the perspex of his cockpit, blinding him with its reflected dazzle, he knew his Lancaster had been selected by the master searchlight as a target. He heard the rattle of the tail turret Brownings and then the urgent shout of the gunner overriding the directions of the bomb aimer. "*Messerschmitt, Skip! Messerschmitt!*" He kicked hard at left rudder to skid the aircraft and pushed the nose down violently to gain speed, feeling simultaneously the explosions of cannon shells on the fuselage that shuddered from their impact and, with it, the abrupt silencing of the Brownings. The aircraft slewed sideways as he lost rudder control and he fought it with stick and elevators, the acrid stink of cordite in his nostrils. Confused cries came over the intercom and, with them, a high-pitched screaming from the tail gunner. He caught a glimpse of the twin-engined night fighter, a black silhouette, as it passed through the beam of the searchlight and beneath the nose of the wounded Lancaster, streams of tracer from the dorsal guns following it as it banked to renew the attack.

"For Christ's sake, Skipper!" The gunner's voice echoed his rising panic as his guns fell silent with the disappearance of the Messerschmitt. "The starboard rudder's gone! The bastard's coming again!"

There was no longer the security of powerful and sustained lift from the Lancaster as he struggled with the controls, the rudder pedals slack and unresponsive under his feet. He sweated behind his oxygen mask as he pushed the stick forward and steepened his dive to lose the Messerschmitt he knew would be lining up on his illuminated belly for the kill. Encapsuled in brilliance and blinded to the outside darkness, he could fly only by the dials of his instrument panel.

"I'm jettisoning!" he called into his microphone, speaking above the moaning of the tail gunner, his mouth dry. He nodded to the flight engineer, who reached forward and pulled at the jettison control handle.

He felt the bounding lift of the aircraft as the bombs fell away and then the dorsal gunner shouting, "Starboard beam, Skipper! Starboard—" and the sharp rattle of his Brownings swamped in the detonation of cannon shells behind him, a shocking blow against the armour-plating of his seat and, within his vision, the tearing of metal skin from the wing, its inner engine nacelle erupting into flame, the propeller tearing free and smashing into the perspex canopy above him. Something hit his head and he felt stunned and sick, losing momentarily in sudden darkness the jiggling instrument panel. Cold air rushed into the cockpit, reviving him to a realization that the aircraft was turning sharply on its wing and out of control, the flames from the burning engine streaming back in its wake. The cockpit was no longer illuminated with blinding whiteness but with the hellish orange of the fire.

"Bale out! Bale out!" he yelled into his mask, thumbing frantically at the fire extinguisher pushbuttons yet knowing them to be useless against the inferno that would soon reach the fuel tank. The outer engine died in a stuttering of choking jerks, leaving the propeller to windmill uselessly as he fought to bring the falling aircraft back into a controllable dive against dead engines and the drag of the ruptured wing. He would have no more help from the flight engineer. It took no more than a brief glance to see that he was dead in his seat, the top of his skull a sodden mess of leather helmet, blood and white bone.

He heard the tail gunner crying out incoherent desperate words and knew that he would be unable to desert him, to bale out and leave the stricken Lancaster and those remaining of his crew. He seemed to have lost the Messerschmitt which had destroyed them and the flak was being left behind. His head hurt him where it had been hit and blood pulsed in his ears. His arms were curiously leaden as he held back the stick, frightened that he would again lose consciousness. The biting cold air streaming in through the shattered canopy was reaching through his fleece-lined flying jacket, chilling his body and numbing his hands. They were wooden and nerveless as he throttled back the remaining engines, feathering the propellers to revolve slowly in the airstream and stop. Then he lowered the flaps and reached down by the side of his seat, feeling for the fuel jettison control, pulling it in his urgent need to empty the main tanks before the fire reached them. He lifted the nose gradually, the airspeed indicator falling back as the aircraft settled into a shallow spiralling dive. It had weight now, metal tons of it with an incapability of doing anything but descend to the earth below.

The burning wing showed its skeleton of shattered ribs and stringers through the stripped skin. To his heightened imagination it appeared on the point of collapsing and he turned on it to reduce the lift of solid air beneath its surfaces. Apart from the quiet whimpering of the rear gunner, there was silence on the intercom. The barrels of the Brownings in the nose turret pointed motionless to the sky. He couldn't see what damage had been done to the fuselage, but the crew were either dead or had baled out. Cannon shells exploding in the confined compartment behind him would give neither the navigator nor wireless operator much chance of survival. Nor, he felt, had he much himself. Even unloaded of its bombs, a dead-engine landing in the darkness on unseen territory promised only a destructive impact of over sixteen tons of burning metal and death for the two still-living bodies of smashable flesh and bone. He felt an urgent need to empty his bowels. And that, he realized, was the squalid symptom of the fear in him of approaching death. He wanted to bale out–there was still enough height – but his captain's duty to his injured gunner would not allow it.

The Lancaster was shaking badly and he could hear the airstream of his descent, see the bending of the fractured spars that held the wing just short of its folding, could feel the heat of the flames from the burning engine that licked close to the cockpit canopy. The dead flight engineer at his side lolled backwards and forwards against his safety harness. He had died with his eyes open and they watched Philip without expression as he nursed the dying aircraft in its last moments, straining to peer through the oil-covered windscreen and thinking of Laura whom he would never see again. It made bitter the inevitability of his coming death. That part of his mind not seeing the shadowed and indistinct fields rising to meet him, which indistinctively controlled the almost unmanageable aircraft, visualized with the acuity of a man who knows he is about to die the familiar loveliness of her face, imagination reliving in small coloured pictures their last being together. And following them, flickering shadows from his twenty years of living; the final self-awareness, he remembered, of a dying man.

The ground was approaching now, sliding swiftly beneath as he forced the Lancaster to level flight with hard-on stick and elevators, fighting the drag of the wing. Vague formless masses of blackness appeared in front of him and he pulled back to stall her, praying *Dear God, please help me* and then whispering "Laura! Laura!" into his microphone, seeing in lethargic slow-motion the wing drop and slam into the ground to crumple in corrugations with a thunderclap of tearing metal and, pin-sharp in the explosion of the fuel tanks, the dials of the instrument panel moving sluggishly towards his face and then the abrupt darkening of his consciousness... He found himself standing unsteadily in the yellow light of the burning Lancaster, an almost unrecognizable mass of crumpled flaring metal, its skin already melting in curling black flakes and writhing as if in sentient agony. It had cut a swathe of smashed fir trees in the wood on which it had fallen and they burned with wind-blown flames. The twin rudder planes had vanished, the tail turret impacted into the fuselage giving the wounded gunner no chance of survival. Philip could see nothing of the cockpit from which he must have been flung, bursting free from his restraining safety harness and incredibly, miraculously, escaping death or injury.

He could hear nothing of the burning, of the explosions from the aircraft that threw out flaming debris in uncanny silence. He was dazed and confused, his mind a chaos of vivid impressions reliving the anguish of his fall from the sky, hearing again the destructive explosions of cannon shells, the cries of the gunner, seeing the terrible mutilation of the flight engineer's skull. He looked up into the overhanging blackness, hoping to see the drifting parachutes of what might be left of his crew. There was nothing other than a red glow from a burning Nuremburg and the distant blinking of exploding flak among the departing bombers.

He was still wearing his flying helmet and oxygen mask and he pulled them off, feeling his head for the wound he had suffered when the propeller had broken loose. His fingers felt nothing and there was no pain. It surprised him that there were no after-effects from what had been a hard blow.

When he saw the headlights of an approaching vehicle flickering through the tree trunks he shook himself free from his dazed inertness and threw the helmet and mask into the burning Lancaster, then left it for the deep shadows, moving into the concealing safety of the wood. When the flames were no longer visible he stopped and hid himself in a thicket of bushes, his shaken mind numbed with the need for sleep and rest.

One

They lay together in the scented grass, the sun warm on them, replete from having made love. Not many yards away an occasional car passed behind the hedge concealing them. The May evening breeze had a fresh edge to it, but both had removed their jackets. Hers had on each of its sleeves the narrow band of a WAAF Section Officer. His was identical, denoting the equivalent rank of Flying Officer. For him, there were cloth wings stitched over the pocket of the left breast. Known, their sexual intimacy would not have been approved.

She was a plump woman who, when standing, would have been shorter than average. Her reddish-brown hair was cropped to fit beneath a service cap. She possessed a small nose that should have been freckled and was not, unusually dark green eyes and a mouth loose and soft from his loving. Her breasts were large, straining against the fabric of her shirt and, even when disciplined beneath her jacket, a distraction to the members of the Officers' Mess. She was married – but not to Flying Officer Oliver Missen, the man with her.

Oliver reached for his tunic and took cigarettes from a silver case. He lit them and passed one to her.

"Poor James," she said, looking away from him. "I always feel so bloody guilty."

James was her husband, a captain in the Royal Artillery somewhere in India. If Oliver felt guilty also, he could shrug it off. She had told him that her husband was at a supply depot and not within shooting distance of the Japs, and to Oliver that made his use of her not so bruising to what little conscience he had about making love to a married woman. There was a war being fought and his own future was precarious enough not to refuse what opportunity had offered as a recompense for his celibate iron bed in a requisitioned manor house and a likely early and violent death.

And he wasn't taking; only borrowing. Borrowing a body and not reciprocating the emotions she apparently needed to justify what she was doing. He had never understood why women always wanted more from a man than a mutual release of a sexual need. He had met her at a Mess dance in the first week of his posting to Wallisham. She had introduced herself as Morwenna Howis with a Welsh lilt in her voice, making it as obvious with her eyes as only a woman could that in a squadron of virile and woman-hungry officers he was the one on whom she had set her sights. She had later asked him, bluntly enough and without euphemisms, to make love to her. He hadn't been particularly interested because there was a woman in the nearby town whose bed, when he could reach it, was his. But Morwenna was readily available and lustful and the first woman he had met to be so honest in her need. He wasn't within miles of being in love with her and had no wish that she should be serious about him. He needed her physically, but no more than that. Her body was a drug to dull his fear of dying, a drug that could calm him after his daily sorties over France; each sortie haunted by the certainty that it would be his last. That morning he had returned with the skin of his Typhoon punctured, his sweating body trembling from the stress of forcing his faltering will to dive into the barrage of flak from the armoured column he had been attacking. Although he was one of a flight of three aircraft he had felt isolated in his fear, the hail of hot metal searching for him alone. He knew he wasn't the stuff of which VCs were made, willing to die for intangibles like honour and glory. His instinct was for survival and this he fought for when he had to, concealing what he felt with a brittle flippancy. He was born, he was sure, with *Please God, let it happen to somebody else* etched on the inner aspect of his skull where only he himself could read it.

"Yes," he agreed, "poor old James. If it's any consolation to you, he's probably doing the same with the local memsahibs. I've got it on good authority that most of the Army bods do."

"Don't be nasty, Oliver. I'd hate that and it doesn't help at all." She turned back to him, holding his gaze. She knew she was making an idiot of herself over him and she didn't care, other than that she would not be held cheap. He had been an instant attraction to her with his dark handsomeness and strong personality, the elegance and panache with which he wore his uniform. He made her husband a pale and insubstantial ghost from her past. "You probably think I'm much too available. I'm not really. Only with you."

"I wouldn't be flattered if I thought I was one in a NAAFI queue." He thought she was going to be serious and he put his hand between the buttons of her shirt and held her breast, warm and smooth and pulsing gently, in his fingers. "Wenna, sweetheart, don't get all self-analytical and guilty. It'll only give you problems."

"You don't give a damn, do you? Not really?" There was no bitterness in her voice. "You're never very serious, are you?"

"Only when I'm making love."

She shook her head. "You've the same expression you have when you're driving your car .... wondering if I'm going to get you to where you're going."

There was an approaching rumble of an engine that grew louder as a climbing Typhoon thundered over them, low enough to show clearly the undercarriage folding up into the zebra-striped wings, the ground vibrating from its passage. He frowned, twisting his head to follow its diminishing outline into invisibility against the pale blue of the sky.

"I give lots of damns. I wouldn't be dicing with disciplinary disaster if I didn't." He smiled. "I imagine that what we've been doing could fairly be regarded as conduct unbecoming a war-substantive officer and temporary gentleman."

"And me, too." She stubbed her cigarette in the grass and reached for her jacket. "I should get back now. I've things to do with my section, even if you haven't." She stood with him and held his hand, pressing it, her eyes worried. "If I don't see you before tonight, please be careful." She made it light. "You don't know how it is with us poor women left behind."

"A piece of cake," he said cheerfully, fingering his moustache into order and smoothing his black hair. "Only the dim clots get clobbered." He didn't want her worrying about him either. It made him feel as if he belonged to her. One day, if he survived, he would need to detach himself and return her to her husband. The last thing he wanted would be an embarrassingly emotional scene and tears.

His car, parked at the entrance to the field, was an orange open sports which had long lost its canvas hood. It was a squadron heirloom, taken over from successive owners as they were severally posted killed in action or missing. It ran exclusively on stolen 100-octane aviation petrol with the minimum of documentation.

With Morwenna at his side he reversed into the road and pointed the nose of the car in the direction of the airfield, a short mile or so away. He was turning his head and speaking to Morwenna when the long shiny bonnet of a Daimler appeared from around a bend in the centre of the narrow road. He jabbed at his brake pedal and wrenched at the steering wheel with a fighter-pilot's instinctive reaction, too late to do more than hit the steep grass bank with a front wheel that collapsed and turned the car on its side to slide with a grating of metal on the road surface into the front of the braking Daimler.

With Morwenna tumbled on to him, a weighty blue-cloth bundle with painful brass buttons, he had a glimpse of the horrified faces of a man and woman behind the bonnet before there was a bone-shaking stop and a shower of fragmented windscreen glass falling about him. He lay motionless for a few moments with Morwenna, her mouth open in soundless panic, scrambling on him with her heavy service shoes to get out. The engine had stopped and there was an anticlimactic quietness. He could hear the two wheels spinning above him and the splashing of water running from the smashed radiator, and smell spilled petrol. Lying there, his shoulder resting on the road, he began to laugh. It was bloody ridiculous. He could have been killed in this sardine tin of a car with its undersized engine. Ridiculous when he thought of his daily landing of seven tons of 2000-horse-power Typhoon at a hundred and ten miles an hour. He pulled himself free from behind the steering wheel he was still holding and stood up. Morwenna, leaning against the grass bank with her cap gone and with dust on her uniform, watched him with frightened eyes, obviously shaken but unhurt.

"Sorry about that," he said, grinning. "Are you all right? All in one piece?"

She nodded, managing a tiny smile. "And you? You're not hurt?"

"Only where you trod all over me."

He slapped road grit from the arm and shoulder of his jacket and went to the Daimler where it had stopped with its front wheels straddling the bonnet of his overturned car. Its massive bumper had absorbed the force of the collision with no more than a few scratches on its stainless steel surface. The man and woman were still in it, the man holding a handkerchief to the woman's forehead. He was an old man, gaunt-faced with an eagle's beak of a nose and a pleasant mouth that softened the overhanging arrogance. She was much younger, greyhound-lean and country-house elegant in smooth tweed, her narrow features tanned and free of cosmetics. Her eyes were closed and a trickle of blood ran down the side of her face.

Oliver looked in through the open window. "I'm sorry," he apologized for the second time. "I really had no chance to avoid you."

Their reaction astonished him. She opened her eyes at his words and he saw in them a startled recognition. Her mouth opened and she whispered, "Philip," staring at him as if she couldn't believe what she saw. The man held the folded handkerchief poised motionless as he also stared from eyes that age had paled and set back in their sockets.

"You're hurt," Oliver said to the woman.

She shook her head, her gaze not leaving him. "It's nothing," she said. Her voice was cultured and one used, he thought, to telling under-gardeners and kitchen maids whatever it was they had to do.

The man said, "It was my fault. I was drivin' too fast."

Their combined attention on him was so marked that he felt that there must be something odd about his appearance. He rubbed at his mouth, suspecting he might have Morwenna's lipstick on it. Or dirt on his face. "Is something wrong?" he asked. "Apart from the accident, I mean."

"Forgive me," the man apologized in his turn. "You . . . it's just that you remind me of somebody." He handed the handkerchief to the woman and climbed from the car. "Is your lady friend all right?"

Morwenna had recovered her cap and was standing, brushing dust from her uniform with the flat of her hand.

"We both are," Oliver said. "It's my car that's bought it." He looked glumly at it, an orange beetle-like thing on its side, its free wheels turning slowly, lying with its nose bleeding a spreading puddle of rusty water on the glass fragments of the windscreen.

"D'you want me to fetch a policeman?" the man asked him. Although his voice was pleasant, it was also the voice of a man used to authority over subordinates.

Oliver considered the expired insurance cover and the non-existent road fund licence. "I'd rather not," he said, giving him a disarming smile. "Not unless you do. There might be complications and, frankly, I'd be in trouble."

The man was still regarding him with his curious stare, ignoring what damage might have been done to his expensive car. The woman, too. Her eyes had not left his and it was beginning to irritate him. And yet, there was something in the manner in which they did it that was a bafflement; almost, he thought, as if they both knew him from somewhere and he hadn't remembered it. Certainly he had never seen either of them before in his life.

The man withdrew a slim leather case from his waistcoat pocket and gave him a card. "My name is Woollgar," he said, "and this is my wife. I'd be grateful if you'd allow me to be responsible for the repairs to your car. It was my fault and I insist."

Oliver held the card in his hand without looking at it, but his fingers felt that it was engraved. Despite the austerities of four and a half years of war, there was a rich smell of money about the couple.

"That's generous of you, Mr Woollgar, but it isn't necessary. She's an old crock and I doubt that she'll be any good after this." It was true in a way. Although only a 1934 model, the car was prematurely aged. The engine used almost as much oil as it did petrol. Left out in all weathers, it had had too many uncaring drivers and too little attention for it to be anything but a potential breakdown on journeys longer than from the airfield to the nearest pub.

"If you change your mind, I'd be happy to." Woollgar seemed disappointed that his offer had been refused. "Are you stationed here?"

"Yes. Both of us."

"May I give you a lift?"

"The station's only half a mile away. And I'd better stay here until I can organize some bodies to move the car." He looked at the woman. "I think your wife might need a doctor for that cut of hers. She's probably shaken up as well." He turned to rejoin Morwenna. "My name's Missen, by the way, if you need to contact me."

He watched the Daimler being reversed and then edged past his car. Mrs Woollgar had kept her gaze on him until the last moment.

Almost, he told himself, not very seriously, as if she saw in him a younger man with whom she might like to go to bed. Which didn't explain why her very much older husband should have looked at him as if he had seen a ghost.

Two

The moon shone its cold fire through a thin layer of high cirrus cloud. It was a Hunter's Moon, a dangerous night-fighter's moon that reflected on the polished surfaces of the wings and engine nacelles of the three Typhoons streaking over the phosphorescent slick of sea towards the dark mass that was France.

Oliver maintained his position behind and above Flying Officer Sandison, the No 1 of the Section. His own rear was covered by the No 3, Sergeant Bevis. He flew the bellowing 24-cylinder monster with an easy practised efficiency and, flying her, she was a part of him: her pounding engine his heart, her smooth metal sheathing his skin, the stringers and spars and cables his bones and sinews, the petrol and glycol the life-sustaining blood in veins and arteries. She was beautiful to him, a substitute for the Bentley racing car he could never have afforded. A ton of Napier Sabre engine housed in a sleek nacelle and driving a three-bladed propeller with its 2000-plus horsepower could pull him through the air at over four hundred miles an hour. She was a beautifully dangerous female monster – for he chose to think of her as female – her wings lethally armed with four Hispano cannon and eight solid fuel rockets that could blow a locomotive from its tracks and brew a Panzer to molten metal. As with all female monsters, she could be as dangerous to her lovers as she could be to her enemies, possessing both an eagerness to kill and an urge to self-destruction in returning uncontrollable to the earth. Oliver had an empathy with her that stopped short of sharing with her an unawareness of the fear of pain and death.

He moved his head from side to side, searching for the night fighter that would be a dark silhouette either blotting out a patch of the stars or appearing as a menacing shadow against the luminescence of the sea. With the drag of eight rockets and full magazines of cannon shells on board, the Typhoon's flying speed and manœuvrability were reduced. So encumbered, they could be shot from the sky like exploding pigeons by the faster Messerschmitt 109s which hunted the night air searching for their prey.

This, he thought, could be the night he would be buying the chop. Before changing into his flying kit he had looked around his small, sparsely furnished room, telling himself that it might be the last familiar thing he took with him into the darkness. He had smoked too many cigarettes and, before leaving, had opened his Flying Log Book in which he might never make another entry, cursing his unloseable morbidness in doing so, wondering if he was the only one. He couldn't guess how his fellow pilots really felt about their dangerous sorties over enemy-occupied territory, for most made much of the opportunity of killing the Hun, never considering that they might themselves finish up as a burning heap of smashed metal. Those who did were silent and introspective as if already feeling the cold kiss from bony jaws.

He feared fire most of all. He had seen those who had unfortunately survived, disfigured and maimed, their faces bubbling horrors of fried flesh, their hands peeled of skin like rotting fish. His own face mightn't be much, but he wanted to keep it, to live with it a bit longer. Women were attracted to it and he hadn't yet had his fill of physical passions. He would wish himself dead rather than live on as a suppurating and corroded monstrosity. In thinking of that, Morwenna came into his mind. He found it difficult to realize that a few short hours earlier he had been making gentle love in a sunny field under a blue sky. The transition from civilized love-making to the imminence of a killing violence had been too abrupt.

Tonight, their target was an ammunition train reported by intelligence sources in France to be travelling between Amiens and Dieppe. With a Flakvierling multiple gun at each end, it would be an iron caterpillar with a bite in its head and a sting in its tail. If the gun crews had the courage to keep firing at three Typhoons spraying them with rockets and cannon shells in a steady undeviating dive they could hardly miss. More often than not, they didn't. The prospect frightened Oliver.

He knew that it wasn't courage he lacked. It was the intent to suicide at which his mind baulked. In fighting a Focke-Wulf 190 or a Messerschmitt 109 there was a chance of survival. He could use his skill at flying to avoid their fire and to return it. Brewing up a defended train was something else altogether. It was a deliberate act of recklessness, a flying into the biting teeth of death.

The sea gave way to the darker configuration of land and a thin scattering of flak from coastal defence guns came up at them, too late to do anything but trail behind the tails of their aircraft. High above were the chalk-lines of condensation trails made by heavy bombers heading for Germany and as visible to the Luftwaffe as they were to Typhoon pilots below them. There were other Sections of A Flight flying on independent missions somewhere in the darkness, but they could not be seen.

Sandison banked and Oliver turned with him, his leader's aircraft clear in the brilliant moonlight. His altimeter read 2000 feet and the fields slid smoothly beneath them. He could identify villages and isolated farm buildings, the silver gleam of rivers, and pick out hedges and clumps of trees. When the railway lines showed below as parallel threads of shining metal, Sandison broke radio silence. "Red Two and Three line astern." His voice came over edged with eagerness.

"Roger." Oliver made his acknowledgement curt, concealing in it the stifling pounding in his chest. He heard Bevis's laconic 'Roger, Red Leader' and read into it the diminutive sergeant's reckless bravery that had already earned him a DFM.

They had been briefed in detail on the attack and Sandison, he knew, would follow it to the last shell in his magazines; inflexibly, regardless of what was flung against them. And the leader would have the advantage of whatever surprise there was in the attack, but alerting the gun crews to Oliver and Bevis following behind. Bevis, as third man in, would get it the worst.

He first saw the train as a wisp of trailing steam in the far distance, emerging from the shadow of a cutting in the darker ink-blot of surrounding trees, then the caterpillar-like train of wagons taking a curve in the lines. He dimmed the annuluses of his gun-sight and fused four of his rockets with the selector switches, seeing his features illuminated in the soft glow from the instrument panel and reflected in the curved perspex at each side of him as grotesquely misshapen, the oxygen mask elongated into a demonic snout. His mind scampered with thoughts of the hail of steel shells into which he would soon be flying, each capable of tearing chunks of flesh from his body or exploding him into a falling ball of fire.

Feeling his mouth dry and acrid he gave himself a deep breath of oxygen, holding tight to the throttle lever he was going to push through its gate as soon as the rockets left his wings.

The train was large now, filling the annulus of his sight, and Sandison's aircraft had started on its dive. Oliver pushed his stick forward and followed him, bouncing in the turbulence of his wake. He saw the trail of the rockets leaving Sandison's wings and sparks spraying from the wheels of the locomotive as it was braked. A storm of flame and smoke erupted from the wagons behind as the rockets hit and flashes winked from the flak-wagon pushed in front. As Sandison vanished into the darkness on a climb over the train, tracer hissed in burning yellow streaks towards Oliver and he knew that he was in the convergence of shells seeking him out. He contracted his belly and hunched his shoulders as if to make himself a shrinking target, his whole world the narrow cockpit, a vibrating metal coffin moving at 250 miles an hour towards a waiting firing squad. And then the fear came; nightmarish unrepressible fright that churned his mind into a need for panic-stricken flight and, remotely, a shaming contempt that it was there. It bulged his eyes and opened his mouth for the shout that was paralysed in his throat. He felt sickness in his stomach as his body reacted to his panic, his foot banging hard on the rudder pedal and skidding the Typhoon sideways to get out of the stream of murderous steel. He released his rockets, knowing that his deflection would cause them to miss the train and not caring. As they exploded harmlessly in the field alongside the now motionless locomotive he fired a burst from his cannon without aiming and pushed open the throttle, climbing over the tail of the train and pulling the shuddering Typhoon round in a steep turn.

He knew he would have to try again, to fight the raw animal fear that took possession of him when faced with almost inescapable destruction. Looking back he saw Bevis's Typhoon on its approach in a steady undeviating dive, his rocket and cannon firing in the face of the flak concentrated in its turn on him. As he watched, so a flash of light came from the nose of the aircraft, swelling to a bursting flare of fire that streamed backwards like spilled golden entrails as it carried on like a meteor to explode into the flak-wagon and locomotive, hurling its debris along the track.

Oliver tightened his turn until the wings fluttered, aligning the Typhoon with the rails as he straightened her for the run-in at the rear of the now distant train. The locomotive and wagons were blazing furiously, explosions rippling along its length, billows of smoke rising like a dark fog. As he drew nearer he could see that the rear gun platform was silent and men were running, foreshortened pigmies silhouetted against the orange glare. He held the burning train in his sight and released his remaining rockets as it rushed towards him. Simultaneously he saw the trail of the rockets curving over Sandison's Typhoon below his nose as they streaked towards the target. He pulled back on the stick, centrifugal pressure heavy on his arms and legs as he climbed and turned again, coming at the stricken train on a quarter approach and pouring cannon shells at the running men, conscious he was now firing at a target no longer capable of defending itself and meriting nothing for courage.

He was sweating, his shirt wet on his back, his mask clammy on his face. As he kept climbing on a course for home his legs felt weak and he was trembling from the few seconds he had tried and failed to fly cold-bloodedly into the killing flak. But it only took seconds to die and Sergeant Bevis had died where he would have been had he not skidded his own Typhoon out of it. That was some justification, but not enough. Not enough to justify his moving to one side, knowing that Bevis would inevitably take the full brunt of the stream of shells. However he looked at it he had lacked moral fibre and LMF was the most degrading offence with which a pilot could be accused. What he had done afterwards had been instinctive, leaving a corner of his mind knowing that there was then no real danger.

He had lost touch with Sandison and he pressed his transmitter button, calling for him although knowing that he could be locating himself for any night fighter sent to the scene of the attack. He almost welcomed it, wanting to blot out his belittling pusillanimity against an enemy on no better terms than his own.

When he received no acknowledgement from Sandison he held on course. He felt exposed, an easily seen silhouette against the moonlit sky but not fearing now the approach of a dark shadow beneath his tail, weaving the Typhoon and looking behind and below with his thumb on the firing button, seeking for it to ease his self-induced humiliation.

He came in from the circuit to line the nose of the Typhoon between the twin rows of dimly seen purple flares on the airfield rising to meet him, lowering the flaps and letting her settle to a safe approach speed. With the wheels skimming the moonlit grass he eased back on the stick and throttle lever, feeling for the steel mesh runway. She touched and bounced as she lost lift, rolling and bumping as he held her straight with the rudder and slowed her breakneck speed with the brakes, the battering roar of the engine giving way to the banging of her tons of metal returning to the stresses of weight.

Turning on to the parking apron and the waiting mechanics and armourers, he idled the engine and then opened up to a clearing roar against the brakes. Switching off the ignition he sat for a few moments, dazed by the sudden quietness. He felt himself vibrating inside like a nervous dog, the sweat cold on his body. It had been less than an hour, yet he was deaf from the noise of the engine and the buffeting of the airstream, mentally disorientated by the nervous tension of the fear he had been unable to control, the taste of burned cordite and exhaust gases harsh in his mouth. He had survived once again, but he wasn't proud of the way in which he had done it.

Climbing down from the wing he felt the ground an unsteady and shifting platform after the shut-in cramped confines of the cockpit. Four other Typhoons were ticking away the heat from their engines on the apron. As he walked past them he checked their code letters. None was Sandison's. He should have been back or in the circuit preparing for his landing. There was a creeping suspicion in Oliver's mind that his leader, unexpectedly appearing below him in his second attack on the train, could have been caught in the blast of his salvo of exploding rockets. He put the thought away, not wanting to load himself with any more guilt.

The Squadron Operations Room, bleak and uncomfortable and converted from what had been the bar of a pre-war flying club, was as makeshift as the field from which the Typhoons flew. It was the temporary annexe to the dangerous skies of northern France. The squadron, relieved of its former air fighting capability, had been absorbed into 84 Group of the Second Tactical Air Force and re-formed as a rocket-firing squadron, converted to airborne artillery for the pre-invasion disruption of German rail, road and sea communications. It had not been a welcome change and the majority of the pilots, trained and habituated to air-to-air combat, resented their new role. None more so than Oliver.

The Squadron Intelligence Officer was already debriefing a pilot in the Operations Room. Two others waited their turn to recount in detail what they could recall of their danger-filled minutes of violent action. They held cups of tea and smoked cigarettes. One looked as if he had just returned from seeing a man hanged; the other wore an air of satisfaction and was obviously bursting to get whatever it was he had off his mind.

"Good show?" the second said to Oliver, asking for both of them.

He turned his mouth down. "Bloody dicey. We lost Sergeant Bevis. And I'm not too sure about Jimmy Sandison. He hasn't returned yet."

It sobered his questioner, but only momentarily. It was the form not to be seen to be emotionally affected by the death of a fellow pilot.

Oliver sat, withdrawing himself behind the nonchalance with which he smoked. He had composed his body and the fingers holding the cigarette were steady. He turned his thoughts to Morwenna. She would be lying in her bed awake and counting the aircraft landing, fretting that he might not be returning. She would have to wait until morning to know, it not being one of the duties of a WAAF Section Officer to enquire of the well-being and safety of operation pilots at one-thirty in the morning. Even given the opportunity, he wouldn't want her at this moment. She would wish to know things about what had happened which, in his present condition, he couldn't hope to disguise against her female perceptiveness. Nor, he lied to himself, was he wholly a man walking behind permanently eager loins. His ego was shrivelled and a shrivelled ego was nothing to take to bed with a woman. He couldn't appear less than a man to her. What he needed was a bellyful of conscience-drugging, ego-dulling whisky and some sleep to blot out his cowardice and the recurring picture in his mind of Bevis dying in his disintegrating Typhoon.

Bevis's name would still be chalked in on the Squadron Formation Board under A Flight, Red Section, with that of Sandison's and his own. A quick rub with the grubby brown duster hanging at the side of the board, the return of his personal effects to a relative together with a brief telegram from the Air Ministry, would be his requiem. It would be followed by a letter of condolence from the Squadron Commander telling whomever he had left behind what a wonderful chap he had been and how he had inspired the squadron with his devotion to duty and ability to kill Germans. It might be true of Bevis, Oliver thought, but it would be said equally of the most reluctant and uninspiring of them as each in his turn got the chop. Every man had to die as a hero.

While he waited, he heard two aircraft circling the airfield and then, in quick succession, landing. One of them had to be Sandison, he convinced himself, realizing at the same time that the Section Leader could have seen his turning away from the flak and wasting his rockets in an empty field. If he had, Sandison would know or guess his poltroonery even if he couldn't prove it. Oliver would see it in his manner, in the inflexion of his voice when he spoke to him. He would feel his shame like a splash of yellow paint. A suspicion that he lacked moral fibre would make him the squadron leper.

Summerbee, the elderly and wingless Flight Lieutenant IO, had the Form D authorizing the A Flight sorties in front of him. He had never flown himself other than as a passenger, but he knew what Group wanted from those who did. Oliver took a chair opposite him and lit his third cigarette.

"A good trip?" the IO started him off.

"No. Sergeant Bevis bought it. And I don't know if Sandison has got back yet."

"I see." He looked at his watch. "He's still got a bit of time before we need start worrying."

"I don't see him stooging around France in the dark looking for trouble without any rockets or ammunition."

"We'll see. You intercepted the puffer?" He made a note on his clipboard.

"Yes. We picked it up a few miles west of Amiens, did a line astern approach with Sandison leading and Bevis behind me. We attacked in a dive from two thousand feet." Oliver made his voice unemotional. He was the battle-weary warrior who had been there and seen things. "Number One made rocket strikes behind the locomotive. I came in on his tail – about a thousand yards behind – when the flak started up. There were fore and aft flak-wagons with multiple pom-poms." He drew deeply on his cigarette as he prepared to lie. *Christ*, he told himself, *this is where Sandison should come in and make me a liar.*

"Yes." The armament had been known to the IO and the pilots when the operation was laid on.

"I hit the locomotive with my first salvo and brewed it up. Then I did a turn to come in from the rear. That's when I saw Bevis hit with the flak. He was on his approach and dived straight in. I shouldn't think he knew what hit him."

Poor ham-handed Bevis. His fellow NCOs called him "Bouncer" because he landed his Tiffy like a lorryload of old iron that could be dumped down on the deck irrespective. It was inevitable that he would have written himself off by his own clumsiness if he hadn't been killed by the Krauts first. His DFM had been earned for shooting down two of seven Messerschmitt 109s that had jumped him from a cloud and were tripping over their feet to get him in their sights. He said that all he did was to keep his thumb on the gun tit while he tried to find a way out of the mêlée, shooting down the two Messerschmitts that appeared fortuitously in front of his cannon. Oliver knew he wouldn't have been frightened for he didn't possess enough imagination to be. He needed only to have his nose pointed at a target and he went for it like a rabid terrier. He was only nineteen and without a war intervening would have been riding a motor-cycle at a reckless speed to the nearest seaside town with a girl on the pillion seat.

"You're certain he was killed?" Summerbee was pedantic, and patient with it. He would want every detail he could screw out of a pilot whose brain was still disorganized from being the target for lumps of exploding metal.

"He was on fire, disintegrating before he went in and too low to get out," Oliver said shortly. He wanted to be done with it and get to the whisky. "There can't be any doubt."

"And Sandison?"

"I saw him on the second run-in from the rear. He was in front of me and below. I didn't see him release his second salvo of rockets but the whole train was popping off and I imagine he did. I let loose mine and then shot up the rear gun crew who were running for it. I called him over the R/T and heard nothing so I set course for home, keeping a few rounds in the magazines in case I got jumped."

The door opened and two pilots came into the room. Neither was Sandison and Oliver guessed that now he wouldn't be returning. Accepting his probable death, half of his mind regretted it, the other half was relieved that, with it, went the only possible witness of his poltroonery. Set against the deaths of Bevis and

Sandison and the loss of two Typhoons, the destruction of the locomotive and its train of ammunition wagons and two flak gun crews seemed a not very profitable exchange.

When he had completed his debriefing and was stood down from Readiness, Oliver returned to his room in the Station Duty wagon with the surviving pilots. Four of the twelve who had taken off such a short time previously had failed to return.

The manor house requisitioned by the Royal Air Force stood in its own grounds on the perimeter of the airfield, far enough away to need transport to it. It had been neglected and even at night looked slovenly and down-at-heel. The furnishings had been removed and stored in locked rooms, leaving an uncomfortable shell whose bare boards boomed and echoed against walls bare of everything but Squadron Orders and Notices and stained patches where paintings had hung. The commissioned pilots and WAAF officers slept, ate and drank in it. Although two truckle beds had been squeezed into it, Oliver slept alone in what had been called the Green Room. The former occupant of the second bed had dived his Typhoon into the Channel a few days back and had not been replaced. For Oliver, being alone was a luxury.

The windows of the room were mullioned and overlooked a garden of straggling unpruned rose bushes. The room was reputed to be haunted by the ghost of Sir John Jarvis, an eighteenth-century rakehell and libertine who had died unshriven there in his pox-ridden debauchery. It had not manifested itself to Oliver but he had often sensed, or imagined he sensed, that he was being stared at by Jarvis's invisible brooding presence. Whichever it was, it was nothing that disturbed him.

In between ridding himself of his flying kit he drank a full glass of whisky from the bottle he kept concealed in the wardrobe. It did nothing to slow down the racing of his mind, but did help him in rationalizing what had happened. Bevis had died because he flew bull-headed and unnecessarily into the flak when it would have been more sensible, less foolhardy, to have avoided it as he had done and attacked around the defences. A fighter-pilot – and that was what he had been until the squadron had been delegated by some wooden-headed brasshat to the task of shooting up ground targets as an adjunct to the artillery and armoured divisions soon to be in France – avoided his opponent's fire where he could and, in his turn, manœuvred to get behind and give the bastard a lethal squirt in the back. The whisky made it seem as acceptable as his wish not to commit suicide against a wall of flak. That Bevis had done it was of his own choice. If Oliver was to die, he could not be expected to go out of his way to anticipate it. He had already proved his courage with a confirmed score of two Focke-Wulf 190s, four Messerschmitt 109s and a Heinkel 111 he had shot into the ground as it was taking off from a French airfield. And that didn't count the ground targets he had brewed up with his rockets. It wasn't necessary to die a hero's death to underline it. And there was Sandison. If he had, indeed, flown into the explosions of Oliver's rockets then the fatal mischance was as much of his making as of Oliver's, for the trails must have ben easily descernible in the moonlight. But the knowledge that he could have been responsible for his leader's death was a nagging guilt.

He took his towel and soap and padded naked to the bathroom at the end of the uncarpeted corridor. The cold wet needles of a shower did more for his well-being than had the whisky, his mind having justified his avoidance of death as much as it ever would. Towelling himself, he studied his face in the wall mirror, trying to read in it what other people saw. A lean face with the jaw muscles prominent, the wide mouth and sharp nose separated by the black bar of his moustache. The dark brown eyes under thick eyebrows might, he admitted to himself, indicate a certain softness of purpose when set against the blue or grey of reputedly harder characters. A womanizer's eyes, he had been told, and he was honest enough not to argue against his being a gross feeder on female flesh. He hadn't been born with an easily erectible appendage for it to deteriorate from non-use of its primary function in the darkness of his trousers. Not when it might be so short-lived. Not when the prohibition of its casual use was inspired by a religion out of which he had long opted. And with his promiscuity, his thirst for women, mitigated in his own mind, his ego reinflated, he thought of Morwenna warm and excitingly smooth-skinned in her bed and staring at the dark ceiling, uncertain about his return.

He dressed and left the house by the front door, walking silently on the unkempt lawn to the rear. That the WAAF Officers' Quarters were Out of Bounds to all ranks had always seemed of minor consequence against the larger issue of his continued physical survival. He tapped on the glass of a curtained window with his fingernail and waited, a darker mass in the dark shadow of the wisteria overhanging the window.

Even in the act of loving, of expending his lust into her plump enveloping body, he listened for the sounds of returning aircraft that could be Sandison's until the time factor of his flight made it no longer possible that he would return.

Three

Philip Graham opened his eyes and lifted himself to a sitting position in the shrubbery. It was daylight and his watch showed the time as five-twenty. He had been sleeping for seventeen hours. The sun, a glowing crimson coal, was dropping behind purple clouds, the trees darkening to silhouettes. Between the clouds an invisible high-flying aircraft left a contrail like a pink-tinged scar scratched against the darkening blue.

He was on the edge of a plantation of fir trees and they stretched behind him in regimented rows. In front were bare brown fields rising to softly rounded grass-covered hills. In the middle distance a red-tiled church spire and the roofs of buildings with smoking chimneys rose from a shallow valley. A man rode a bicycle slowly along a dirt road towards a farmhouse at the foot of a hill.

He had awakened to a world without sound, to the eerie silence of his deafness. When he put a finger into each ear and expanded the canals he felt the pressure but heard nothing of the friction of skin against skin. He was isolated and encapsuled within his head, feeling an odd sensation of apartness, of sad loss and depression.

He thought briefly of returning to his crashed Lancaster, discarding the idea when he realized that almost certainly the Germans would have put a guard on it. His moral responsibility as captain of the aircraft fretted him. The rear gunner and flight engineer were dead. Of that he was certain. Whether the remaining four of his crew had baled out safely only a search of the carcass of the bomber would tell him. And returning to do it would be an act of stupidity. If he wished to avoid capture he had to stay under cover until nightfall. Wearing a leather flying jacket and an RAF flying suit made him a conspicuous incongruity in a hostile countryside. Were he painted a bright orange he would not be more obvious. And his curious deafness – which he imagined the result of concussion when the propeller smashed into the cockpit canopy – made him vulnerable to surprise. It was dangerous to be deaf, unable to hear approaching vehicles or footfalls, not even the warning shout or its following rifle shot. The Germans would have searched the Lancaster. When they found no body they could identify as the pilot's, possibly discovering the metal fitments of his unused parachute and knowing that he hadn't baled out, they would scour the area for him.

The thought of being taken prisoner, of not seeing Laura, perhaps for years, determined him to risk nothing. And being identified as an enemy did not necessarily mean finishing up in a prisoner-of-war camp. He had heard horrifying reports of shot-down crews being mobbed and lynched by infuriated civilians who had suffered their devastating bombing. Nor would being interrogated by the Gestapo be much better. Were he captured he would prefer it to be by the Luftwaffe or the Wehrmacht. They were fighting units and believed to respect the rights of prisoners-of-war.

It reminded him of the silver identification bracelet he wore on his wrist. It had been given to him by Laura when he had received his commission and somehow they both regarded his wearing of it as a talisman against its ever being necessary. She had had engraved on it *P/O 198085 GRAHAM P., Royal Air Force, Blood Group O*, the only information he would be expected to give in the event of his capture. He touched it with gentle fingers for it was the only thing he wore that had been also touched by her.

He had never considered he might be one of those to whom it was going to happen. And now that it had he hadn't a clue about what he should do. He tried to recall the image of the wall map shown to the crews in the squadron's briefing room less than twenty-four hours previously. He had then concentrated his attention more on the assembly area and the thick line of red wool that led in a dog-leg to Nuremburg which had been his track than on the topography surrounding the city to be bombed. Now it was necessary for him to know the position of Nuremburg in relation to the French border. If he managed against all the odds to make France and cross it to Spain, he might somehow get into the escape route to Gibraltar and return to Laura. It was all so bloody confusing, so formidable and unlikely to succeed. Gibraltar must be well over a thousand miles away, the first hundred or so through Germany. He wasn't certain even then where he would hit in

Occupied France. And if, by some miracle, he remained uncaptured there were the Spanish, neutral but Fascistly unsympathetic to being used by escaping English airmen. Switzerland was, he thought, nearer than the French border but, no doubt, its approaches would be more actively patrolled by the Germans than any other. Even were he to make it, he had only the prospect of spending the rest of the war in internment. No, Switzerland was out. He would be expected to try for Gibraltar and from there to rejoin his squadron.

At the moment he didn't know where he was in relation to Nuremburg. He must have travelled miles from it in his falling plane. He tried to remember how long it had been between being shot down and his crash landing, in which direction he had been heading. It could have happened to somebody else for all he could bring back his recall.

The man on the bicycle had reached the farmhouse and had gone inside. There remained only the darkening landscape that looked cold and bleak with now no sign of life in it. He felt that he was the only reality in an unreal and nightmarish world of impending disaster. He shivered, not from the cold he didn't feel but from the hopelessness of his position. As he waited for nightfall, the dream returned to him. It had been vivid and powerful. He had seen his beloved Laura as though he had been standing in the room watching her. The room was nostalgically familiar in all its detail and seeing it had brought a numbing sense of loss to him. The curtains had been closed over the windows and she was sitting in the easy chair by the fire, staring sightlessly into it. She wore the dark green suit he had always liked with a polo-neck sweater. She had been weeping and her face was drawn into lines of grief. His photograph in its silver frame stood on the small table at her side. He had seen it all with a clarity and definition unusual in a dream. So clear that he had called 'Laura!' to her, trying desperately to make her understand that he was there, that he was alive and well. The door had opened and Cynthia came in. Her stepmother's lips had moved, saying words he could not hear but which he nevertheless understood as if he were reading her mind. He felt the compassion and anxiety in it, too; as much as he could feel the bleakness of Laura's sorrow. She said, "Laura, are you coming to eat?"

Laura had shaken her head. Her words, too, were soundless

although he knew what she was saying. "I'd rather not. Later, perhaps." Banal words, but they had disturbed him deeply.

Cynthia sat on the arm of the chair and put a hand on her shoulder. "Laura", she said, "I'm sure he'll be safe. They would have said had he . . . had he been killed. Please don't sit in here on your own."

"He's dead, Mother, I know he is." Her eyes had brimmed over with tears and she turned her head away.

In his dream, Philip had shouted his frustration and anger, trying to get through the invisible wall of silence that separated him from their grief, of Laura's burying him before he was dead. There was a reality about it that had none of the oddness and shifting distortions of dreams previously experienced; like, he thought, the running through of a silent film into which he was unable to penetrate, but only to watch.

The soundless movement of their lips continued without his understanding and the picture had faded abruptly, there supervening the nightmarish reliving of his falling to the black landscape that rose to meet his dying Lancaster, the battering of the airstream and roaring of burning fuel not deadening the moaning of the rear gunner in his ears, the final impact into the ground that had brought darkness to his consciousness until he woke.

While he suspected that there must be a mental trauma, he felt nothing but a physical well-being. He was neither hot nor cold, neither hungry nor thirsty, his bodily functions and sensations suspended by the shock of his experience. The weariness was all in his mind and he thought that he could sleep for ever.

As he waited impatiently for nightfall, sitting motionless in the deepening twilight, leaves stirred in a bush and the sinuous brown body of a weasel appeared, moving over the bare earth almost within his reaching distance. It halted and sat upright, combing paws over its blunt whiskered muzzle. Philip kept himself still. Although the weasel appeared to have him within its vision it showed neither awareness of him nor fear of his presence. When it had completed its toilet it sniffed the air and dropped back on its four legs, running silently across the small clearing only inches from Philip's flying boots and not once acknowledging his existence. It was a triviality but it disturbed him, making him feel that he was a non-being, an inanimate thing of no more consequence to the weasel than the trees surrounding them.

When it was fully night with the moon not yet risen, he took a bearing on the North Pole star and left the shrubbery, walking across the fields in a south-westerly direction. Because he could hear nothing, not even the sounds of his own movement, he turned his head frequently to ensure that he was not being watched.

Four

Oliver had left Morwenna before first light and slept in his own bed until ten o'clock. Eating the late breakfast served to him by a sour WAAF waitress not too sympathetic with the inconvenience caused by night-flying pilots, he retrieved from his wallet the card Woollgar had given him the previous afternoon and read it for the first time. Woollgar was not only a retired Lieutenant-Colonel, but a knighted one as well. And with a DSO and Military Cross to add to it. His address was shown as Saxinge Hall, Dunsham St Michael. It decided him against reading newspapers and dozing in the Mess anteroom for the next few free hours before the next briefing. He changed from the battledress he was wearing to his No 1 dress uniform and borrowed a car.

Although he welcomed the freedom of "Released" state from the "Readiness" and "Available" states too often imposed when the Squadron's main function was air combat and when emergency take-offs were the rule, he found it paradoxical that on the eve of the invasion of Europe pilots could virtually opt out of the war between sorties and the few training sessions they now had. Some boozed away their uncertainties in the Mess and local pubs, some killed birds and rabbits in the surrounding park and others hunted for accommodating women in the nearest town. It smacked to him of clocking-on and clocking-off in a routine job at a factory.

He had been intrigued by the reaction of Woollgar and his wife to his appearance and he thought the courtesy of an enquiry about Lady Woollgar's injury was a good enough reason to find out why. Before he left he called in at the Operations Room to check on Sandison. His name had already been scrubbed from the Formation Board and, despite the guilt he felt, there was a small warmth of relief in him. And the relief was made acceptable by the thought that Sandison was as likely to have made a forced landing and survived as he was to have been killed.

Dunsham St Michael was nine miles from the airfield and his short journey through the narrow roads was made longer by columns of tanks and personnel carriers moving towards the coast.

The approach to Saxinge Hall impressed him. Behind two massive stone pillars surmounted by black-painted greyhounds and supporting large ornamental iron gates that had escaped being commandeered and melted down was a small lodge, obviously unoccupied. The drive was lined Italianate fashion with dark-foliaged cypresses and if it all looked a little untended it was, nevertheless, very manorial. The house, in Queen Anne style, was large enough to accommodate a school. Where not covered with ivy it was a mellowed pink brick with gabled eaves, the tall windows stone-mullioned and leaded. It was a house that would have stabling and a servants' quarter separated by a *cordon sanitaire* of green-baize-covered doors. A high-walled garden extended from one side and, behind it, attached to the house, was visible the roof of an iron-ribbed conservatory. Surrounding it all was a parkland of acres of grass and clumps of oaks and elms.

Oliver closed the door of the borrowed car that looked anachronistic in the forecourt of the house and climbed the steps leading to a panelled oak door flanked by pillars and large enough to ride a horse through. He pulled at the bronze bell-rod and waited, already feeling out of his normal milieu of service discomforts and austerities.

An elderly woman in a black linen dress and obviously the housekeeper opened the door. "Is Colonel Woollgar in?" he asked her. He wasn't certain about calling him Sir Clive. It sounded over-familiar and he played safe with his military title. "And is it convenient to see him? My name is Missen and we met in a car accident yesterday."

He stepped inside the spacious hall and she left him feeling that he should have produced a card for her to carry somewhere on a silver tray.

Holding his cap beneath his arm and smoothing his moustache, he looked around him. Gilt-framed paintings covered the walls and among them he thought he recognized a Canaletto, although he had not seen an original before. A sheaf of flowers in a copper bowl the size of a footbath stood at the base of a plinth bearing the marble bust of the Roman Emperor Vespasian. He knew this only because the plinth had TITUS FLAVIUS VESPASIANUS carved in it. It was all as he had imagined it would be, the reflected image of cultured wealth with little there that wasn't antique. Balustraded stairs rose in a wide sweep past more paintings and verdigrised tubs of palms and hot-house plants.

It was Lady Woollgar who came down them. Although she must have been prepared, there was still an initial look of puzzled disbelief in her eyes when she saw him. She wore a tweed skirt and woollen pullover as if about to go out and kill a few pheasants and was followed down the stairs by two black Labrador dogs. Her pale-straw hair was drawn back from her fine-boned face in a ponytail, showing a small strip of plaster on her forehead.

Oliver's first impression of her was confirmed. She was attractive, cool and poised with a little more than a share of natural arrogance. And a woman who wouldn't care too many damns about how she appeared to the peasantry. He was certain that he would hesitate twice to cross her in anything. She didn't smile and he had the uncomfortable suspicion that his call was unwelcome.

She held out her hand and he shook it, feeling it warmer than her expression. The dogs sniffed at his trouser legs and sat, looking, he thought, as if they too were reserving judgement on him.

"I hope it's not inconvenient, Lady Woollgar," he said. "I called to see if everything was all right after the accident. Your head," he added lamely. She was a woman who made him take care to enunciate correctly and to avoid the service slang he had cultivated.

"That's very kind of you, Mr Missen." Her voice was well-bred and modulated to a pitch that reminded him irresistibly of women who ran Charity Balls and who could put a parvenu firmly in his place by admitting to having been educated at Cheltenham Ladies' College only as a preliminary to a Swiss finishing school. "I'm perfectly well, thank you. And you?"

He smiled. "Too trivial to mention. A few bruises."

She didn't smile back and it discomfited him further, making him feel a graceless clod. Had he discovered his fly-buttons to be undone he could not have felt more gauche and he cursed her in his mind for her calm and unblinking staring at him.

"And your lady-friend?"

"A service colleague," he answered ambiguously. "She's quite well too, thank you."

"Should I ask after your car?"

He shrugged. "It was an old banger. It should have been put down years ago."

She moved towards a door, the dogs following immediately behind her. "Come into the drawing-room. I'm sure my husband will wish to see you." Her gaze had not left him and he turned away from it with relief when she asked him to sit. She put a crystal box of cigarettes on the table at his side. "If you smoke," she said, "please help yourself."

She left him and he took a cigarette from the box which was comfortably stuffed with cork-tipped Du Maurier and plain De Reszke, neither brand easy to find in tobacconists. As he smoked it, he took in the room. There were three settees, a chaise longue and four easy chairs like the one in which he sat and felt lost, engulfed in its huge brocaded and padded depths. There were painted portraits of Victorian and Edwardian men and women who looked at him with the calm certainty of superiority he had received from Lady Woollgar; silver and porcelain in glass cabinets and period furniture with curved legs and clawed feet. The carved stone fireplace with its massive fire-dogs supporting the best part of a sawn-up tree was big enough to stand in. The powder-blue drapes at the wooden-shuttered windows were faded and beautifully ancient. For all its looking like a museum set-piece, the room was lived in. There were newspapers and magazines and a sideboard with bottles and glasses on it; black dog hairs made a patch on the fabric of the chair opposite him.

He found it difficult to believe it was a household that acknowledged the existence of whale meat, reconstituted egg and Spam or the rationed austerities of two ounces of cheese, a shilling's-worth of meat and a weekly egg laid by a hen. The whisky, brandy and sherry on the sideboard were evidence that money could still circumvent a war's shortages. It didn't affront any patriotic morality in him. In their position he would do the same.

When she returned he pushed himself from the easy chair and stood. "My husband," she said, "will be with us in a moment. Would you care for a sherry?"

"Thank you." He hesitated as she moved away from him to the sideboard. Sod it, he said to himself. It can't be half as bad as flying into a load of flak. Then he spoke to her back as she poured into two glasses. "Forgive me if I'm wrong, but is there something about me that ... well, that you don't approve?" He smiled as he said it, making it a small pleasantry.

She didn't answer immediately but finished pouring the sherries, then turning and holding out a glass to him. Taking it, he kept within reaching distance of her. She was a woman after all and if he could think of her in sexual terms – he could smell her perfume and see the small mounds of her breasts beneath the woollen pullover and that was a sufficient stimulus – she would be less belittling to his masculinity.

"It's not that, Mr Missen, and I'm sorry you think it is." She took a cigarette from a flat pink packet and put it in her mouth, waiting. He thumbed his lighter at it and smelled the Turkish scent of its smoke.

"Your husband said that I reminded him of someone."

She was clearly reluctant to answer him. "Yes. It was a shock to see you, Mr Missen. You have a quite remarkable resemblance to our son-in-law."

"I hadn't thought God could make the same mistake twice." He winced when his wrongly phrased flippancy evoked no response but a slight raising of her eyebrows. He had intended his remark to be self-deprecatory but realized, too late, that it was deprecatory to her son-in-law also.

"He is dead, Mr Missen." She put the sherry down and picked up a silver-framed photograph, holding it out to him.

He took it, his face expressionless, and said, "I'm sorry. I had no idea."

It could have been a photograph of himself, a few years younger and with the moustache shaven. He wore an RAF uniform and cap with pilot's wings just visible on his left breast above the edge of the frame. There was an uncanny familiarity about the shape and structure of the face. Only the eyes were strange and they made the personality of the man different. It gave Oliver an odd kind of shock to be confronted with this image of a man so very like himself and now so dead.

He handed the photograph back to her. "I see what you mean," he said. She was sipping at her sherry, regarding him thoughtfully with her unsettling eyes. "And the uniform helps. He was killed in action?"

"Yes. In March, during a raid on Nuremburg."

She made him feel guilty that he was alive instead of her son-in-law. What the hell was he supposed to say? He couldn't be expected to weep tears of grief about somebody he hadn't known. He'd got the chop in a service where the chop was a commonplace incident.

"I'm sorry," he said again. "It's pretty rough being a bomber pilot. Lancasters?"

"Yes. I don't imagine you'd met?" As if she thought he had been doing his own time at an Elementary Flying School.

He shook his head. "Different job, different squadrons. And I'd have naturally remembered someone looking so much like myself. What was his name?"

"Philip Graham. Flying Officer Philip Graham." She wasn't, he thought, exactly chatty about her son-in-law and he was finding it hard going.

"No, it doesn't mean anything."

The door was pushed open wider and Woollgar came in. The suit he wore was expensively soft and beautifully tailored, but shabby and soiled. He looked tired and very much his age, his nose jutting out more than Oliver remembered, the veins in his face and hands prominent and blue, the flesh shrinking to show the structure of the underlying bones.

"Sorry I kept you waitin'," he said pleasantly. "I was repottin' in the conservatory and you can't just drop it." There was a gentle amiability about him and he seemed pleased to see Oliver. He offered his hand. "I'm glad you called," he smiled. "I've been worryin' about you'.'

"There's no need, sir. No bones broken."

"Sit down, my dear chap, and make yourself comfortable. I'm havin' a whisky." He looked at the sherry on the arm of Oliver's chair. "I'm sure you'd like something stronger than that."

"I'll join you, sir."

Woollgar spoke to his wife. "You too, Cynthia?"

She shook her head. "I told Mr Missen about Philip." It was a small warning.

"Astonishin'," he murmured. "You really are like him. Amazin' coincidence." He was pouring out generous measures from a bottle. "Shook me rather. Thought I'd seen a ghost. A queer feelin'."

"So Lady Woollgar told me. I'm sorry if I remind you too much of him." Oliver could feel the woman's steady gaze on him and something about it chilled him.

"Not at all. Never seen anythin' like it. Bar that moustache of yours, of course." He gave Oliver his tumbler of whisky. "Cheers," he said, "and damnation to the Hun." He waited until his wife was seated, then took a chair opposite Oliver and relaxed himself in it, looking like a benign and weary eagle. "Been up nearly all dam' night," he said. "Wastin' time. No need for the Home Guard now. Too old and too bloody useless." It wasn't clear whether he was referring to the Home Guard or himself. "You flyin' those Typhoons we have racketin' around?"

"We do an odd spot of rhubarbing in them now and again."

"Fighter boys, eh?"

"We were." Oliver didn't think he was giving aid and comfort to the enemy by disclosing that, but caution was necessary. Woollgar was, or had been, a lieutenant-colonel and might have strong views on what he thought was careless talk. He was a man, he judged, who would prefer to eat his Germans alive and raw. "We now shoot up trains and Panzer columns, flak-boats and radar installations. Airborne firing squads," he said deprecatingly with a downward turn of his mouth. "If we barge into any of the Luftwaffe boys we think we're lucky. Your son-in-law was on bombers?"

"Yes. A fine young fella. Didn't give a damn for the danger." His face saddened. "That's the curse of war. Takes all the youngsters with spunk and leaves us old veterans doin' nothing."

"Not so very old, sir, if I may say so." He could see that Lady Woollgar was displeased about something.

Woollgar snorted in the back of his nose. "You tell that to the Staff-wallahs at the War Office. All I could screw out of them was a commission as major in the Home Guard. Well, it was the Local Defence Volunteers then. A *major*," he repeated with disgust. "I was a major back in 1916 in a real army and ..."

"You were going to speak to Mr Missen about his car, Clive," Lady Woollgar interrupted. She sounded as if she had heard it all *ad nauseam* and wished to stop his launching into infinities of nostalgic reminiscences.

Inconsequentially, Oliver wondered how accessible a wife could be – she wouldn't be more than forty-five and still emanated a sexual attraction – with a much older husband who must have reached the end of his working married life. Now and then he thought he could recognize a weighing-up of his potentialities behind her cool regard of him. Cynthia. Just the name did things to him. It fitted her perfectly and he had not fornicated with a Cynthia before. Given the opportunity, he could think of no good reason why he should not. Beneath her aloof chilliness he chose to recognize her as a real ball-breaker of a woman given the right man. When their eyes met he let his interest show, believing she couldn't help but be flattered by the admiration of a younger man. There was nothing unusual in his attitude. On meeting any woman not unsuited to his taste by age or physical grossness, his mind automatically stripped her body of its clothing and put her naked in bed with him, savouring in imagination the fleshy pleasures of her. It was, he assumed, what any normally equipped male would do.

Woollgar stood and reached for a small cedarwood drum on a table and opened it, taking from it a slim green cigar. "You care for these things?" he asked Oliver. He hadn't looked at his wife or acknowledged that she had spoken.

"No thank you, sir. I'll stay with the cigarettes."

Woollgar returned to his chair and began to pierce the cigar carefully as though it was the last one he possessed. "How did you get here?" he asked amiably. "Your car back on the road?"

"No. It's a write-off. I borrowed one."

"From what you said at the time, I take it you weren't insured."

Oliver grinned. "One of those little things that slips the mind."

Woollgar grunted behind his cigar. "That brings me to the point. I feel responsible for what happened – I was usin' most of the road – and I hope you won't be offended." He chose his words carefully, squinting at the rising smoke from his cigar. "There's an old car of mine in the garage that Philip used and I wouldn't be seen dead in it myself. It seems a pity it should stay there and rust. I'd be happy if you would take it away. Truthfully, my dear chap, I can do with the room."

Oliver was surprised and showed it. "That's very generous of you, sir," he said, "but I couldn't poss—"

"Dammit! Of course you can." He was brusque. "Borrow it if you must, but use it. My daughter . . . it'd be better out of the way. Can only bring back memories, you know. Eh?" He spoke to his wife. "I think Laura would like to meet Mr Missen, my dear."

She looked from him to Oliver and back again, not managing to conceal the beginning of a frown before he had seen it. "I'm sure that Mr Missen will understand, but would that be a good thing?"

"That's dam' silly," Woollgar said mildly. "She can't hide away for the rest of her life." There was an echo of a previous domestic discord in his words. "Be a good girl and bring her in."

There was a firm insistence in his voice and she stared at him with warning signals in her eyes, her lips compressed, the presence of Oliver obviously acting as a constraint to her objections. She stubbed her cigarette out in an ashtray in a gesture of annoyance and rose, leaving the room without a further word.

Oliver felt that he was the innocent bystander in the middle, being neither able to say he didn't mind not seeing her and possibly offending Woollgar, nor to say he would like to and certainly earning his wife's displeasure. Of one thing he was positive. Had he been out of earshot, she would not have submitted quite so tamely to Woollgar's gentle insistence.

Five

When Laura had seen the Telegraph Messenger cycling along the drive towards the house, she had gone to answer his ringing at the door like a woman going to the scaffold. That she had expected it hadn't made it any easier, but she was glad her father and stepmother were out. She had given the boy a shilling before opening the telegram, refusing to show her inner perturbation but knowing that the blood had drained from her face.

IMMEDIATE FROM AIR MINISTRY KINGSWAY. REGRET TO INFORM YOU THAT YOUR HUSBAND FLYING OFFICER PHILIP GEOFFREY GRAHAM IS REPORTED MISSING AS THE RESULT OF AIR OPERATIONS 31ST MARCH 1944 STOP ENQUIRIES ARE BEING MADE THROUGH INTERNATIONAL RED CROSS GENEVA STOP ANY FURTHER INFORMATION RECEIVED WILL BE IMMEDIATELY COMMUNICATED TO YOU STOP LETTER CONFIRMING WILL FOLLOW.

At first she had felt numb and incapable of anything but the awareness of stumbling to her bedroom, the telegram still held in her shaking fingers. There, the strength went from her legs and she sat on the edge of the bed and wept. She knew he was dead, the telegram only the confirmation of a premonition of tragedy she had lived with for the weeks Philip had been on his operational tour.

The letter came two days later, telling her that Philip and his crew, engaged in a night bombing raid on Nuremburg, had failed to return. It added that this did not necessarily mean that he had been killed or wounded and that if he was a prisoner-of-war he should be able to communicate with her in due course. It had been an official optimism that did nothing to shake her conviction that he was dead.

When the second telegram came she was already living in a melancholy world of shades of grey and white, of muffled sounds and a need to be left alone with her misery like a sick cat. She had nightmarish dreams of Philip screaming from a distorted face as he plunged from a black sky in his burning bomber, feeling his terror and the final agony of his mutilated body burying itself in the ground. This recurred nightly and she lived in its shadow in the days that followed.

FROM AIR MINISTRY KINGSWAY. DEEPLY REGRET TO INFORM YOU THAT YOUR HUSBAND FLYING OFFICER PHILIP GEOFFREY GRAHAM IS NOW REPORTED HAVING LOST HIS LIFE AS A RESULT OF AIR OPERATIONS ON 31ST MARCH 1944 STOP LETTER CONFIRMING THIS TELEGRAM FOLLOWS STOP THE AIR COUNCIL EXPRESS THEIR PROFOUND SYMPATHY STOP UNDER SECRETARY OF STATE AIR MINISTRY.

That had added bitterness to the bitterness already in her and she had refused to read the letter that she knew could only increase her anguish. With an odd sense of resentment, she found that Philip's death did nothing to lessen the appetites of her body. There was still a hunger for good food, a thirst for her pink gins and a continuing addiction to cigarettes. Seven brief months of marriage with only an occasional forty-eight-hours' leave from his squadron had aroused in her a need for the sublimities of her husband's body that had derived from the warm and loving personality now gone from her. She was a young woman with unexpended physical passions in her, not an elderly and used-up widow left with the withered memories of a lifetime of diminishing needs. Faced now with a lonely sterility, there had been occasions when the urgings of her body had almost taken control of her mind, when she had been tempted to give it without affection (and that was necessary) to the first available man, partly to subdue its hunger for thrusting masculinity and partly to exorcize the desolate sense of loss she thought would be otherwise always with her.

For a month she had stimulated her memory of him by using the things he had used, brooding over his photographs and the letters he had written to her. She had gone to the garage and sat in the driving seat of the car he had used, holding the steering wheel and stabbing herself painfully by knowing that it had last been touched by his hands, that its leather-covered rim must still have on it some of the essences of his body. After that her own contact had nullified its association with him and there had been no second time, the car ceasing to mean anything to her.

She remembered saying light-hearted things to him about the obituary columns in the *Daily Telegraph*; that nobody ever had the moral courage or honesty to describe anyone as being other than devoted, everloving or so sadly missed, and that those who had died seemed to have done so conveniently and neatly in alphabetical order. Death had happened to other people then. Now the reading of casualty lists gave her a perverse sort of comfort of which she was ashamed, a shared satisfaction that she had not been singled out alone.

Chambers, the kindly and well-meaning Rector of Dunsham St Michael, had called and in between sherries had tried to console her with remote platitudes about heaven and angels and Philip's being in the presence of an everloving God. It had been no comfort at all and she had been repelled by his complacent certainty of a state in which she could not believe. There had been nothing in what he said to compensate her for Philip's lost love and the tenderness of his physical presence. Chambers had offered to pray with her and she had refused, telling him that she thought it was a little late for that and where had his merciful and compassionate God been when her Philip was dying his terrible death. Certainly not, she said, with Philip or with any of the other thousands of men slaughtered in a war not of their making.

She had gone to a spiritualist medium, an elderly, fat, white-haired man with a calm and assured manner whose wife left them together in their sitting-room while she made tea for them. That had been no good either, the man confessing his inability on that occasion to contact Philip's spirit, although he thought he had sensed him trying to make contact. He told her that there was no death as she understood it and that if she persisted her husband would make himself known to her. He refused to take the fee she had offered him and asked her to come again. But she hadn't.

When she had finally accepted that it really was happening to her and that Philip had gone irrevocably, an inner anger fed her bitterness and she became brittle and hard. She had never worn black as a sign of her mourning and she began to cultivate the outward show of a woman who had now accepted that she could no longer live with the dead.

She heard the car being brought to a halt outside and the slamming of its door with no interest at all. It was pink gin time and a good enough reason not to get out of her chair to see who was calling. Whoever it was would probably be boring and she preferred the company of Salchen, her black-and-tan dachshund bitch, who shared the chair with her.

Drinking gin and angostura bitters in the late morning could give her a gritty irritability with people which was quite different from the floating smoothness induced by her drinking of it in the evening. Because of it, she chose to do her morning drinking in her own room, away from the careful conversation of her too-solicitous father and stepmother who ostentatiously avoided any but the most necessary references to Philip.

When her stepmother came in, her second glass was half-emptied.

"We have a visitor, Laura," she said. "That RAF pilot we told you about. The one in the car accident. He's in the drawing-room and your father thinks you should meet him."

Laura pulled a face. "Bloody hell! Need I?"

"No, you needn't. But I'm afraid your father's in one of his insistent moods." She hesitated. "We didn't tell you before, but I should warn you that this man looks very much like Philip." Her face was expressionless. "If you aren't feeling well I can give him your apologies."

"You don't think I should see him?" She resented her stepmother suggesting an excuse for her against the wishes of her father. There had been a coolness and constraint between the two women since Laura had realized that her stepmother held her father in barely concealed contempt and that whatever love had been in her for him had long since dissipated into their sleeping in separate rooms and treating each other with unemotional politeness. Philip's death had warmed briefly a sympathy between Laura and her stepmother, but that had cooled after a few weeks. She now felt the first prick of her irritability and it altered her immediate inclination not to see the man.

"It may upset you. It hasn't been all that long, has it."

"Mother, I'm not a little girl. He *isn't* Philip and I'm not likely to be upset."

"It rather upset your father and me." Then she added, "He wishes to give him the MG."

Laura shrugged her indifference. "Why not? And why does father want me to meet him?"

"I suppose because he's a guest and he feels that you should."

"And you don't?"

"I think it better not. We aren't likely to see him again."

Laura stood and lifted Salchen to the floor. "Don't worry, Mother, I shan't go into a swoon. I agree with Father. I think I should meet him. What's his name?"

"Missen. He's a flying officer." She was tight-faced with disapproval. "I don't think he is quite . . ." Which meant that despite his having been commissioned, she had labelled him not the product of a public school and therefore someone to be kept at a distance. Although she would never say it so bluntly, she would have called him a temporary gentleman destined to be relegated to the *hoi polloi* with the ending of the war.

"For heaven's sake," Laura said sharply, her irritation rising, "you're being so bloody snobbish. And please stop trying to put a wall around me."

Despite her assurance that meeting the man would not affect her, it did. He lifted himself out of his chair as she entered the room behind her stepmother and turned to her.

Dear God, she moaned to herself, *Philip*. There was a sudden weakness in her legs and her heart seemed to trip and then thump loudly. Nothing of it showed in her face as she walked towards him.

Without the moustache he could be Philip standing there, his back to the fireplace where he had so often stood. The same achingly familiar features: the narrow cheeks and nose, the black brows over eyes that were a deeper brown than Philip's. Not, she felt, quite so frank and forthcoming and with cynicism in them. A stranger's eyes and that stopped her from making a fool of herself. The moustache made him look older than he probably was. He wore his pale blue uniform with panache and she knew that on his head his cap would be tilted sideways and not square over his forehead.

Her father, benignly as though giving her a present, said, "This is Mr Missen, my dear."

She gave him her hand and smiled, feeling nothing in it that would distinguish it from her holding a glove.

He held it a fraction longer than he need have. "Hello," he said. It was a moment in which he normally worked at projecting his masculinity. With a recently widowed woman he was at a loss and he returned her smile only briefly. He saw her as a slim girl in a plain white dress, her deep blue eyes heavy-lidded, her black hair hanging loose and glossy to her shoulders. Her skin was pale and smooth, her only make-up the red paste on her mouth. The scent she wore disturbed him as, always, it did on a woman and he knew immediately that if he could he would have her.

She made her voice steady with an effort, conscious of her stepmother watching. It provoked in her a lightness of manner. "You don't look any the worse for it," she said.

"I'm sorry?" She had baffled him with her very first words.

"The accident. I thought you'd be done up in splints and things." She was studying his face. "You are like him, you know. Very much so."

"You mean, like your husband?" He was cautious with no more flippancy.

"Yes, but in a different kind of way. As if you were a twin. No, perhaps more a brother." She held his gaze calmly. "I'm embarrassing you?"

"No." But he wanted her to drop it, beginning to feel like a freak with peculiar abnormalities. He was himself and owning to enough ego to resent looking like somebody else. "I was sorry to hear of your loss, Mrs Graham."

"Yes," she said, frowning slightly as though resenting being reminded of his death by him, and added nothing more.

That discomposed him also. He should have remembered that condolences from a stranger were usually an intrusion. "Your dog doesn't appear to like me." He smiled to make his remark a humorous one. The dachshund behind her had been growling softly at him. "The other two didn't seem to mind."

"She's forgetting her manners, but she's like that with strange men." She spoke to her father. "Would you pour me a drink, darling? And shut up, Salchen," she said to the dog. She returned her attention to Oliver. "What do you fly?"

"Tiffies – Typhoons. We probably keep you awake at night."

"I've heard you going over," she said, "and that's an understatement. You're at Wallisham?"

He grinned. Off the subject of her dead husband, he thought he could get on with her. "For my sins. It's a bit of a dump."

"And operational?" Something perverse in her wanted this man to be living as perilously as had Philip. There were no decoration ribbons under his wings and he would have been less in her eyes were he to be non-operational.

"I do get shot at occasionally," he admitted, "and the food's bad in the Mess."

Woollgar handed his daughter her drink and said, "I hope you don't mind, my dear, but I've offered Mr Missen the use of the MG to replace his own."

"Of course not." She lifted the glass of pink stuff and said, "*Gott mit uns*. I'll show it to you." She spoke to her stepmother: "Perhaps Mr Missen would care to stay for luncheon?"

"We would be delighted." She had said it after only the briefest of hesitations and Oliver wasn't sure how delighted she actually was. He thought she might be over-protective towards her daughter against a man with as little a future as the dead Philip.

"Thank you," he said, "but I do have to be back on duty this morning." He looked at his watch. "In fact, I'll have to be leaving soon."

"Then you'd better look at the car now," Laura said.

With the dachshund following close at her heels, she made polite conversation with him on their way through the house to the courtyard at its rear, drawing from him that his home was in Dorset, that his father was a partner in a firm of architects and that he had no intention of returning there should he survive the war. It was a civilized, peripheral curiosity and not the stuff on which he could start to build a sexual understanding.

He was impressed with the evidence of money in the house, realizing that he could do worse than to get established there. He knew the old boy approved of him; being an officer in one of the fighting services was enough. That he could mollify and disarm Lady Woollgar's apparent disapproval he had few doubts. He had fewer still about the woman at his side. Looking at her as he talked, he made naked in his mind the mounds of her breasts beneath the austere white dress, the soft swelling of her hips and the long smooth curves of her thighs. There was a sensuality in her mouth that invited masculine exploitation – what he called tuft-hunting – and he was certain that he could have her. He sensed that she was interested in him, showing it in her eyes above the banality of their conversation. He understood women as he understood the aerodynamics of his Typhoon. They were the two accomplishments on which he prided himself: the techniques of flying and of making love. For him, they had much in common. He let her see and recognize his sexual awareness of her. That was the basic cockpit drill, the requisite of pushing the right buttons, making the necessary contacts for a smooth and coordinated take-off. He accepted without false modesty that he looked good; his hair black, his teeth white, his slim and muscular body smoothly shaven and manicured. Women were attracted by his charm and modesty and by his obvious interest in them. He was deferential to their wishes, attentive and well-mannered. He flattered, often with a creamy liberality, and never omitted the small gift, chosen carefully to underline his sincerity. He spent money on them in other ways for he had learned early that women had a distaste for penny-pinching men, that they considered it their privilege that a man should unload a ready wallet for their pleasure. Above all, he had an unblushing readiness to allow them to believe that he was in love with them. This, he had discovered, was the essential armament needed to penetrate a woman's defences. There was little else he needed to do to provoke in them the decision to permit his access to their bodies. That he resembled this woman's dead husband was fortuitous, his death a gap in her life into which he was preparing to insinuate himself.

The courtyard was paved with old, dark red bricks, moss-covered in patches from the lack of horses to walk on them. Unflowered geraniums in earthenware pots stood in carefully tended rows at the foot of the enclosing walls. There were three stable doors, all needing repainting. She unlatched one and he moved quickly to open it for her. Inside, it smelled of long-gone hay and horse manure. A green MG Midget looked tiny in the loosebox in which it stood, its nose beneath the empty hay-rack. It was a familiar enough model to him with its folded canvas hood, long upswept mudguards over wire-spiked wheels and a slabbed back with a spare strapped to it. A two-seater, it would be used to its best advantage in getting to a roadhouse with a heavy wallet and in the company of a woman who didn't mind the rush of wind through her hair. It was Oliver's sort of car.

"May I sit in it?" he asked.

"Of course. That was the general idea." There was a faintly amused expression on her face.

He put on his cap and fitted himself into the cramped seat, holding the steering wheel and reading the dials on the instrument panel. The speedometer went to 70 mph, but he knew that she wouldn't do much more than 60 flat out. The mileage was recorded as just over 8000 so, although five or six years old, she hadn't been used much. Petrol rationing had done that. Against Emergency Regulations, the key was in the ignition. He turned it on, pumped the accelerator pedal and pressed the starter button. The engine made a satisfactory clamour in the confines of the loosebox and he switched it dead, before climbing out.

"It's very generous of you," he said. "I had to borrow the one I came in." In case she thought him unable to do so and to minimize any suggestion of patronage that there might be in the giving, he added, "It seemed hardly worthwhile considering buying another." He lowered his voice. "Come invasion and we shall almost certainly be moving to France. After that ..." He pushed out his bottom lip wryly.

"You sound as though you don't expect to survive. Isn't that rather defeatist?"

He shrugged. "Statistics are against it. You've only got to be in the wrong place at the wrong time. I'm sorry, am I being pessimistic?"

"Rather. Philip never doubted that he would survive." A shadow crossed her face. "Not that it altered ... well, it happened."

"I'll go on being pessimistic." Because her parents had probably mentioned he had been with Morwenna at the time of the accident, he added, "Which is why, I suppose, I've not married. But I'm engaged," he smiled. "To a seven-ton lady with wings who's a very demanding mistress. She's also very beautiful and fast and all I have."

She was serious, not responding to his flippancy. "You should be grateful you are not."

He understood what she meant. "I am. It's no job for a married man." He hesitated. "Does my resemblance to him disturb you?"

She regarded him expressionlessly. "I've come to terms with his dying, Mr Missen. Why do you ask?"

"Only ..." He hesitated again. "I was hoping that it wouldn't stop my seeing you again. No," he cut himself short, a man who had realized that he was being too brash and who was angry with himself. "I'm sorry. I shouldn't have said that." He wished he could have said bluntly that he wanted her; wanted her scented desirable body because that was how he reacted to beautiful women. And so much more with this one because there was a war on and he could – probably would – be killed doing his stuff for Merrie England and was it too much to ask that she should send him on his way with the memory of her naked body having been given to him?

"Perhaps you had better make up your mind one way or the other," she said, almost as though she had read his thoughts.

"We've only just met, Mrs Graham, and I'm very conscious of ... frankly, I let my own wishes run away with my discretion. I'm sorry if I've embarrassed you."

"You haven't." But she wasn't helping him either.

He put sincerity in his voice and looked away from her. "Do you mind if I say that I find you unsettling?" Before she could answer, he said, "That must sound infernal cheek but it's meant sincerely. I hope you don't resent it.'

"No, I don't, but I'm not quite sure how to take it." Her expression was neutral, giving him no encouragement to continue.

He gave her the impression that he was groping reluctantly for the right words, but wanting to say much more. "You don't need me to tell you how extraordinarily attractive you are to a man." He grinned. "Dammit, I'm not very good at this, am I?"

"You haven't done too badly so far. And you don't need to flatter me." There was a hint of mockery in her voice and he could sense that she was studying his face. "I'd rather you didn't assume that because ... because I'm a widow I'm also a recluse."

He returned his gaze to her. "No, I won't. I didn't mean to. Look," he said impulsively, "could I take you out for a drive in the car sometime? I do get off duty now and then. I know a place not too far from here which still has some decent food and wine."

Letting him wait for her answer, she thought of the bleakness of her aloneness, of her need for physical masculinity. The chemistry of her body was attracted to him by his resemblance to Philip and, on his own account, by his poorly concealed admiration, evident in the way in which he had eyed her breasts and thighs. He was nothing if not obvious in what he wanted and, given the right circumstances and an acceptable approach, she knew that she would give herself to him. He might be the anaesthetic she needed to numb the pain of her loss.

"You'll find me in the telephone directory," she said coolly, not intending that he should find his taking her anything but difficult. "And now you'd better see my father about collecting the car."

Six

When Philip woke there was a greyness that was neither darkness nor light, its thin opacity a hangover from the previous night. The tumbledown ruins of the farm shed in which he had taken shelter looked down on a mist-enshrouded valley of brown and green fields and clumps of trees coming into leaf. A small river, grey and sullen, ran through a huddle of houses not far below him. There were people moving and doing things, but no sound of their activity penetrated his deadening deafness.

Periodically and without effect he would pinch his nostrils between finger and thumb and blow to clear the eustachian tubes in his ears. His inability to hear anything worried him for, apart from being a danger to him in his present predicament, permanent deafness would finish him as Air Crew and leave him with a crippling impairment in almost every aspect of his life; never to hear Laura's voice again, the music they both loved or the words of his fellow men. With the isolating apartness was still a mental confusion, a sense of displacement, of acute sorrow and depression. At the back of his mind was a vast unease which he fought against bringing forward and recognizing.

Before finding the shed in which he had slept there had been long interminable hours of walking through a dark countryside, sleeping and anonymous in its strangeness. When he came to buildings and roads he avoided them where possible. Occasionally he saw lights and, once, had stumbled away in sudden fright from a railway track as a locomotive and train of carriages rushed silently at him from behind. He had felt only the vibrations of its coming through the sleepers on which he had been walking. Later, a large Alsatian dog had come upon him and barked without sound, showing its teeth and bristling its neck hairs as if it were as frightened as himself. When he stood still, unbreathing and trying not to let it smell his fear, it backed away and left him. He had run then, blindly and awkwardly in his flying suit and boots, for although he had not heard the dog's barking others could and they would come searching for him with guns and more dogs.

He had lost count of time, his watch having stopped and refusing to restart. Sometimes his memory of leaving the scene of his burning Lancaster made it a few hours ago; at other times, days and weeks back in the past, separated from his now-ness by the seeming endlessness of his confused wandering. Even though an enemy in a strange and hostile country, he needed to talk to somebody. He knew, as he had never known before, that the ultimate wretchedness was to be alone. When this nostalgia for human companionship hit him, he was tempted to allow himself to be captured. If that was to be his destiny then whatever he did or did not do wouldn't change it. If it was intended that he should return to Laura, then he would. He recognized it as fatalism, a flaccid surrender to events, but it eased the conflict in his mind.

When he saw the lights of a Panzer column moving along the road on which he was walking – one of the few occasions when forced to – he had been tempted. He stood in the darkness on the verge, not attempting to conceal himself but allowing chance alone to decide his capture or otherwise without doing anything about it. The tanks rumbled past him silently, although he could feel the vibration of their heavy passage through the soles of his boots, near enough for him to see the helmeted heads and shoulders of the observers in the open turrets, to read the insignia and numbers painted on the steel flanks. He had not been seen or, if he had, not recognized in the darkness as an enemy airman. It gave him a brief confidence that he was not to finish in a prison camp.

In the near dawn of the past day with the lightening of the sky, he was skirting a copse high on the edge of a cutting through which ran a road. With a shock of surprise he saw three men in the mist, walking away from him towards a bend in the road. They were shapeless in flying suits and jackets, their leather helmets showing only the tops behind turned-up collars, but easily recognizable as RAF aircrew. They walked openly with no attempt at concealment, purposive in where they were going. Although they were some distance from him, by concentrating his vision he could see clearly the stitching in their helmets and jackets, the zip fasteners in their flying boots. They were real enough and each was staring fixedly ahead. Like, the thought came to him, the walking dead: if they turned he would see their faces as skulls. He had imagined for a wild moment that they were his own crew safely parachuted from the falling aircraft, although reason told him that from the number of Lancasters and Halifaxes he had seen shot down over Nuremburg they need not be. He had shouted, silently to his deafness, but knowing they must hear him as he scrambled down the steep bank in frantic haste. When he reached the road and looked for them, they were rounding the bend and apparently unaware of him. He ran, calling to them that he was an Englishman. '*RAF! RAF!*' he had shouted desperately. When he reached the curve around which they had vanished there was only the mist and an empty road and he was not certain that his disordered mind hadn't materialized them from his imagination. But his sense of loss was acute and he had wept in his wretchedness.

That the men he had seen, or imagined he had seen, had been so easily recognized as aircrew made him even more aware of the impossibility, dressed as he was, of escaping capture. He needed civilian clothing. And, with it, identification papers. To get both he would have to break and enter a house at night and risk almost certain capture; or to find and kill with his bare hands an inoffensive non-combatant civilian. If he could. And were he able to screw himself morally into doing it, which he knew to be impossible. He could never kill in cold blood. He checked himself at that assessment. It wasn't correct. He *could* kill, had killed, civilians in cold blood. And in their hundreds by dropping high explosives and incendiaries on their towns and cities. But not killing as he had been thinking. Not singling out a man he could see and feel as a warm living being and in strangling him – for he could think of no other way – to experience the paroxysms of his death, to suffer his agony with him. And, afterwards, to undress him and put on the still-warm clothing. He shuddered his disgust. There was another reason why he couldn't do it. Speaking no German and caught in the guise of a civilian, he would inevitably be treated as a spy and as inevitably handed over to the Gestapo. There would be no Stalag for him with the companionship of fellow prisoners-of-war, but torture and an ignominious death in the courtyard of a prison. And, thereafter, no Laura. Not seeing her again, nothing but an everlasting night without her.

He had dreamed of her again during his last sleep. It had been as vivid and as frustrating, more incomprehensible, than the other.

He had found himself standing in a small room he didn't recognize. It was furnished as a sitting-room, comfortable and unostentatious. The curtains in the single window had been drawn, shutting out the daylight. Laura sat in a chair, her gloved hands resting on its arms, wearing her hat and coat which, even in the dimness of the room, he recognized. She was pale with an unhappy expression, looking at a man sitting opposite her. He was white-haired and flabby fat and his eyes were closed. As if peering into the man's skull, he saw a small red glow in his brain, waxing and waning like a pulsating ruby. His lips were moving with words Philip could not hear. He had tried desperately to speak to Laura, to tell her that he was coming back to her, but it was as though there was thin glass between them, a barrier neither his voice nor body could penetrate. As he tried to make her hear him the glow in the man's brain began to expand, growing larger like a bursting red sun. He felt irresistibly drawn to it and had fought against being engulfed by it. There had been a heart-stopping jolt and he was running in cold terror across a moonlit landscape, pursued by flickering black shadows he knew to be demonic dogs. His terror woke him to the reality of the debris-cluttered shed on whose floor he had been sleeping. It had been nightmarish and frightening and for minutes he had lain and panted as if he had, in fact, been running for his life.

Laura! Laura! Laura! He repeated her name urgently in his mind, hoping she would receive it telepathically. The dream had filled his brain with her to the exclusion of his terror. He knew she must be thinking of him and it was an insistent pull to be back with her. He could feel it like the exertion of a physical force, overriding what he recognized now as his defeatist impulse to seek capture. She would be suffering, certainly having been informed that he had failed to return from his mission. And if his dreams were anything to go by, believing him to be dead.

He had met her on one of his forty-eight-hour leaves in a first-class compartment of the train to Euston. They were the only occupants and the black-out blinds had been lowered over the windows, the dimmed blue lighting inside making reading painful. This lack of something to occupy him on the journey had made him intensely conscious of her presence. Her eyes had attracted him first when he found her regarding him with a frank and interested stare that had nothing of a sexual challenge in it.

Illuminating their depths he had seen a warm and lovely personality, an inner something that disturbed and excited him. He had met the one other person in the world he knew would be complementary to his own loving. It would have mattered nothing had she been other than the beautiful and elegant woman she was. When the train had been halted outside the station because of an air-raid warning and the lights switched off, he had taken advantage of it and spoken to her, finding a release from the first-class carriage conventions in the sounds of the sirens and the following explosions that bound them to a common danger. He had later escorted her to her hotel and that was the beginning. Since his marriage he had heard the word "uxoriousness" spoken in derision and had been stung enough to check it in a dictionary. "Foolishly or excessively fond of one's wife. Doting on her." Excepting the word "foolishly" he couldn't disagree with the description as applied to himself, not knowing any other that would define his complete identification with her. Without his love for Laura to draw him back to her, he suspected that he might have remained with the carcass of the Lancaster and surrendered himself tamely enough to the prospect of a prison camp.

Because of the comparative security of the mist and the thought of spending more frustrating hours in the squalid shed, he began walking. If the mist cleared then he would find cover until nightfall. He kept to the fields, hidden from casual observation by hedgerows and stone walls, reconnoitring the ground to be covered from the vantage points of coppices and small woods. When he came to a forest he travelled through it, its fir-tree gloominess made more eerie to him by the complete silence, but giving the confidence of concealment. Occasionally he saw people – mostly farm workers – in the fields and vehicles moving along distant roads. Once he saw four men in waterproofs and jackboots, all carrying shotguns and coming towards the wood in which he was resting. At first he had thought they were hunting him until he saw one of them fire at a disturbed rabbit. It had been nerve-racking for him and, because he could not locate their whereabouts in the wood either by the sounds of their moving or the firing of their guns, he had remained hidden in shrubbery for what he judged to be three hours.

While crouched there, a cock pheasant had flown on to a lower branch of the tree overhanging the shrubbery, startling him with its sudden appearance. Like the weasel, it acted as if completely oblivious of his presence although he was clearly visible from above. He thought there might have been a mental togetherness in their both hiding from men with guns. He tightened his stomach muscles and held himself as motionless as the trunk against which he was leaning, frightened that the pheasant would attract the hunters to his hiding place. When it finally flew away, he relied on its instinct for safety and followed it, but still wondering why it had not reacted to his presence.

He came to the river as daylight began to die, first crossing a two-track railway after putting his hand on the lines to detect the vibrations an approaching train would make. The ground sloped steeply and became spongy as he stumbled his way through outcrops of rock and clumps of reed-like grasses. The mist had thickened so that when he reached the river's bank he could not see its further side. He stood in the gathering gloom, baffled by this impassable barrier. Physically he wasn't fatigued, but his mind felt as though at any moment it would slide sideways into a black chasm. He tried to re-create a map of southern Germany with what imagery it was now capable. This was a wide river that could be the Rhine. If it was, he thought that he could remember that it originated in the mountains of Switzerland. Or was that the Rhone? He had always been so bloody useless at geography. No, it had to be the Rhine. It was flowing from his left to the right so now he could orientate to Switzerland and France which should be in front of him. He was certain – almost certain – that in this part of Germany the Rhine marked the frontier with France. If this were so, how had he reached it so quickly? Or had he? The unknown number of days and nights he had been walking had merged into a formless and timeless grey blur with interludes only of sleeping his anguished and nightmarish dreams. Now he couldn't be sure of anything other than the compulsion of his irresistible need to return to Laura.

Fighting against his desire for sleep, he turned and followed the river against the flowing of its water. It was close to being dark when the bridge loomed above him, its iron stanchions and girders wet and reflecting the dying light of day. It was narrow and appeared to carry the railway he had earlier crossed. He could see the outline of the top of a guard post hut at its nearer end. As he studied its structure for a means of crossing without passing the hut, the head and upper trunk of a German soldier appeared between the spandrels of the parapet. He had an automatic rifle slung over his shoulder and his helmet obscured the face that was turned in Philip's direction. There was a fixity of attention in the way his body was held like a gundog pointing.

Philip held himself rigid and unbreathing, his fear drying his mouth. Although standing in the shadow of the bridge, he knew that he must be visible as a darker mass to the guard. If he shouted at him, challenged him, he wouldn't be able to hear and that would provoke a firing of the rifle. Part of him wanted to step out from the shadow with his arms above his head in surrender. Instead he closed his eyes, believing that it would make him less conspicuous were their whites not showing, retreating within his mind and bracing himself for the killing impact of bullets in his body.

Seven

The Crew Room was warm from the black Tortoise stove standing between the windows with its iron pipe rising through a hole in the ceiling. Coloured models of German fighter planes hung by thread from exposed unpainted joists and the walls were papered with profile and plan silhouettes of armoured vehicles and flak-ships. Blackout curtains kept from the night outside the yellowish light from unshaded bulbs. The thin walls vibrated with the sounds of engines being run up and tested.

Oliver was with seven other pilots, officers and sergeants, who sat on wooden chairs and on the large table in the centre, sharing it with parachutes that had been pushed to one side to make room. Tobacco tin lids were used as ashtrays and the air was thick with cigarette smoke.

Flight Lieutenant Poxton remained standing with his cap on to indicate his apartness and that what he had to say was as their newly appointed Flight Commander. A rufous-haired man with foxy features and daunting grey eyes, he wore a brass A in each lapel of his tunic to signify his was a pre-war Auxiliary commission. The faded purple-and-white ribbon of a DFC was stitched beneath his equally faded wings. He was unsmiling, looking as if about to be unpleasant.

"Right, chaps," he said brusquely. "Settle down and listen to me. I've one or two things to say before the pre-briefing." He let his hard stare meet the eyes of each of the assembled pilots. "Intention. This is a Mark One rocket. I'm not happy with your performance as a Flight. Bluntly, you're scruffy, bloody idle and your morale is nothing to write home about." He bared his teeth and that made him look even more foxy. "And that's a reflection on me. Which I'm not going to accept. You're acting like a shower of pricks with your fingers well in. We've got too many kites unserviceable due to sheer bloody carelessness and bad flying discipline; too many ops scrubbed or going off half-cocked because we can't get enough of them off the ground. Group is asking what the hell is going on and I have had to make excuses for you."

If the pilots were resenting his tearing them off a strip, they weren't foolish enough to show it, keeping their feelings behind impassive features and for the most part convincing themselves it was the others he was talking about.

"All right, so you think you've come down in the world. So you're fighter-pilots bellyaching about being airborne artillery. Well, you're it, you're going to stay it and you'd better get used to it. I know you don't go mad on brewing up trains and knocking out flak-ships. Who the hell does? So we've lost more than a few doing it. If any of you think that's a good argument for not giving your damnedest, there's always a way out." He glared at them challengingly. "And I know none of you would want to take it. What we're doing is more essential to the strategy of the invasion than the knocking down of a few bandits. You can't argue that every ammo train we clobber means less for the Krauts to chuck at the brown jobs when our own Der Tag comes. And the more flak-ships we can send to the bottom, the easier they'll get across the Channel." He was visibly winding himself up. "Our kill–loss ratio isn't anything to boast about either. The flak's bad. Of course it is. It's bloody murderous at times and it's meant to be. But that's no reason for not pressing home our attacks. You know as well as I do that you're more likely to be hit turning away from an attack than going straight into it."

That was sophistry, but he was the sort of man who would do it himself without giving a damn for all the flak the Germans could fling up at him. Oliver, for all the heroics, knew that he preferred being a very-much-alive and undecorated Flying Officer than being the recipient of a posthumous DFC.

Poxton regarding them sombrely. "Sometimes I believe that all you think about is getting back to your boozing and to how many women you can bang off before you get the chop. And when you aren't doing that, you sit around like a lot of bloody grandmothers because some of us have bought it. Let me remind you. The bomber squadrons are losing more men than we are or ever shall, so thank your lucky stars you aren't with them." His voice sharpened with all the authority of his two rings. "*Pull your bloody fingers out!* I mean to have a flight that hasn't got half its kites lying around useless on the tarmac and, when they do get in the air, aren't piloted by banged-up layabouts."

He waited until he thought it had all sunk in, daring any one of them to contradict him, then continuing more amiably. "All right, chaps, you know what I mean. We're supposed to be the cream of the Air Force, so let's prove it." He looked at his watch. "We've a very special sortie for first light tomorrow morning. We shall be taking some Tiffy-bombers with us to do a demolition job on a château. It's heavily defended, so it's no cushy number. I shall be going and I want five volunteers."

As he put up his arm with the others, Oliver thought wryly that to ask for volunteers like this was a no-option demand. Nobody would have the stomach not to. He decided that he didn't like Poxton. He was the personification of men who charged dumb-headed into barbed wire and bullets, willing to die and to have other less stupid men die with them.

Poxton looked them over critically. He hadn't flown with them long but, so far as their records showed, he knew what each should be able to do. "Kelham," he said, "Missen and Rogers. Sergeants Mitchell and Tunnard. You other two", he added as though apologizing for their omission, 'will fly with B Flight, so get genned up on the puffer-trains that've been lined up for tonight.'

When the unchosen pilots had gone and the door closed behind them, Poxton moved one of the chairs nearer to the group and sat. He accepted a cigarette from Rogers's proffered packet to show that there were no hard feelings on his part.

"Right," he started, "this is a short pre-briefing session that'll not be discussed outside this room. The full briefing will be at 03.00 hours and you can get some rest in between now and then. It's a beautiful little job," he said, almost with affection, "with a target that'll make your mouths water. Field Marshal von Rundstedt." He paused to enjoy the surprise on their faces. "He's a very good reason for our keeping it under our caps. Apart from the hot reception we'd meet if the Krauts got to know."

"He's got his headquarters in Paris," Oliver said. It didn't make it anything like a mouth-watering target.

"So he has." Poxton obviously thought that Oliver was being too clever. "But we've good information that he and his Chief of Staffs are visiting the 12th SS Panzer Division Headquarters at ..." He looked at a piece of paper he had taken from his pocket.

"... at the Château Coulmier. Which is a few kilometres south-west of Versailles. So far as we know, he and his staff are staying overnight. With a bit of luck, the top brass of the Panzer Division will be there, too." When Rogers started to say something, he said, "Just a minute, Hugh, let me give it to you first." He smiled at Rogers, which he hadn't done at Oliver. "We shall be escorting four Bomphoons from 207 Airfield. They'll be carrying two 500-pounders each and will be doing most of the dirty work. You, Charles," he said to Kelham, "will be leading the way in with me. Our job will be the initial knocking out of the flak guns they've set up on the château. Oliver, Hugh, Sergeants Mitchell and Tunnard, you'll be riding guard on the Bomphoons; line astern in twos on starboard and port. You'll be dealing with any enemy interception there might be *en route*. If you do have to, we shan't be waiting. Just keep them off our backs until we're safely on the run-in to the target. Once we are it's essential that you keep the flak guns around the château under control, draw their fire away from the Bomphoons."

He looked at the paper again. "We shall be flying a diversionary course to a place called Drieux as a feint, then turning to approach the château from the west. There's a lake, the Etang de St Quentin. It's about two kilometres long and leads us virtually to the front door of the château. Which makes it a piece of cake for navigation. We'll be going in at zero feet so that the bomber boys can drop their loads through the windows, when we hope the bastards are all in bed and von Rundstedt gets one of them right up his backside." He smiled happily. "Not forgetting our rockets and shells. Because of the diversion we'll need extra fuel and we're being fitted with drop tanks. Which means only two pairs of rockets each, but they'll be enough to half flatten the château and all who sail in her."

"The Frogs'll love us busting up one of their châteaux," Oliver murmured. It wasn't really meant for Poxton.

"So bugger the Frogs. They'll be putting up with worse than that before we've finished." He put the paper back in his pocket. "You'll be shown photographs of the château and the approach to it at the briefing. I told you that it won't be a cushy number and I mean it. The photographs were taken this morning by a PRU Mosquito from 20,000 feet and show that the Krauts have at least six flak positions in the grounds. More if they've been well camouflaged." He shrugged. "It might mean only the Panzer Division's normal set-up. If we can catch them with their trousers down it won't be too bad. One other thing. There's a squadron of FW 190s based at an airfield four kilometres the Versailles side of the target." He grinned maliciously. "You chaps who've been itching to get at the Luftwaffe again should save yourselves a cannon shell or two. You might very well need them. Any questions?" he ended abruptly.

There weren't many for he had laid it on the line only too clearly and when he had settled the few raised he stood and they stood with him.

"By the way," he said as he moved towards the door, "the op is on, come rain, snow or whatever, so don't get praying for bad weather. No creeping off the airfield or I'll have your skins nailed to the hanger doors." He said it humorously, but nobody was in any doubt that he meant it. "And no boozing tonight. You're off it as from now. I'm not going in with any bugger who's half-squiffed or suffering a hangover."

He hadn't mentioned consorting with women – no doubt because it hadn't occurred to him that any officer or NCO would risk it on his own doorstep – and Oliver, not having been looked at meaningly, accepted it as an indication that his association with Morwenna was as yet unsuspected.

Back in his room, Oliver went to the brown plywood coffin-like box shown on the room's inventory sheet as *Wardrobe, wooden, officer's one*. He had inherited its use from a long line of previous officers, most of them now dead. One had believed Hedy Lamarr to be the Ultima Thule of female desirability, lining the inside of the door with photographs of her. Oliver scarcely glanced at them. Black and white images had never done anything to relieve his itch for warm living flesh or to promote his need for it.

He retrieved the bottle of whisky from where it lay beneath his folded shirts and underclothing and poured an undiluted half-glass of it. Taking it with him he stretched himself out on the bed, a pillow supporting his shoulders against the metal bedhead. He had things to worry about. Poxton's pre-briefing session hadn't filled him with enthusiasm for the forthcoming sortie, although he had adopted the let's-get-in-and-bash-the-bastards attitude expected of the chosen volunteers. It was a natural masculine camouflage, more so for those who felt fear and whose pride would not allow it to show. For Oliver, too many of these optimistically briefed operations had ended in disaster with the pilots getting the chop and he had had a bellyful of them. If there was one man, he told himself, who would do his damnedest to avoid finishing up as a chiselled name on a small town war memorial, it was Flying Officer Oliver Missen.

He drank another whisky, convinced that he flew as well with a couple of glasses of it running through his veins as he could on the tomato juice he had been drinking in the Mess. Alcohol and sex in their proper quantities were the only prophylactics he knew against the fear of death, bridging the period between the anticipation of the event and its actuality. He understood why brothels and booze had in the past been so often included in the logistics of an army.

What the whisky had not done yet was to drown his thoughts about Operation von Rundstedt, due for take-off in seven hours' time. Although they had been given their orders to kill him, it remained an impersonal execution. He could only recall his likeness from photographs, a faceless thin man, corseted and bloody Prussian-rigid in his Wehrmacht Field Marshal's uniform hung about with gold braid, medal ribbons and an Iron Cross with diamonds in it. A man important enough to be hedged around by at least six flak positions. Oliver's mind brought them to the surface in all their menace. Probably heavy stuff, 88 mm or 105 mm that would slice off a wing almost with the wind of their passage, make a smashed shambles of the engine and cockpit if it hit and send a Typhoon hurtling into the ground at over 300 miles an hour with the pilot having no chance of baling out. Whatever else the Germans were short of, it wasn't flak shells. Or quadruple flak guns that could pump them at attacking aircraft at 700 or more rounds a minute. Going in at a defended ground target like the château was the equivalent of an infantryman advancing at a steady walk into the concentrated fire of a cluster of heavy machine-guns.

None of Poxton's happy and confident assurances were of any comfort. This was suicide stuff. For a fighter-pilot, the parachute had been a psychological crutch in combat at thousands of feet upstairs. For airborne artillery, it was merely something soft on which to sit one's backside. Upstairs there had always been the chance of baling out if you were clobbered and your jinking around to get out from under still put you on the losing end of a dog-fight. But you couldn't argue with multiple streams of HE shells coming up at you as you dived towards them.

Death, he told himself, wasn't anything in itself that he feared for the Holy Joes might be right in saying that it might even be an improvement on this life and, at its worst, a state of absolute nothingness. It was the body's painful transition to it that frightened him. He had heard men about to die falling to the earth like burning torches, screaming their agony over the R/T to other men who were still in danger of the same terrible end. He had once heard one calling for his mother and that futile pathos had been the worst of them all.

He groaned and reached down by the side of the bed for the bottle, cursing his over-active imagination. He needed the solace of company in his fears. Returning to the Mess from the pre-briefing, he had tried to read the faces of Poxton, Kelham and Rogers while eating the dehydrated potato and the grey lumps passing as meat. If they had the same forebodings of possible death and disaster as he had they weren't showing it and he envied what he thought was their unimaginative insouciance. At least one – possibly two or three – of them was going to be dead before his meal had been digested and passed from his body. One or two of *us*, he included himself morbidly.

Afterwards, in the makeshift bar, he had sipped at his tomato juice as a token of his compliance with Poxton's orders. Morwenna had been there and, after a period of neither acknowledging the other's presence, she had manœuvred herself to within conversation distance of him.

Behind the uniform there was a clean freshly scrubbed look about her and he caught the faintest whiff of the discreet scent she wore. Her green eyes were troubled and she was unsmiling.

"You're flying in the morning." She made it a statement, her voice low.

"Yes. First light," he answered her. She probably knew that something special was in the offing and was worrying about him. "Briefing at 03.00 hours."

"I have to see you." She was looking away from him. "Can you come?"

"Yes. Twelve-ish?" He was certain they could not be overheard in the hubbub of voices at the bar, but he smoothed his moustache to allow his hand to cover his mouth. "That's not too late?"

She hadn't answered but moved away from him, leaving him to wonder why the hell she had to be so solemn about it. He hoped to God she wasn't going to be tearful and possessive as if this was to be his last night on the bloody earth. That she was apparently so unhappy about his coming operation might mean that what she had heard – and she did occasionally have access to such information through her WAAF channels – was something that worried her. It wasn't anything that gave him confidence.

As he lay on the bed he let his imagination anticipate the marshmallow softness of her pale body, hot and yielding beneath his own. She was a demanding lustful woman on her own admission, unambiguous in her need for him and, until now, had been enough for him. But the image of Mrs Graham – Laura – supervened like a photographic double exposure and he knew that given the choice he would prefer the unexplored strangeness of her harder slimness. If he did make it with Laura, then he had to find a civilized way of detaching himself from Morwenna. It was one of nature's dirty tricks that a woman's intuition could usually detect a man's promiscuities and he was determined not to allow it to cripple the opportunity he had made for himself.

He was feeling more relaxed now, less guilty about the necessity for drinking alone. His eyeballs felt as though they were swimming in their sockets, the skin of his face drum-tight. He had had enough of the whisky were he to be an adequate lover with Morwenna. There was half an inch of it left in his glass. He raised it to the emptiness at the end of the bed, choosing to imagine that the invisible presence of Sir John Jarvis stood there regarding him. Probably balefully because Oliver was still alive, still able to enjoy the pleasures of the flesh.

"Your good health, Sir John," he said, careful with his articulation. "You pox-ridden old bastard!"

He drained the glass, knowing that he must be partly sloshed at least to talk to the ghost of a man who had probably never existed. And, if he had, his death not calling for commiseration. His dying of the pox had been less painful than it would have been had he been shot out of the sky. At least he deserved his pox and had, no doubt, enjoyed his earning of it. Shifting his mind forward to the image of Morwenna – he saw her lying naked and waiting in her bed – he laughed, his tongue feeling large in his mouth. Freud – he thought it was Freud, but some bloody psychologist – had said that the sexual act for a man was a repressed infantile wish to crawl back into the safety of his mother's womb. "Mummy," he said thickly and laughed again, "here I come." He would ask Morwenna what it meant for a woman.

Already he was aware of an anticipatory fluttering in his loins and he swung his legs carefully from the bed, standing and replacing the bottle in the wardrobe. When he had rubbed his teeth with his handkerchief and put on his cap, he opened the bedroom door and listened with the exaggerated caution of a man who had had a quarter of a bottle of whisky too much.

Eight

Morwenna was neither naked nor waiting for him in her bed. He had tapped his fingernail on the window and opened it slowly and noiselessly, holding his unsteadiness together and climbing through the drawn curtains into the room illuminated only by an electric fire. She was sitting in an armchair at its side, fully clothed but for her jacket.

He was surprised and, for a moment, nonplussed. Throwing his cap on to the bed he went to her, holding her arms and stooping to kiss her. Her kiss in return was so lacking in its usual intensity that he had a premonition of impending trouble.

"Sit down, Oliver," she said. "I want to talk to you."

Her husband's on the way back, he thought, as he took the chair opposite her, and she's about to throw me overboard. Despite his own intention of doing the same thing, the immediate prospect didn't please him. Not until he had made sure of Laura. Or – and he went cold at the thought – their sexual intimacy had somehow been discovered. "What's happened, Wenna?" he asked.

In the glow of the fire her expression was sad and lost. "I've been to town today."

"That was nice for you. You enjoyed it?" When she manifestly had not.

"No. I went to see a doctor."

He was confused. "You mean the MO? Why?"

"Not the MO. I was hardly likely to. A civilian doctor." She drew in a deep breath. "I'm pregnant, Oliver." Her eyes were large as she waited for his reaction.

He stared at her, shocked into soberness, the taste of whisky in his mouth suddenly bitter, his heart feeling as if it had dropped into his stomach. Inside he had shrivelled to a smaller man, a resentful man. *You bloody stupid bitch!* he shouted in his mind and, with it, went his desire for her, her body now to him squalid, bloated and disgusting.

"For Christ's sake! How could that happen!" His voice was harsh with anger despite his attempt to soften it.

"I don't know," she said miserably. "I thought you ..."

"I did." But he knew that he hadn't been all that careful on occasions. One spermatozoon, the one tiny malevolent tadpole in a million others had made it to her uterus and it could ruin him. "How certain are you? What did the doctor say?"

"I'm almost certain. So is he. I have to see him again tomorrow." Her eyes brimmed with tears that glistened red, reflecting the bars of the fire. "I'm frightened, Oliver."

"How the hell do you think I feel? You'll have to get rid of it. Have an abortion."

She shuddered. "I can't. I don't want to."

"Don't want to? Christ, you'll have to." His mind searched like a hunted rabbit for a bolt hole. "There are ways. A hot bath, lots of gin, a jump off a bloody chair, slippery elm. And chemists sell pills for this sort of thing. God almighty! What a mess you've got me into!"

She shook her head. "No, I can't." She hesitated. "Do you really love me, Oliver?"

"Of course I do." The lie came automatically and he had told her he did a hundred times. "But you're married and I'm thinking about you. And," he added, "you've got to think about James."

"I am," she said. "I can't go back to him. Not after what we've been to each other. I thought you knew that."

"No, I didn't." He felt trapped, suffocated by her demands on him. He couldn't drag in another man to account for her pregnancy for he knew that he had been her only lover. She was too palpably honest to be promiscuous.

"I'm going to write to him ... tell him."

He groaned. "That's not being fair to the poor bugger."

"And our loving each other is?"

"What he doesn't know won't worry him."

She looked anguished. "That's a terrible thing to say."

"For God's sake, Wenna, don't be so bloody selfish. This isn't only you." He was frustrated with her obstinacy. "I'll be court-martialled, cashiered, Christ knows what!"

"I wouldn't tell them it was you, Oliver," she said simply. "After James has divorced me we can get married. I love you so much."

He stared at her. She had got it all worked out. She was insane! Divorce, marriage, a child! He felt trapped in an imprisoning cocoon of sentimentality and mawkishness. The thought of napkins and talcum powder and drooling toothlessness, of a squalling red-faced shrimp feeding on the breasts to which he had made love revolted him.

He shook his head, compassion in his expression. "That would be wonderful, darling, but I'm not going to allow it to happen. First of all, I could never take another man's wife away from him, no matter how much I loved her. No," he said as she started to speak, "I do have some decency left. The second thing is this." He chewed on his bottom lip, choosing his words carefully. "You know – I know – what the casualty statistics are in this squadron. We've only two pilots left who were with it in '39 and they've been shot down and lucky to walk away from it. So I'm not a good bet for survival." As if to emphasize what he was saying, the sound of approaching engines reached them as Typhoons took off and passed over the building in a thunderous roar that blotted out his words. He waited until their noise had died away and said, "If you go through with this, it'll probably be on your own where I shan't be around to do anything for you." He made his voice earnest. "For your sake. For *its* sake. If there really is an it."

"Don't," she whispered. "I won't believe that. But if you were ... if you were killed, I'd still have something of you."

A fat lot of good that would do him were he dead. He could have hit her in her stupid adoring face. She didn't understand what she was doing to him, that any prospect he might have had with Laura would go down the drain with his fathering of a bastard.

"Ask this doctor of yours, sweetheart," he coaxed her. "Tell him what you do. Persuade him that your having a baby now would be against your absolute indispensability as a WAAF officer. There's a war on and there're millions of people being killed. What's the difference with something that's not yet even a human being?" He felt bitter towards the fœtus held in the darkness of her belly, a mere scrap of jelly yet seeking to claim the rest of his life.

He rose from his chair and knelt before her, putting his arms around her, his face against hers. "*Please*, Wenna," he urged her. "For your sake."

Her arms tightened around him and her mouth sought his. He felt the wetness of her tears on his cheek. "Be kind to me darling. Please love me."

For the first time the softness of her flesh did not stir him and his body remained unresponsive. "No," he said, avoiding her lips, "that's making things worse. Much as I want to, you've made me realize that what we've been doing is wrong." Had there not been the fear that she might still name him as the father of her bastard he would have let his anger explode and told her that she could stew in the juice of her snivelling obstinacy on her own. He wondered whether she had deliberately allowed the conception to trap him into marriage. To hell with her. It wasn't as though she'd cut off an arm or leg for him. She hadn't given him anything that she hadn't wanted herself. The trouble with bloody women was that when they'd made love with a man they thought they owned him, that they'd done him a favour.

He chose his words so that she wouldn't misunderstand him. "Under different circumstances I would want to marry you. Of course I would. I can think of nothing more wonderful. But we have to get things straightened out first." He unwound her arms from him and stood. "Will you, darling?" He reached and smoothed her cheek with his fingers. "Other women have got themselves into this trouble and they've got themselves out."

She must have sensed it in him. "You're angry," she said with a small show of spirit. "Isn't it me who should be?"

"Yes, angry enough to get rid of it."

"It's my body, Oliver, and you're expecting me to have horrible things done to it. Women can die having abortions."

"I'm sure that you're exaggerating it."

"I don't think I am. And it's not you who happens to be pregnant."

"If I were, I'd damn soon do something about it." Not waiting for an answer and not expecting one, he looked at his watch and said, "I'd better go. I have to get some sleep in before three o'clock."

As he left he took with him the picture of her sitting as if incapable of movement, a sad and desolate expression on her face, her eyes like those of an abandoned dog. "Be careful, Oliver," she whispered to his back as he climbed through the window.

Back in his room he knew he couldn't sleep for the couple of hours before the briefing and he needed to fight the shrivelling dismay in him. He swallowed two benzedrine tablets, washing them down with whisky before changing into his flying kit. He lay on the bed to wait for the drug and whisky to accelerate his mind into a smooth-edged and uncaring clarity.

When his pulse began to pound erratically, he laughed without humour. He felt light-headed, his body featherweight, his brain stimulated and squirrelling around in his skull. "You stupid bastard, Missen," he said aloud. He saw himself standing before the President and members of the Court, the President a group captain at least and armed with *The Manual of Air Force Law* and *King's Regulations & Air Council Instructions*. In fornicating with a fellow officer he had committed the most heinous of service crimes. No, he corrected himself, it would have been worse had she been a WAAF Other Rank. Or had he committed sodomy with an airman. But bad enough. They would have the set-faced stony expressions of men who either thought that putting it into any woman not one's wife was disgusting or, if they didn't, hadn't been caught out doing it. He spoke to the polished toe caps of his black shoes at the far end of the bed, squinting to identify his reflection in each.

"Flying Officer Missen, O., you are charged that on a date unknown, being on active service and outside the sublimities of Holy Wedlock, you caused a spermatozoon to be deposited in the uterus of Section Officer Howis, M., she being the property of the Air Ministry, where it conjoined unlawfully with an ovum of the said Section Officer Howis, M., causing a cessation of her menstrual discharge and rendering her unfit for duty in the service of His Majesty King George VI, by which act you behaved in a scandalous manner likely to bring comfort to the King's enemies and to bring the Service into disrepute."

He groaned, wondering what the hell he had to be so bloody flippant about. But everything would be all right. Trouble was something you somehow got out from under. Something you looked back on from a safe distance and laughed about.

Nine

With the first sickly gleam of grey light the Typhoons took off, filling the air with the shattering roar of their engines. Poxton and Kelham first, then the four Typhoon-bombers. Oliver and the three others followed in the turbulence of their slipstreams, turning wide over the sleeping countryside and formating on the navigation lights moving like fireflies in the dark sky towards the Channel. Poxton's quiet voice came over the R/T, shepherding them into position then ordering the lights switched off, their only points of reference against accidental collision being the mauve flames from the exhaust ports. With eyes growing accustomed to the darkness they could be seen dimly, a group of black sharks streaking through a black sea with fiery breath coming from their gills. There would now be radio silence but for emergencies and each pilot rode lonely with his own thoughts, concentrating on keeping in touch with the other aircraft.

With his body harnessed in the narrow confines of his cockpit and reacting automatically to the mechanics of flying, Oliver's mind felt well-oiled and bird-quick, thoughts pressing into it in a disconnected confusion of Morwenna below in her bed, her belly nurturing the growing seed of his careless lust, brooding on it to his belittlement. Of Laura in hers, her slim and elegant body waiting unknowingly for him to possess it. He saw her now in his mind's eye, not in detail but her grape-coloured eyes staring into his and then nothing until his imagination visualized her breasts, belly and pubic hair. They were his if he survived this bloody stupid and suicidal mission. The smooth vibrating rhythm of the engine passing through the metal stringers and skin reminded him of the ultra-high frequency oscillations that the Sabre engine induced in earlier Typhoons, sending men into battle so the pilots alleged with painful erections and with no means of subduing them. He had never needed that mechanical aphrodisiac. Thinking of Laura's nakedness was enough.

Having taken another benzedrine tablet, he had been able to hold his physical and mental instability in undetected check during the briefing which, for him, made nonsense of Poxton's enthusiastic optimism. Blown-up photographs showed the Château Coulmier as a slab-faced building with a high-pitched slate roof and narrow windows, only a strip of grass and trees separating it from the lake. In addition to the six flak gun positions Poxton had mentioned – and they had been menacingly obvious – staging had been erected on the roof pediments for what appeared to be heavy machine-guns, but which could be multiple light flak guns. The château was clearly prepared for, and capable of, defending itself against just the sortie on which they were now engaged. They were going in at a suicidally slow 250 miles an hour to allow the Bomphoon pilots a precision placing of their bombs. There would be daylight enough to see the château and, Oliver reminded himself, correspondingly enough for them to be seen on the long and unobstructed approach. Unless God was saving him for something even more nasty, he was being carried towards almost certain destruction by his own volition, a lethal bee that could only sting at the cost of its own life.

They were passing over a darker mass that was Eastbourne with its faint white edging of the Channel's water-line. There was a lighter grey beneath his port wing, the forerunner of a rising sun that would strike glinting light from the polished surfaces of the aircraft and expose them to the enemy. The smell of hot metal, rubber and petrol fumes was strong in his nostrils and already he felt stifled behind the rubber of his mask, sweat trickling from behind its edges. He gave himself a deep inhalation of oxygen to numb the fears crowding in on him, that his forced thinking of Laura's body had failed to banish.

He knew that his terror of flak, if known, would be judged a despicable and cowardly disinclination to risk his life, to die, for his country. But, he argued with himself, he wouldn't be the only one. It wasn't within his imagination to accept that anybody would be anything but a reluctant sacrifice when the odds for being slaughtered were so heavy. Excluding Poxton, he doubted that the others with whom he was streaking low over the sea, now glaucous and streaked with dimly seen foam, were happy warriors with no fears of a screaming death in a wreckage of falling, burning debris that had been an aircraft. They would have to feel as he felt, their bowels liquefying in a cold black fear of dying. Or would there be one who was gallant and courageous, single-minded in his eagerness to kill the Hun at whatever risk to himself? He could admire self-immolating heroes but still believe them to be bloody fools. That he had this terror of flak was something he accepted, that he had to live with. With some it was heights and vertigo, or closed-in spaces and claustrophobia that made them nerveless and frightened. He possessed a discriminating fear, not of danger itself - he had proved that - but specifically of this horrifyingly devastating flak pumped in such quantities at attacking aircraft and with such destructive accuracy. This time, he told himself, I have to. I've got to. But, Christ! Only another twenty minutes and we'll be in it. Were they jumped by a flock of Focke-Wulfs or Messerschmitts before they got there he would thank God on his bended knees, burn a bloody candle if that did any good.

The other Typhoons were visible as silhouettes now as they rose and fell in keeping station, their exhaust flames dimming in the growing light, each occasionally shuddering as it hit the slipstream of the one in front. The four Bomphoons, boxed in by their escorts, their green-painted bombs slung under the wings, followed Poxton and Kelham, the helmeted and goggled heads of the pilots insect-like beneath the bubble hoods.

With Dieppe a dark blotch against the coastline of France, Poxton began to lose height until they were bellowing at two hundred feet above the fields, a few late bursts of ineffective flak from the coastal defences following behind their tails. Their course would now be plotted and, were there any Focke-Wulfs or Messerschmitts in the air, they would be intercepted. Oliver scanned the clouded sky, almost praying for the black specks to appear. He brightened the annulus of his gun-sight and switched on the weapons selector box. He was combat-ready, the rockets fused in their rails beneath the wings, the 20-millimetre shells waiting in their belts for the four cannon. Finally, he lowered his seat and pulled down his goggles to protect his eyes.

The landscape had grown grey with skeins of mist in the valleys, the villages in their path approaching, growing larger and sliding beneath the engine nacelles in a swift blur of roofs and trees. "Firebugs. Slow and drop." Poxton's voice, unemotional and scratched by static, came over the R/T as he reduced speed. Oliver watched his Air Speed Indicator. When the needle dropped back to 200 mph the drop tanks would be released to give them greater speed and manœuvrability when it was needed. He transferred the fuel supply line to his mains tank and, when he saw the small silver cocoons fall away from Poxton's Typhoon, pulled down at his own jettison lever.

His mouth was dry and he stretched himself against the tightness of his harness. They would soon be on the final approach. Dear benevolent God, his mind pleaded, if you're ever going to help me let it be now. He wondered if he had a guardian angel flying station on him. He would have to be a bloody fast mover. And if they all had one there would be ten of them, all busy flapping their wings and making good air speed to keep up. If there were such beings, they fell down on the job more than they did it. And their Boss, too. He grimaced behind his mask. Did anybody ever joke on the scaffold? Perhaps they did. Anything but thinking about the agonizing death to come.

"Firebugs. Port to ground zero." Poxton's quiet voice again as his wing dipped. The others followed and Oliver, turning on his wing in a tight bank, looked through the side of the hood at the small town he knew to be Drieux below. A brief glimpse of narrow streets and tiled roofs and an open square with trees around its perimeter, of parked cars and a man in a black beret looking up at them, then flattening out to straight and level with a final view of two horses galloping panic-stricken across a field. Frog horses, he thought inconsequentially. A wonder the poor buggers hadn't long before been eaten.

Almost full day now and light enough to read the jiggling black and white dials on his instrument panel without screwing up his eyes. Raindrops splashed on the windscreen and were carried backwards in runnels over the curved perspex of the hood, distorting his vision. The palms of his hands were sweating and, closer to him than the bellowing of his monstrous engine, he could hear the blood pulsing staccato in his ears. His eyes watered and there was pain behind them. The uplift given him by the whisky and benzedrine had dissipated, leaving him in the greyness of impending doom.

The Typhoons were strung out, Poxton and Kelham a thousand yards ahead and skimming above the road that led to the lake and château. A car approaching them skidded into the verge as the aircraft thundered over, two men scrambling from it and flinging themselves into bushes. Then they were over a wood Oliver knew must be the Forest of Rambouillet, a dull greyish-green in the dawn, its foliage lashing and tossing in their wake and sending birds flying.

Under thirty miles to the target and steady at 250 miles an hour. Oliver felt hypnotized by the ground streaking beneath, the airstream rumbling along the belly of his Typhoon. Four miles a minute, seven or eight minutes to go. Perhaps all the time left for him to live. The bastards would be ready for them, their bloody Nazi fingers on the triggers ready to blast them out of the sky. Where were the Focke-Wulfs? There wasn't much time now, the seconds carried away in his slipstream and nothing that could stop the impetus of this roaring monster carrying him to the death that waited.

The lake. Pale grey-blue in the rain, thin and foreshortened by distance and, behind it, the solid outline of the château and its scattered trees. Forbidding, even in matchbox size. And then, Poxton's even voice: "Right, chaps, let's go."

As if the Germans had been waiting for his word of command, sparkles of light appeared from the trees around the château and fireballs in bright clusters came horizontally over the lake towards them. Oliver's legs were soft rubber and he knew his eyes were staring his fear. Sweat poured from him and he felt his bowels moving. Suddenly, the air around them split with explosions that bloomed small clouds of brown smoke and whipped away behind. Broken lines of tracer filled the air, curving towards them, leisurely at first then streaking past like burning wasps. Oliver was low enough over the water to ripple it with his passage, his Typhoon bumping and tossing in the turbulence of the explosions, the château looming larger in his windscreen. Puffs of white smoke appeared in a blizzard of flak in front of them through which it seemed impossible to penetrate. Thin red tracer came from the roof stagings and his port wing jolted, a line of ragged holes tearing its upper surface. Time was expanding for him and everything moved in the languorous slow motion of his heightened fear, his vision pin-sharp, his hands paralysed on the throttle and spade-grip of his stick. The leading Bomphoon erupted in a gigantic yellow chrysanthemum of slowly expanding flame and gouts of burning petrol marked its fall with a comet's tail. As it plunged, so its companion flying on its wingtip flipped over, showing its black-and-white striped underside for a brief second before cartwheeling into the lake to explode in a spouting upheaval of foam and flaming debris.

Poxton and Kelham had fired their rockets, the white trails dropping down towards the flak stations, followed by cannon fire from their wings as they held an undeviating course. Kelham's Typhoon shook as if tripping and the hood flew off, vapour streaming out behind it. Without altering course it continued on and disintegrated with a blinding flash into the storm of explosions from its own rockets.

Through the annulus of his gun-sight, Oliver saw the pink faces of the gunners on the roof as he willed his mind to stay on course, his thumb to press the firing button. The Typhoon at his side was hit and the shock wave of the shell burst lifted his wing, the rudder pedals jerking beneath his feet from a hit on the tailplane. The lake tilted and rushed towards him as he yelled his terror and pulled hard back on the stick, pushing the throttle lever to its limit and ruddering away from the killing flak as though the shrinking man inside had taken over with a frenzied strength, banking fiercely until the aircraft shuddered just short of a high speed stall, climbing over and away with lines of tracer following him. He caught a brief glimpse of Poxton's Typhoon diminishing to a midge as it climbed past the château and turning in a wide sweep with two others following behind him, one trailing dirty vapour from its engine. A pall of flame and oily smoke rose from the front of the château that was fast receding to a tiny square of glistening grey roof.

Still climbing, he reached the murky flocculence of the cloud underbelly and entered its misty half-light, hidden from the searching flak. He was panting as though he had been running, his body trembling, his mind shattered by the vivid impressions of the deaths he had witnessed and which so easily could have been his own. He felt a warm wetness in his trousers where he had urinated in his fear and he groaned his humiliation. He was high enough to need more oxygen and he turned on the regulator, throttling the engine back to cruising speed while he made himself think. He had to go back, to make his second run-in with Poxton and whoever else survived. There were unexpended rockets to account for and a full magazine of cannon shells. His mind fought for excuses he could make for pulling out before making the strike. If Poxton hadn't seen him, the others behind – had they survived – would have. He circled the Typhoon in the confusion of his indecision, fixing his eyes to the instruments, his fingers flexing on the throttle and stick with vacillating impulses, flying blind in the woolly muddiness of the cloud.

What had happened could be measured in the space of a few seconds; seconds in which shaming terror had taken hold of his mind and palsied his body to the extent of his pissing himself like a frightened animal in an abattoir. Lack of moral fibre. LMF. The initials of disgrace that would be recorded on his documents, his ignominious transfer to the aircrew detention centre at Sheffield, the degrading stripping from his uniform of his wings and the contempt of his fellow pilots. He could wish that he had died down there. It would have been over now in whatever waited him after death. Behind his indecision he pictured himself returning there, diving from the cloud and destroying himself and his humiliation by hurling the Typhoon point-blank at the château, to die quickly in a cataclysm of exploding rockets and fuel.

There was a despairing fatalism in him, a something not of the shrunken man inside, that checked the instruments for leaving the security of the cloud. The altimeter read 13,000 feet, the fuel gauge indicating threequarter-full tanks. Hearing a faint call over the radio he was unable to understand in the static, he switched off. The ragged gashes in the wing root beneath his cockpit showed no signs of leaking fuel. He switched off his rockets and fired a two-second burst from the cannon to check that the amunition feed had not been damaged. Unable to see what the flak had done to the control cables and levers in the wing and tail units he waggled the ailerons and ruddered hard, fishtailing the Typhoon and satisfying himself that it might not fall to pieces under violent stress.

Without knowing what he would decide to do, he pushed the nose down and dropped from the cloud, the skin of the aircraft gleaming from condensed moisture. He descended in a shallow spiral, searching for the lake and the plumes of smoke that would identify the château. The huge sprawling mass of Paris lay away to his starboard, darkened by pewter cloud and being rained upon, the sodden greens and browns of the countryside swinging below him as he circled.

When he first saw the aircraft through the blur of his propeller, he thought they were the Typhoons he had seen leaving the château. There were three of them, tiny in the five or six thousand vertical feet separating them and flying in echelon line astern, crossing diagonally beneath his nose. As they grew larger he recognized them as Focke-Wulf 190s, camouflaged green on their upper parts with black crosses distinct on the wings.

With his fear forgotten he activated his camera-gun, his mind canalized on their destruction. "O Lord," he breathed, "deliver them into mine hands." There was nothing in him now but the growing savage exhilaration of a release from nervelessness, the prospect of expunging his humiliation in the killing for which he had been trained. He took his hand from the throttle lever and pulled at the body webbing of his parachute for its reassurance, then searched the sky above and behind against the possibility of his being jumped in his turn. He filled his mind with hatred for the German pilots even as he started his dive.

They had not seen him, so intent, he thought, were they on looking for the low-flying Typhoons that had attacked the château. He held the stick forward as the needle of the Air Speed Indicator swept round the jiggling dial to 400 miles an hour, the aircraft shaking as if racing over a cobbled road as it plummeted down. With the rockets on their rails spoiling the airflow the ailerons and elevators fluttered, vibrating the wings and shuddering the stick in his grasp. Carried along by the impetus of his need to destroy, he didn't give a curse about the possibility of the damaged wing folding up on him and he heard himself shouting obscenities as the Focke-Wulfs grew larger in his gun-sight.

He could now pick out the unsuspecting heads of the pilots beneath their angular cockpit hoods, a glimpse of goggled and masked faces peering down to the ground below as they banked in a gentle curve. They looked so complacent and unaware of his intent to kill them that he yelled, "For Christ's sake! Can't you stupid buggers see me!" into the dead microphone of his mask. Although he did it when he had the chance and it was the accepted norm of air combat, he had a repugnance against shooting men in the back. He lined the red spot of his gun-sight to a point in front of the rearmost Focke-Wulf on a diagonal that would take his fire across the three of them, seeing the figure 12 on the side of the fuselage and the swastika on the conspicuous yellow tail fin as he controlled his plunging monster and measured the deflection. With his teeth bared to nothing but the darkness inside his mask he pressed his thumb on the firing button, the recoil of the cannon shaking the Typhoon and filling the cockpit with the smell of burnt cordite. The four streams of tracer shells converged to the point of an elongated V and curved towards the rear Focke-Wulf, exploding on the wing and tearing it off in a shower of burning pieces, the engine nacelle erupting in flames. The second Focke-Wulf, hit almost simultaneously, reared sideways to show its pale-blue underside, an undercarriage leg falling free before smashing into the leading aircraft in a tangle of shattered framework and burst metal, and then exploded abruptly into a ball of fire that fell in a curving arc as Oliver skidded his Typhoon violently to avoid colliding with them, overshooting with his cannon still firing.

The ground was rising dangerously fast to meet him and he pulled back with both hands on the stick, his goggles sliding down over his nose, his body flattened painfully against the armour plating of his seat under the pressure of centrifugal force. Growing darkness deepened to blackout as the blood left his eyeballs and sounds became muted and for a few blind seconds he imagined himself flying into the falling Focke-Wulfs. As he climbed, so his vision returned, gradually lightening to a world of photographic grey and white, then to the seeping back of colour and, with it, a cracking in his eardrums to bring back the roaring of his engine. Rolling out of the climb and orientating himself, he saw the two Focke-Wulfs still locked together and falling in a fiery mass that spilled out entrails of thick smoke and shredding metal. The first Focke-Wulf he had hit was spinning violently as it dropped, flames spouting backwards from its engine and Oliver thought he saw in them a blackened figure struggling to climb from the cockpit and then falling back. He could have imagined it and it didn't matter. There were no parachutes opening in the sky.

The sudden appearance of balls of brown smoke in front of him jolted his attention from the final impact of his victims into the ground. He turned and saw the lake and then the château from which the flak was being fired. He was furious now, the lust still in him to destroy overriding his fear. He switched on his selector box for the rockets and pushed the nose of the Typhoon down until he could see the rear of the château in his gun-sight and then with the flak still rising to meet him releasing the salvo of rockets. Without waiting to see where they struck, he heaved at the stick to climb in a spiralling roll into the safety of the clouds. With the foggy obscurity around him, the moisture misting his hood and forcing him to fly on instruments, he held his climb and broke through to a brilliance of blue and a sun that splintered gold light on the disc of his propeller and engine cowling and dazzled his eyes.

He turned towards the Channel, invisible to him beneath the clouds, and pushed the throttle lever forward to the gate. There was a kind of exultation in him that submerged what had been to him a now understandable revulsion against a badly organized and ill-timed attack. The deaths he had witnessed of Kelham and the pilots of the two leading bombers were proof of it. They had achieved nothing if what he had seen was the whole of it. He had turned away, yes, but only because he had been hit by flak and blown off course by the explosion of it; too fast, then too late, to recover. He had pissed himself – the cold dampness in his crotch reminded him of that – because of the whisky he had drunk with no thought to empty his bladder before take-off. Then he had spotted the flight of Focke-Wulfs, obviously about to jump the attacking Typhoons, and he had made a decision to engage them. Which he had done and which the film in his camera-gun would prove. Nobody – and he was thinking of Poxton – could now accuse him of lacking moral fibre.

He laughed hysterically and reached forward, patting the instrument panel. "You beautiful bitch," he said, "I love you." Just being alive, he told himself, was bloody marvellous and, reckless of the damaged wing and tailplane, to show that he didn't give a bloody damn for Poxton or anybody else, he put the Typhoon into a victory roll in the canyon between the gleaming white cauliflower heads of the clouds surrounding him.

Ten

Although the mist had dissipated, the shadowless grey dawn that was neither darkness nor light persisted. Philip saw the lane of trees through which he walked as a blurred tunnel, individual trees only resolving into more solid shapes of dark trunks and overhanging foliage as he approached and passed them. The eerie silence of his deafness made him solitary in his confusion and depression. He felt as if he were a caged animal living inside the dark sphere of his skull, his vision the only contact with the greyness of the outside world, the closing of the shutters of his eyelids releasing him to the more vivid reality of his imagination.

He believed his mental incoherence to be increasing for he had no recollection of how he had come to be walking along this lane, his recall like an elusive fluttering moth he was unable to pin down. He could remember seeing the German sentry on the bridge, recall the fear in him that he would be seen and challenged and, unhearing, be shot at for his failure to respond. He had closed his eyes to shut out the danger and, after that, there had been a blankness until he found himself in this twilit avenue of dismal trees in a strange countryside. Either he had somehow crossed the river he believed to be the Rhine or he had retreated, retracing his steps. He couldn't think how he could find out. Of one thing only was he in any way certain. Although not remembering when he had last seen the sun, the moon or the stars, he knew instinctively that he was walking in the right direction. The insistent pull towards Laura was still with him and he followed it blindly.

He believed that after leaving the bridge he had found shelter and slept. There had been dreams, more vivid than the nebulous awareness of his waking consciousness. David, his elder brother killed in Belgium before Dunkirk, had entered his first dream. A lieutenant in the Royal Armoured Corps, he was no wavering shifting phantom of a figure but a clearly defined and fleshly solid of light, shadow and colour in the khaki battledress in which he had died. And Philip had heard the poignancy of his remembered voice. "Old son," he called him, as he had always done. "It's all right, old son," he had said, "Everything's going to be all right." His smile had given him warmth and courage, but when he left him as suddenly as he had appeared his dream-self had wept. And, still weeping his sadness for the brother he had loved, his dreaming moved him to stand in the darkness of the bedroom he had last seen so few nights ago, yet seeming so many eternities of time past.

She lay sleeping with an arm outside the blankets and over the pillow on his side of the bed. As though conscious of his presence she had stirred, moving her lips in silent words. Standing at the foot of the bed and unable to approach nearer, he could sense that she too was dreaming, the pictures she was seeing being formed and dissolved behind the closed eyelids. He recognized images of himself as she saw them and felt with her the loneliness of her loss. He spoke to her, trying to penetrate into her dreaming, feeling that he could be with her but not of her; that while he was conscious of her, she was oblivious of him. Then, the almost imperceptible superimposing of a different face over his own, but not so different that his dreaming mind rejected it as an alien personality in his own likeness. Himself, yet not himself. He was seeing it as she saw it, believing him dead and raising an image, a simulacrum, to take his place. With a sudden shift of emotion he was sharing in a woman's imagery, feeling as she felt the phantasm of a searching moist mouth, of a muscular naked body against her breasts and belly, of wiry male hair and heat and the unutterable sweetness of his entering her, the floating ecstasy of her sexual release as she moaned in her dreaming of it.

In that moment, with the echo of the intensity of her passion making him tremble, he felt himself receding from the bedroom and falling outwards into space, merging after a period of blankness into the consciousness of grey light and tree-lined lane in which he walked. The recollection of his involuntary voyeurism shook him despite his recognizing it as being the fantasizing of a dream, the living with her in her lust for the sexual thrustings of another bringing angry jealousy and resentment to him for this alien usurpation of Laura's body. There was an apprehension of danger for her also; a presentiment he felt of an unhappiness he could neither identify nor imagine.

When he saw the car stationary at the end of the lane where it debouched into a metalled road, his first instinct was to take to the fields to avoid it. But it had the dead waiting look of an unoccupied vehicle, so he put aside his caution and went to it. If it was unlocked and the ignition key left in it, taking it could shorten his journey by days. He would be less conspicuous as a driver than skulking through fields and woods like a fugitive fox.

The car was an old Citröen. There was no carelessly left ignition key and its doors were securely locked. A small square of paper stuck on the inside of the dirty windscreen was printed in French, the words *Passe-debout* prominent and made official with a fiscal stamp showing a portrait of Marshal Pétain. There was a folded newspaper on the front passenger seat and by twisting his head at an angle he could read part of it. What he could see of the masthead read ... RNIERES NOUVELLES D'ALSACE, STRASBOURG: *samedi 2 mai 1944.*

Conceivably, the Citroën could have been driven into Germany, but it was an improbability. He was in France. Which meant that he had crossed the Rhine, something else about which his mind refused him information. If he hadn't crossed it by the guarded railway bridge, he hadn't swum it either. He knew that he couldn't swim so wide a river in his flying kit and his clothing was dry. It was unlikely that a boat, even had he been able to find one, would have been left unsecured or unguarded. He tried to picture himself creeping across the bridge under the menace of the guard and his automatic rifle, but nothing came to confirm that he had. Despite the mist there had been, he couldn't begin to imagine its possibility.

Remembering something about the newspaper that had appeared odd, he peered through the glass at its masthead again. It was there, but it could never be right. Not the second of May. He tried to make order of the confusion in his mind. It made nonsense of the passage of time. He had been shot down on the night of the 31st March. That date would be etched in his mind for the rest of his life and never, certainly, was it more than three or four days ago in recollected time. Yet if he accepted the date printed on the newspaper – he checked again to see that he had read the year correctly – he had been wandering for over a month. That there were gaps in his memory, areas of darkness, he had to accept; a confusing amnesia caused by the blow on his head in the cockpit of the Lancaster. That he had walked from Germany into France, undetected in his distinctive flying jacket and suit, made it a nightmare of unreality.

He left the car and took to the greater safety of a field, moving like an automaton in the silent unfriendly countryside. As he walked, so his mind churned over the thirty-odd days spent as a fugitive, provoking questions he could not answer. He remembered neither eating nor drinking. Nor did he feel the need to do so now. Yet he must have. A man couldn't live and be active for that length of time without doing so. He put his fingers to his jaw, feeling the skin smooth where there should by now have been a beard of unshaven whiskers. His flying suit and boots were as they had been when he took off from the airfield, showing no signs of a month's stumbling over farmlands and sleeping rough in dirty sheds. Where had he been? And where was he now? None of it made sense. Was he insane, the confusion in his mind symptomatic of it? Had he eaten and drunk, shaved himself, in his periods of amnesia? Or was he dreaming a never-ending nightmare that he was accepting as the reality? He touched his body, felt the firm flesh and muscle beneath the smooth fabric of his flying suit. Holding his hand in front of his face he could see clearly the papillary ridges and creases in its palm, the detail of the fingernails and the fine black hairs on the wrist; see, too, the pattern of stitching on the twill cuff that covered it. These material minutiae seemed real enough, but could he be only dreaming that it was so? It might also explain the detail in which he had seen the three aircrew in the cutting, although in his experience a dream was painted with a broad brush of colour and never in such fine and exact precision.

A man's mind could, he guessed, produce fantasms, hallucinations of the non-existing that would appear real to him. The ghost of his dead brother and his visions of Laura could have been such, conjured up by a disordered brain. And everything else he thought he had experienced since his escape from the Lancaster. The weasel and the pheasant that were so strangely unaware of him, the three aircrew who had ignored his calling to them and had vanished so inexplicably, the armoured column that had passed him as though he had not existed. Had they been creatures and things of his imagination, nothing of flesh and blood or structured steel, it would be understandable. It would explain his crossing of the Rhine, for it would not have been there for him to cross. He frowned his puzzlement. If he could remember these things, why not the missing days? The explanation came to him. There were no missing days. If what he had experienced was an hallucination, then so must be the car he had just left and the newspaper in it. So the time factor could be hallucinatory also. As could be the unnatural light that was neither day nor night nor anything else he had ever seen. And his deafness. The deafness of dreaming, for sound had no place in dreams.

In what he realized might be a fleeting moment of sanity, of mental coherence in his clouded confusion, he willed his mind back to his squadron in the hope that it might produce a recognizable reality to which he could hold. He put himself high above the ground in the familiar stark metal interior of his cockpit, seeing in the darkness the squadron's Lancasters, their bellies pregnant with high explosives, taking off in their turn to join the nearly 800-strong bomber raid on Nuremburg, hearing the battering roar of their engines, tense with the anticipation of his waiting, a fullness in his chest which he knew he would lose once he was airborne and too involved with the intricacies of flying his bomber and keeping in station to give room to his fears. He visualized the pattern of what had been, seeing in recalled imagery the instrument panel crowded with dials and switches, the knobs and controls at his side as with Davies the flight engineer he went over the take-off check list. And even that he had always said he could do in his sleep. Autopilot clutch in, compass to normal, pitot head heater switch on, trimming tabs adjusted, propeller controls fully up, master engine fuel cocks and booster pumps on, superchargers to moderate, air intake to cold, radiator shutters to automatic and flaps 15 to 20 degrees down. It was his litany, his Ave Maria against the death that could wait for them in the high darkness. He heard the disembodied voice of the Controller giving him instructions over the R/T, his trundling the ungainly giant on to the runway to follow in the wake of the dark shape of the Lancaster preceding him and already merging as a shadow into the night sky. He relived in his recall the biting cold and the blinding searchlights of their approach to Nuremburg and the German night fighters that harried them ... He stopped his thinking of it before his mind re-enacted the death of Davies and his panic-stricken and helpless fall from the sky. There the reality ended and the nightmarish confusion of being lost and alone began.

Through the hedgerow along which he walked he saw the

first houses of what appeared to be a village and, behind them, the spire of a church. This was the time for proving things. He had to know and he would resolve his confusion by finding a Frenchman and putting himself and his freedom into his hands. Were he not wandering a countryside of his own imagining, there was no other way of getting in touch with a Resistance group and being shuttled through France and Spain to Gibraltar. And he had an overwhelming need to talk with a fellow human, anything to relieve the empty loneliness of his isolation.

When he came to a gate he climbed it, stepping down into the road feeling naked and vulnerable. He saw the village as if it were a photograph, its colouring subdued to a grey monochrome, its single street deserted, the houses shuttered and withdrawn. It was all shabbiness and peeling paint with unswept litter blown into the gutters. Were he able to smell, he guessed there would be a strong stink of chicken and pig manure. Two small vans were parked on the wide footpath and a bicycle leaned against the dirty plastered wall of a single-storeyed bar. A faded sign over its door read *Au Point du Jour*.

He stood there indecisive for minutes, seeing blurred movement through the frosted glass of the door. When nobody came, he turned its handle and pushed the door open. It was dark inside and he stood waiting until his eyes adjusted to the gloom. It was rurally primitive, a small wooden bar counter in a corner with a meagre shelf of bottles behind, a few upright chairs and tables, some advertising posters for vermouth and cigarettes on the walls and a door with a hand-printed notice – *Lavoir* – on it. Near the single window three men sat at a table, two of them wearing black berets. In front of them were coffee cups and small glasses. They talked together, their lips moving and forming words he could not hear. None looked at him or made any sign that he had been seen. He moved closer to them and said, "*Bonjour*, *messieurs*," feeling the vibration of his voice in his eardrums. "*Je suis anglais.*"

Without looking at him, choosing to ignore him, they continued their conversation as if he did not exist. The bloody arrogant, unfriendly bastards! He could have wept his helplessness and there was a sudden rising anger in him. He pushed his face close to the man nearest to him and shouted in English directly into his ear, articulating clearly. "I said I was an Englishman! I need help! I am a Royal Air Force pilot shot down over Germany!"

There was nothing; no involuntary jerking of the head, no blinking awareness of the eyelids as the man lifted his cup and drank from it. Philip unzipped the front of his suit and spread it apart, showing his battledress blouse with the RAF wings over the patch pocket and the whistle attached to the top buttonhole. The man without a beret looked at him without awareness, looked through and past him with nothing in his eyes to show that he was seeing a stranger, an Englishman who had entered his bar dressed in a flying suit. God Almighty! That couldn't happen very often in this flea-bitten ramshackle village in the middle of nowhere. He had to accept now that there was only one answer. They didn't exist. Nor the bar in which they sat. Nor the village. He was dreaming them. Or hallucinating. And if he was hallucinating, then he must be going mad, his mind running from unpleasant unfaceable reality. *Dear Christ*, he prayed, *please let me wake up. Let me be sane.*

He turned and stumbled from the bar back into the road like an ejected drunk. The last vestiges of reality had left him and he was in a strange world of insubstantial nothings, no longer needing to hide. But dreams ended at some time and when this one did, where would he find himself when he woke? In a hospital? Injured from that blow on the head in the Lancaster and drugged into derangement? He made a mental effort to feel behind his dreaming to the reality of sheets against his body and the pressure of a mattress beneath him, but nothing came.

The road stretched before him and he walked it unconcealed, drawn still by the pull in him to Laura. There was a somewhere he had to be and there seemed nothing now that could stop him from being there.

Eleven

Poxton stood behind the table he had to share as a desk with three other Flight Commanders and glared at Oliver. Smears of engine oil on his face outlined the goggles and mask he had taken off and he was pale with anger.

Oliver faced him, holding his helmet in his hand. He had been met on the parking apron with instructions to report to Poxton at once and, despite his earlier regained assurance, there was a heavy lump of apprehension in his chest. "You sent for me," he said.

"You're damned right I did." His words were hard and cutting. "We lost Kelham and Tunnard and two of the Bomphoons."

"I didn't know about Tunnard, but I saw the others buying it." He was already on the defensive, could see Poxton was boiling up for an explosion.

The Flight Commander's voice rose. "You didn't know because you broke off your attack as we went in."

Oliver felt the blood draining from his face, leaving it cold. He took in a deep breath. "Are you saying that—"

"I haven't finished yet," Poxton cut him short. "I know you did because I saw you. And Sergeant Mitchell saw you too."

"You've questioned a bloody NCO about me?" He was angry himself now and truculent.

"I asked him to confirm it. And don't use that tone of voice to me."

"If you're saying I funked it, I'll use whatever tone of voice I choose."

"I'm saying it, Missen. You twitched." There was all the contempt of a man who would fly into the flames of hell if ordered to.

Oliver held his angry stare. Poxton had boobed badly in jumping on him with both feet before asking what had happened, and he knew now that he could demolish his accusation. Insubordination was something he could forget and he allowed his own anger to grow.

"You don't know what you're talking about. Except that it's a load of cock. I was hit by flak and it blew me arse over tit. If you'd bothered to check my kite when I landed you'd have seen the damage. It blew me off course and when I was pulling back I saw three Focke-Wulf 190s coming in high east of the château—"

"I didn't see them. Nor anybody else." Poxton had lost some of his certainty.

"In which case it was just as well that *I* did, or you'd have all bought it." This was the weakest part about which Poxton could have his doubts. "They were going to jump us. I did a climb at full bore, got above them and clobbered all three as they went in. I don't see why you feel justified in tearing me off a strip for stopping three Focke-Wulfs from bouncing you." He pushed hard with his aggression against Poxton's uncertainty. "I was riding guard on the Bomphoons. That was the briefing and that's what I was doing."

"On course. Before we got there. We were on the run-in when you peeled off. You damned well knew what our primary target was."

"If you doubt my word," Oliver said, trying to keep his voice from shaking, "and you appear to be doing so, I'll take this directly to the CO. To Group, if necessary."

"I'm engaged! Come back later!" Poxton snapped this at someone opening the door behind Oliver. When it had been closed, he said, "You will only if I say you will. You can prove these three Focke-Wulfs, I imagine?"

"They're in the camera-gun if that's enough proof for you. When I finished them, I returned to the château and gave it my rockets." His voice rose. "What else was I supposed to do? Get out and fire my bloody revolver at it?"

"You're going too far, Missen," Poxton said quietly. "Any more of that and I'll order you under arrest."

"I'm sorry, but you're provoking me." Oliver damped down his aggression. "All right, perhaps I *was* mistaken in taking off after the Focke-Wulfs. I don't know. Who's to say? I had to make a snap decision and I made it."

"So why didn't you call me?"

Oliver gave him a scornful look. "For Christ's sake! You were already firing your rockets. Did you want me to ask your permission at that point?"

"You can wrap it up how you like, Missen, but you were briefed – ordered – to press home an attack on the flak positions, and you didn't. You disobeyed orders and went tear-arsing off on your own. What the hell would have been the result if we'd all decided to have done that? And who's to say it didn't cause Tunnard's death? You're an officer. What sort of an example do you think you were to the others? I've still a bloody good mind to put you on a charge."

That was now bluff and they both knew it. Three enemy aircraft destroyed in what Oliver was alleging to be an interception on the Bomphoons was unanswerable.

"And I'm willing to answer it. In the meantime, you'll withdraw your remarks about funking out. If you don't, I'll go to the CO with or without your authority."

There was silence in the room as the two men glared at each other. Oliver had choked back harder words only because he knew Poxton was right and that he had funked out, had broken off his attack in uncontrollable fear.

"I'm insisting," he said.

Poxton's features reflected the struggle in him as he weighed the evidence he had for accusing Oliver. Then he forced unwilling words to his tongue. "All right. I withdraw my remarks that you funked out. Think yourself fortunate that I'm not putting you on a charge for disobeying orders and gross insubordination." His eyes were telling Oliver that he hadn't fooled him as he turned away. "Now get out!" he snapped at him.

Although he had successfully defended himself – and he thanked God for the providential appearance of the Focke-Wulfs – he knew that he had by no means disposed of his Flight Commander's distrust and disbelief. It had left him shaken and suspect and Poxton would be watching him, giving him the dirty end of any stick to test his reactions, to break him given another opportunity. He would never be able to get away with it again.

With his Typhoon unserviceable and being repaired in the squadron workshops hangar, Oliver was unhorsed and relegated to being an odd body it was a nuisance to have on the airfield. Like a spare prick at a wedding, he thought without humour or satisfaction, somebody best out of the way and nothing without his aircraft. He needed to fly and felt at a loss at not being able to. There had to be a next time when he could convince himself that he was no coward, that he could overcome his terror of flak.

He was depressed and conscious that he had earned the dislike and contempt, if not the enmity, of Poxton; knowing that his disfavour would spread subtly to the rest of the squadron by the Flight Commander's attitude towards him. Sergeant Mitchell would have no reason to keep quiet about what he had seen or of Poxton's later questioning of him. It would pass from the NCOs to the officers like an infection, being exaggerated and added to as it travelled. His fellow pilots would hear of it and draw their own conclusions. The least he could expect would be to be looked at sideways, spoken to with caution. At the most, treated as a pariah, a man who had funked it and who was therefore guilty of that most belittling of all masculine flaws, lack of guts.

The deaths of Kelham, Tunnard and the two Bomphoon pilots would be partly attributed to his not adding his fire-power against the flak positions on the run-in and, even had he later shot down half the Luftwaffe, it would make no difference to that judgement.

After his debriefing and three hours of unsatisfying sleep, he had joined the Squadron Commander, Poxton, the Intelligence Officer and the survivors of the sortie in the hut used by the Photographic & Signals section. They sat in the darkness with the soft whirring of the film projector and the occasional scratch and flare of matches as they smoked.

The films from the camera-guns, grainy and flickering grey and white, showed a confusion of eruptions as rockets exploded about the flak positions on the first run-in. On the second, when a cannon-fire attack was made on the château, the damage inflicted by the Bomphoons could be seen; huge holes torn in the masonry at the base and a gaping crater in the roof exposing the timbers, all seen indistinctly through a shroud of rising smoke. The château had stood up to it well and Oliver thought that unless von Rundstedt had been unwisely sleeping in front of the building, or admiring the dawn from one of its windows, he was probably still living. From what he could see of Poxton's face he thought so too and would consequently view Oliver's breaking off his attack with even more animus in the future.

Oliver's film, although confirming his claim, was not very rewarding. With the camera-gun oscillating as the cannon shook the aircraft in its headlong dive, the first Focke-Wulf appeared jerkily, jumping in the frames and growing larger as sudden splashes of debris burst from its wing and engine nacelle, shifting sideways out of sight as the second Focke-Wulf appeared. Too briefly, there was a view of exploding shells across a wing and the cockpit hood flying into pieces, an even briefer appearance of the tail of the third aircraft and then nothing but the countryside far below as he overshot. There was no real confirmation that he had done anything else but register hits as he dived past them. At the best, without taking into consideration his own suspect assertions, they would be regarded as "probables".

Before the lights were switched on, Poxton said expressionlessly, "No film of the château, Mr Missen."

Other than for the leading aircraft on the run-in to the château, there had been no instructions about the use of the camera-guns. With one hand on the stick, its thumb on the gun-button, and with the other hand manipulating the throttle lever, it was not always possible to spare a thumb to operate it even if a mind canalized on killing could remember to.

Oliver wanted to smash his face in. You trouble-making bastard! he said under his breath. Aloud, he said, "I boobed there," and left it bloody-mindedly at that. He simmered with resentment because whatever he had failed to do about Operation von Rundstedt he had destroyed three Focke-Wulf fighters and put three German pilots in their graves. Nobody had told him that it had been a good show and he knew that he was hardly likely to be recommended for the DFC because of it. It underlined for him that Poxton had given his own opinion to the Squadron Commander and that it was shared. He hated him now as he had never hated a man before.

Before returning to his room to catch up on his sleep he looked, but not too obviously, for Morwenna. Not finding her was, in a way, a relief. It deferred his facing up to a further problem and left him, he felt, with a clear conscience to telephone Laura.

She would, she told him, be free that evening should he choose to call. If there was any enthusiasm in her at the prospect of seeing him, she kept it concealed behind a casual coolness. But the sound of her voice excited him. She was a woman who wouldn't, he guessed, be the easier to take by standing off and doing a ritual mating dance around whatever doubts she might have about him as a lover. He was convinced that as with the shooting down of an enemy aircraft he would be more assured of a kill were he to hit her with all the armament at his disposal on his first approach, before she had time to prepare her female defences.

Twelve

Cynthia Woollgar was irritated with her husband, a common enough feeling she had at his placid amiability and easy disregard of things that she thought should concern him.

He sat opposite her in the same chair he had used for as long as she had been married to him, reading his *Times* and sucking at his pipe, the dogs sitting at each side of him. His old man's body made occasional small internal noises which abraded her irritation. With a book unread on her lap she stared at the back of the newspaper and fed her irritation with her thoughts. They were not helped by her lack of physical tranquillity.

Although she had, without regret, withdrawn from the ineffectiveness of her husband's failing masculinity and moved into a separate bedroom, the sexual ferment of her body still persisted. She kept it reasonably under control by her uninhibited determination to do something about it when need and opportunity coincided. She made the opportunities by overnight visits to their flat in South Kensington, combining her need for a physical release with whatever shopping she could contrive to justify a rail journey to London.

She recalled the last visit and its recalling was a warning symptom of the approach of her recurring need. In the flat she had bathed and perfumed her body, standing afterwards before the mirror to reassure herself of the flatness of her belly, the tautness of the breasts which had not yet sagged and the unwrinkled smoothness of her long thighs; the citadel, she told herself, before its sought-for despoliation. But not by one of her own sort, for that would be unthinkable. Hers was a basic appetite to be fed by a basic man with no mental or emotional rapport. She had put on her naked body a dark-blue dress, expensive, but simple enough to pass without comment where she was preparing to go. She wore no jewellery, but used more lipstick and scent than she would ever consider suitable in her own milieu. She chose a white mackintosh to wear which she belted tightly around her waist and, finally, removed money from her handbag, leaving only sufficient for her purpose.

The bar to which she had directed her taxi through blacked-out London was in Rupert Street. It was improbable that she would meet either a social equal there or anyone who could know her, it being patronized almost wholly by Other Ranks servicemen. The few women found there would be either disgustingly elderly or those whom she chose to regard as tarts.

Taking the glass of wine which she had no intention of drinking, she sat away from the bar counter where she had been the object of immediate attention of the men crowding it, opening her mackintosh and lighting a cigarette as she scanned the bar. The man she singled out for her calm unblinking reward was huge, a head taller than the others, thick-necked and heavy-shouldered with a powerful body, his wiry black hair shaven to stubble at the nape and over his ears. His khaki battledress was parade-ground neat, the belt and gaiters spotlessly blancoed, his black boots brilliantly polished. He wore the winged badge of the Parachute Brigade and his red beret was folded and pushed beneath a shoulder epaulet, the single chevron of a Lance Corporal on each arm. The beer glass looked small in his big fist. She saw him as a lusty animal of a man with a mind she was prepared to accept as simple and direct, rarely rising higher than his pelvis and brute enough to extinguish the fire burning in her body.

He pushed his way through the crowd to her, confident in his massive masculinity, scenting her with the instinct of a stallion for a mare in season. "Buy you a drink, doll?" he said without preamble, ignoring the untasted wine in front of her. His accent was West Country, his voice deep in his chest. Close to, she saw him as all uncultured sinew and muscle, an uncouth proletarian who had earned his living by it and used it now for the killing of men.

She shook her head and said, "No, and don't call me doll," making him stand there rebuffed with a reddening of his jowls until she added, crushing her own out in an ashtray, "You may give me a cigarette."

He smirked then and lowered his bulk beside her, making the wooden bench creak. Taking a cigarette for himself, he offered the packet to her. "You on your own, then?" His body was near to hers and she could feel the heat of it, smell his maleness. Over the flame of the match he held for her, she studied his features. A hard-planed face with pale-blue eyes and a small mouth in which she read unthinking cruelty. The kind, she judged, who would hit his wife about had he one; a man who would kill another with an ignorant callousness. She was repelled and attracted at the same time, a frisson of anticipation growing in her.

"Are you trying to pick me up?" she asked in the tone of voice which would chill a man of greater sensitivity. It would wither his intentions should he allow it and he would need gall to carry on.

"You're a bit bleedin' cut-glass, ain't you?" he scowled.

"Yes," she agreed calmly, "but don't let that stop you."

He looked around the bar. "There ain't nobody 'ere tha's better."

"We'll see, shall we."

He drank his beer in gulps, his mouth glistening as his tongue licked it. He was searching for something to say. A vulgar man, she considered, but his teeth were clean and white.

"I'm goin' over soon," he said, putting a thick finger on his badge.

She was faintly amused. "And you'll probably be killed. Should you be telling me this?"

He snorted. "I can see you ain't a German spy. Anyway, everybody knows. It ain't much of a secret."

"I imagine not."

His conversation coming to a halt, he emptied his glass and stood. "You 'avin' another one? Somethin' a bit stronger?"

"No. I wish to go." She looked with distaste at the bar where a group of soldiers were singing about hanging out their washing on the Siegfried Line. "I find this place too crowded. Too noisy."

The prospect of losing her had obviously jolted him and he looked baffled. "I know a quieter one. You comin'?"

"No," she said coolly, "I am not." She paused, watching the flush appear again on his jowls. As coolly, she added, "We can have a drink at my apartment if you wish. My husband's away."

His eyes bulged. He had not anticipated being asked so bluntly. "Christ!" he breathed, "Not 'alf." He licked his lips. "Let's go."

"Go out and get a taxi," she ordered him. "I'll wait here."

Opening her handbag she took out a five-pound note, screwed it into a ball and dropped it on the table.

His eyes went from the note to her face and back again. Then he grinned knowingly and picked it up, thrusting the crumpled white paper into his trousers pocket. She could read his thoughts. One of those rich bitches who wanted a real man and was prepared to pay for it. Had he any brains in his thick head he would have felt belittled that she was buying his primitive maleness and nothing more. She had little but contempt for his kind.

He almost ran from the bar, shoving other men aside with his beefy shoulders. When he returned, standing at the door, she rose and went out.

In the dark interior of the taxi, smelling of previous passengers and the leather upholstery cold, he put his arm around her, his wet beery mouth searching for hers. "No, damn you!" she said curtly as though to a refractory dog and pushing him away from her. "Do I look a woman you can fumble in a taxi!"

He had followed her docilely enough into the flat, staring around him with suspicion that there had to be a catch in it, that it was all too good to be true. "My name's Jim," he said as they stood facing each other. He towered above her slimness, her face level with his chest. Globules of sweat glistened on his upper lip.

"Really?" She dropped her emotionless regard slowly over the bulk of his body, observing his need for her, prominent and aggressive. "Come with me."

She led him into the dark bedroom, leaving the door ajar to let in a rectangle of illumination. With a disdainful disregard for his presence she took off her mackintosh and dropped it over a chair, then unbuttoned her dress and stepped naked out of it. She laid herself on the bed and closed her eyes, hearing the sounds of his heavy breathing and his growling curses as he hurriedly removed his equipment and clothing in the semi-darkness. His body was hot and his weight flattened her breasts and forced her deep into the bed, his open mouth and tongue searching for hers. She turned her face away. "No," she said, "Get on with it." Allowing him to kiss her mouth would be too intimate a concession.

Her whole consciousness was now centred in the fire that needed quenching. Urgently. But not so urgently that she would give anything of herself to this organism thrusting into her with its hard maleness. Her need was to be served as she lay flaccid, mentally remote from him, her eyelids shuttering the sight of his grossness from her. So, perhaps, two hundred years earlier, one of her ancestresses might have used a manservant after ordering him to bathe. The small mewing noises she made as his weight pressed breath from her lungs was the only response to what he was doing to her. And the lance corporal, grunting like a pig at its trough, plunging and rearing, spent himself inside her.

Afterwards, she had removed herself from beneath him and stood cool and self-possessed, seemingly unmoved, while he lay exhausted and limp, heaving his chest in wheezing spasms. He was now in her eyes a hulk of sweating white flesh that revolted her, that she wished to be rid of quickly.

"You smoke too much," she said. There was no tenderness in her, no gratitude for her use of him. "I am going to have a bath. My husband will be here shortly so I expect you to be gone when I come out."

The thought that now aggravated her irritation was of the Missen man ingratiating himself into her stepdaughter's life. Into her own life. She considered him not too many degrees socially above the men she used so contemptuously, recognizing him for a parvenu when she first saw him away from the scene of the accident and her initial shock. Good-looking, but brash and with a flashy personality his uniform could not disguise; too ready with his smile and his accent not quite. A womanizer, and she knew one when she saw one.

Despite his unsettling resemblance to Philip he was a poor substitute and she feared that Laura – stupid as she could sometimes be, and obstinate – would become involved with him. She knew her well enough to realize that she had been attracted to him. And if she didn't give too much of a damn about how Laura felt about it, she did how it would affect herself. Philip had been public school, from a good family with the proper connections and had fitted. Missen patently had not and would not. He was impossible and probably had no money. He would be an embarrassment, his presence in the house as a member of the family a disaster. At her social level he was nearly everything she disliked in a man. That he might conceivably take Philip's place with Laura was a danger she would do much to avoid.

"Clive," she said sharply, "Will you please put down that paper and listen to me."

The *Times* came down and he stared at her. He could anticipate from the tone of her voice that she was set for any opposition he might make to whatever it was that she had in her mind. "Yes, my dear," he said, "I'm listening"

"That Missen man of yours. You've to do something about him."

"So you said before," he said mildly. "What had you in mind?" He knew, but admitting it wasn't going to help him with Cynthia.

"He's calling here this evening. Laura's invited him." She made it his fault.

His eyebrows lifted. "I see. Is that bad? He seems a decent enough young fella to me."

He would, she thought. Any man in an officer's uniform and on active service would have his approval. She said, "I'm not so certain that he's a decent enough young fella as you put it. I don't like the way Laura was looking at him."

"I didn't notice it." He didn't necessarily believe it either.

"You wouldn't. You're a man." She made it an indictment. "She's going to fall for him unless we do something."

"You said that before, too. And, even if she did, I don't follow your objection." Putting the newspaper down he began to refill his pipe, doing it with a methodical care that further irritated her. "What is it you have against him?"

"I've a lot. He hasn't the right background. Which should be enough. If I'm any judge he's a common womanizer. Would you approve of their marrying? His being in the family?" Her eyes regarded him without affection, seeing the stringy neck and prominent larynx, the tiny veins that had burst in his nose and the trembling in the fingers that were pushing tobacco in his pipe.

"I don't know him well enough to say," he temporized, knowing that he was wasting breath saying it when she so clearly had the bit between her teeth. "Aren't you jumpin' your fences a little early? I can't imagine it's all that serious. She hasn't known him for five minutes." He yawned and blinked, a sign that he was becoming bored with what she was saying. He wished he could think of something urgent to do in the conservatory. Or to be able to say that he was due for duty with his Home Guard platoon.

"Do you wish to wait until he's made a fool of her? And of us?"

She wanted to shout at him. "Your giving him Philip's car encouraged him. It wasn't the most intelligent thing you could have done."

"Laura had no objection." She was blaming him for that also, but he had anticipated it.

"That's precisely the point. She should not have been put in the position to object or otherwise."

He felt anger stir in him against his wife's shrewish implacability. He hated arguments, always lost them anyway and was inevitably left with the feeling that he had done something wrong. "God dammit!" he swore. "She's my daughter and she's twenty-two. She's got a mind of her own and she knows what she's doing."

Her lips had compressed at his outburst, his remark that Laura was his daughter and not hers. "I don't need reminding of that. But you need reminding that she's not in a state to know what she's doing. She hasn't got over Philip's death. It's indecent. That this man Missen looks like him is the worst thing that could have happened. It's bound to affect her judgement. God knows, though, he's no Philip." She was scornful. "He's a scrubby little architect's clerk or something who'll go back to being that when the war's over. If he isn't killed by then. And you wouldn't wish Laura to be widowed a second time, would you? She should have learned from Philip's death that ... damn you, Clive, do I have to tell you how stupid it would be?"

He lifted himself from his chair, wincing at the pain his bursitis gave him. Bloody woman, he said to himself. Making problems, stirring up trouble where there had been none. He fixed her with a blue-eyed glare that had, in his day, frozen subalterns into speechlessness. "No more of it, Cynthia," he said sternly, "I'm not going to interfere in what Laura chooses to do. Do you know what you're doing? You're trying to treat her like a blasted schoolgirl!"

"You don't propose to do anything about it?" Her irritability had grown into cold anger.

"No, I don't."

"If you don't, I will."

"Don't push me too hard, my dear." He was mild again, picking up his *Times* and walking away, leaving her with her woman's frustrations and well aware that he would make no difference to her future intent.

Thirteen

"Laura! Laura!" It had been Philip's voice, recognizably its timbre and the inflexion of love he had always put into it. The call was so clear, echoing still in her mind, that for a shocking moment she thought he must be standing there. She had been sitting at her dressing-table shaping the red paste of lipstick to her mouth when she heard it, and it was as though he had spoken from behind her.

"Philip?" she whispered and the words came again, so insistent that she turned and looked around the room. Then she stood and went to the door and opened it. There was nothing, only the empty corridor leading to the head of the stairs and, from below, the sounds of somebody moving. She trembled with the shock of it, feeling him near to her, yet knowing he could not be.

She returned to the dressing-table and stared at her face in the mirror, trying to control herself. She felt that she was dangerously near to being unbalanced, letting her imagination take over in raising a simulacrum off the dead who should be allowed to rest in the peace of his nothingness. This subconscious calling him back to her was morbid and unhealthy. The rational part of her mind accepted that he had gone like a leaf blown prematurely from a tree, now withered and dead and incorporated back into the soil. Accepting it did nothing to ease the pain and ache of his leaving her. There was no faith from which she could obtain comfort, nothing in the Christian God to which she could turn for a belief of a living after death, nothing more than was given to a squashed beetle or a slaughtered pig. If he existed – and she wanted him to exist so that she could hate him – he was cruel and without compassion, a vast indifference to pain and suffering. Philip was gone and she hadn't even the solace of numbing grief. Instead, there still came the recurring nightmares of his plunging to the earth, his mouth open as he screamed silently from an agonized face. The echoes of it were carried over into the grey lack of interest of her days and, with it, the raw-nerved black organ of loss that quivered and hurt piercingly when touched with a recall of him. She despised her body for remaining alive while his, that warm and loving flesh which had so easily and smoothly brought a unity of responses from her own, was dead. She despised it for its appetites that still needed satisfying. He had awakened her sexual desire from a pre-marriage virginity and then left her with it. Its future satisfying would mean nothing to him and almost as little to her.

"We are the dead," she told her reflection, finishing the putting-on of her lipstick, "for I am dead, too."

Oliver had applied for permission to leave the airfield for the evening, driving to Saxinge Hall in the green MG he wasn't quite certain had been given or loaned to him. That he had used his ration of petrol coupons was no problem, the tank being filled illicitly with the 100-octane fuel on which his Typhoon flew. Resting on the seat beside him was a bottle of under-the-counter gin and the angostura bitters he had noticed Laura drank with it. He drove slowly, unused to the controls of the tiny car and restricted by the masked headlights that threw only a feeble yellow rectangle of light a few yards in front of the bonnet.

When he came in from the blacked-out darkness of the forecourt, Woollgar had greeted him with a special warmth and shaken him by the hand. Lady Woollgar, although not so genial, had smiled and said, "You'll stay for supper, of course?" That was the first indication that he was not expected to take Laura out as he had intended, for which he had gone to the limit in cashing an extra-large cheque. Although he thanked her and accepted, he felt disappointment. It wasn't his métier to sit around making polite social noises with a father and mother putting the brake on what he wanted to do. He took it to be the preliminary vetting of him as a suitable escort and he thought he had misjudged Lady Woollgar's earlier antagonism.

When Laura came down from her room, he sucked in his breath. She wore a woollen dress that fitted her like soft moss and a gold rope necklet encircled her throat. Her black hair gleamed and swung easily about her face. She looked freshly-bathed and made-up and he noticed that there were the faintest of smudges beneath her eyes. There was no smile for him, but she stared hard and he knew that she was seeing again his resemblance to her dead husband.

He gave her the gin and bitters. "You might find it difficult to obtain," he said keeping irony out of his voice, knowing that the sort of money she and her parents must have could always overcome a war's shortages.

"You've a practical mind, Mr Missen," she told him gravely, "that rises above scent and flowers. You'll help me drink it, I hope." To her father she said, "We'll go into the conservatory out of your way, darling."

There were brass lamps there with white globes, twin moons floating in a miniature jungle. The glass in the walls and roof reflected them, throwing sharp black shadows from the green foliage. Small palms and stiff-leaved trees with spiny outgrowths, stumpy cacti and tall yuccas grew from pots in crowded profusion and climbing plants grew up the iron ribs of the structure. A tree fern arched its spiky fronds over a white-painted table and four chairs. The clean smell of wet peat filled the warm moist air. It was, Oliver thought, the sort of place which Victorians used for their assignations and it cheered him. Through the glass was darkness and the dim foliage of the outside trees.

She had carried two large cut-glass tumblers in with her, placing them on the table to join the gin and bitters. Then she sat and gazed at him gravely. "I feel like getting drunk," she said. "You can either join me or just pour as I need it."

"I'll join you." He was surprised at her directness. "I need anaesthetizing, too. Heavy or light?" He unscrewed the bottle and began pouring the gin.

"Heavy-ish. I'll do it in stages. And it's not an anaesthetic for me. It's an analgesic."

"I'm sorry." He added the bitters until the gin turned pink, handling her one of the tumblers and sitting down. "Now and then? Or only when you entertain importunate men?" He smiled to show he was being humorous.

She didn't smile back. "Are you importunate? I hadn't noticed. Every night," she said expressionlessly. "I need to, otherwise I wouldn't sleep. Does that shock you?"

"No." He thought that he understood women who smile rarely if at all. Their seriousness concealed the damped-down forces of unreleased emotions he could exploit. Lifting the glass, he said, "*Prosit.*"

She sipped at her gin without acknowledging his salutation. "Damn you!" she said, "You *are* like him. In appearance, I mean. As if he's hiding there behind that moustache you wear."

"It upsets you?"

"It ... it disturbs me a little. It reminds me of him. But, of course, you don't resemble him otherwise."

"I suppose not." He wasn't sure how she meant that, but it sounded slightly belittling. "What can anyone say?"

"Nothing," she said flatly.

"I suppose had I not resembled him, I wouldn't be here."

"Possibly not."

He felt deflated. "I think I need my drink."

"Forgive my saying so," she said, "but you look as if you've had a bad time."

"It shows?" He wasn't going to deny it and he touched his face with his fingertips, wondering how it could. It would be almost as good as wearing a medal ribbon.

She shrugged. "If you're worried, I assure you that it doesn't detract from your looks. I heard them going over this morning," she added, "and they woke me up. Were you with them?"

"Yes. A bit of a do near Versailles."

She waited and, when he didn't add to it, said, "Are you going to be all coy about it?"

"I usually am until I'm well tanked up." He guessed she would be scornful of line shooting and he was conscious of the lack of ribbons in the unused space beneath his pilot's wings. "Some of my friends bought it and I was a little bloodied."

"But unbowed?"

He grinned boyishly. "No, frightened to death." She wouldn't believe so easy an admission.

She pushed her empty tumbler towards him. The gin had been a large one and she had drunk it quickly. As he poured more into it, she said, "You have heard how my husband died?"

"He was shot down in his Lancaster on a bombing raid?"

"Yes." Her eyes were dark and large on his. "Do you think he was frightened?"

"Frightened?" What sort of a question was that?

"I mean ... dying as he did."

He thought she had been aching to ask someone like himself that question and she hadn't waited long. It would be like a tongue touching always at the hole where the tooth had been extracted. He pushed the tumbler over to her and then finished his own in one swallow, feeling the heady stuff like fire in his throat. "Is that why you can't sleep?"

She closed her eyes briefly. "One of the reasons. I have this dreadful picture of him in my mind . . . falling . . . screaming all the way down. It's not anything I can forget, not anything I can live with."

He knew that before he could have her he would need to exorcize this ghost that was haunting her. Her telling him was an intimacy of a sort, although she was making him feel like a psychiatrist. It wasn't the role in which he had seen himself. He shook his head. "I'm sure that wouldn't be so. Of course I don't know the circumstances, but there are a couple of reasons why it's unlikely. If his aircraft was so badly damaged that it was uncontrollable and he wasn't killed immediately, he would have baled out with his crew and been taken prisoner." He didn't tell her of the other possibilities: of his being wounded and unable to, of his parachute being damaged or failing to open anyway. "If he stayed with it, he would be too involved in bringing it down in one piece to have time to be frightened. And with a shot-up Lancaster and a crew to worry about, he'd have his hands full. Believe me, you just don't have the time."

"There had to be when he knew."

"Yes, there possibly would be. Look," he said gently, "don't think I'm shooting a line if I give you an experience of my own. And I've had a couple. I mean, when being killed seemed inevitable." He drank more gin, thinking out his words. "It was my third or fourth flight in the Typhoon, after I'd done my circuits and bumps and was stooging around to get used to handling her in different situations. I was a bit cocky, I suppose, although she's a difficult kite to fly at the best of times. I took her up to 16,000 feet to do practice recoveries from spins. I didn't have a care in the world and I'd genned up on the Pilot's Notes until I knew them backwards. A spin in a Tiffie is usually vicious, although that isn't anything that's advertised. She bounces you around in the cockpit and knocks you silly, scrambles your brains. And you have to start to bring her out of it – if you can – after she's done her first twist. I thought I'd done everything right – full opposite rudder, centralizing the stick, that sort of thing – but she stayed in it. And I knew she wasn't going to come out. By that time she was dropping like an aerodynamic brick and the ground was beginning to come up pretty fast."

Her eyes were steady on his face, unrevealing of what she was thinking.

"I lacked all the things you need to fly: weight, stability and coordination," he continued, "and there was nothing I could do about it. I needed to bale out and that's something I've always had a fear of doing. Ever since ... well, ever since. And it's not easy in a kite that's spinning you around and keeping you off-balance. I managed to push back the hood and unbuckle myself. That's when the airstream comes in and you have to fight to get out against the pressure. And all the time you're conscious that you are running out of height. Running out of enough of it for the brolly to open before you hit the deck. And I was stuck, half-in and half-out, pushed against the hood by the wind with the breath knocked out of me, mesmerized by the ground whirling around and coming up to meet me. That's where the point comes in. I knew I'd left it too late, that I was going to dig myself a hole in the landscape. If I felt anything it was that I was angry, furious at the stupidity of it... flattened in the cockpit like a pinned insect. There was no real fear, no regrets. I wasn't even sorry about having to die. I never had any thoughts of my parents, or anybody. It could have all been happening to somebody else. True, I still had some sort of instinct for survival, but it seemed detached somehow. I suppose the old adrenalin was pumping away. There was nothing I could do and I *knew* that I was going to be killed. I make the distinction between the future prospect of death and recognized imminent death, the point where you can no longer do anything to avoid it. I'm frightened when the prospect is there, and who isn't? On the two occasions when it was imminent, I wasn't. I suppose nature steps in to save you too much horror. I've read that animals and birds captured by a predator get this detachment from reality effect. Anyway, I obviously didn't die. When we were definitely too low for me to jump – even had I been able to – she came out of the spin of her own accord, straightened herself out and started to climb up towards another stall and spin." He grinned. "Cross my heart, it's true. I had a harder job getting back into the cockpit before she did than I had in trying to get out. When I'd finally got her under control I suddenly had the shakes and I must have been as white as a piece of paper. I know I wanted to be sick. I never did another practice spin although I faked my Log Book to show I'd done my quota." He paused. "Is all that any help? Believe me, it's true. Every word of it."

She remained silent for a long time, looking abstractedly out through the dark glass. Then she turned her head to him and said, "Thank you."

What he had told her was the truth and had happened to him. What he didn't tell her was that he had watched an army parachutist falling from a troop carrier with his parachute unopened. He had screamed all the way down until hitting the ground, but perhaps that anticipation of imminent death had lasted too long.

Oliver saw that her tumbler was empty and he poured more in, then refilled his own. It was beginning to have an effect on him and he realized that he was next door to being garrulous. He felt also the stiffening of a need for her. He looked at her, imagining the underclothing that would be revealed beneath the dress. It would be silky and clinging and crackle with static electricity, its taking off the unsheathing of warm ivory skin. He saw her naked body in his mind's eye and used it even as he spoke to her.

"Your mother asked me to stay for supper," he said.

"She's my stepmother."

"I didn't know." He hesitated and gave her a half-smile. "I was surprised to be asked. I had the impression she didn't approve of me."

"She probably doesn't. It bothers you?" Her words were beginning to be slurred, her dark-blue eyes glistening like, he thought, the sea seen from above. She lounged lax in the chair, her attitude as if waiting for him to say or do something she was expecting.

"I would prefer to be liked, naturally," he said cautiously.

"I can't offer you any comfort on that." She was a woman who could always make him feel that he had said the wrong thing. "Is it because you are trying to make me one of the women in your life?"

Her words jolted him, but he felt that he had to jump in with both feet or be taken for a timid mouse of a man. "This isn't like me at all, Laura," he said, putting earnest sincerity into his voice, "but I think I'm in love with you. No, I *am*. And I've not said that to a woman before. Am I being presumptuous?"

She thought about it for a moment or two, her face showing nothing. "I'm flattered," she said drily, "but I hope you aren't expecting it to be reciprocated. Oh, don't worry. I'm not about to tell you that I don't wish to see you again."

"I've offended you. I'm sorry." But he knew that although she had shrugged it off, it would have its effect. Few women ever told that by a man could be anything but warmed to him.

"To the contrary." The slurring in her words was more pronounced. "I told you that I was flattered, although I don't necessarily believe you. And what do you propose doing about it? Get into bed with me?" She laughed without humour.

He swallowed. "You're a very direct person."

"Why shouldn't I be? Isn't that your intention? But I warn you that I'm very much an empty shell and if that's what you want you're welcome to it. You might," she said sardonically, "bring something back – give me something I need. On the other hand, you probably might not. It's a chance I shall have to take."

"Only if you wanted to." Damn her! He thought she might be mocking him, making him feel a scheming womanizer. For a very brief second he felt like telling her to go to hell. She was safe enough here in the conservatory with her father and stepmother in the house and could afford to exercise her mockery on him.

Seeing his face stiffen, as if she had read his thoughts, she said, "I don't mean to tease you. Gin makes me very outspoken."

He smiled with an effort. "I was going to ask you if I might see you tomorrow."

"I shall be in London. With my father," she added. "I may stay there overnight in our flat. He would be returning earlier. Would that fit in with your war effort?"

"My kite's temporarily unserviceable, so I possibly won't be going over. Can I telephone you?"

"At the flat, if you can get to South Kensington. Not here. Have you a good memory?"

"A photographic one."

"Then remember Kensington 7530. If you get no reply, it's possible that I've changed my mind about you. And now," she told him, draining her tumbler and standing, "having made our rather despicable clandestine arrangements, we'd better go into supper."

He rose too and stood before her, holding her arms in his hands and looking into her eyes, seeing in them only her infuriatingly cool self-possession. He kissed her gently, feeling her mouth moist and warm on his, tasting the gin. Although her closeness, the heat from her body and her perfume did things to his breathing, there was no discernible response from her and her arms remained passive at her sides. There was no rejection either. She turned away and he followed her.

Fourteen

After checking in at the guardroom, Oliver lifted the bonnet of his MG and removed the rotor arm. Not in obedience to the regulations requiring a motor vehicle to be immobilized against what was now an improbable German invasion, but against its being taken and used by a fellow pilot. He walked because he had a visit to make and a reason, should the Duty Officer become aware of his return, for not returning immediately to his room.

His Typhoon, silvered with a fine mist of dew, stood outside the workshop hangar from which he could hear late-night activity. The starboard tailplane and elevator had been removed completely, the damaged wing and rudder patched with bare metal plates not yet camouflaged. It was sobering evidence of his stupidity in doing his victory roll and it could have killed him.

He found the Flight Sergeant fitter in the hangar and was told that subject to his being able to cannibalize another Typhoon for a tail section, it should be back in the air by the morning. The flak and cannon shell damage to it was of too common an occurrence for him to comment on in terms of sympathy for the pilot. His concern was to get his machines back into service and not to worry about the men who had to fly them.

Oliver returned to the Typhoon, checking his watch. It was a little short of 10.45 and too early to be certain that Morwenna had returned to her room. Mounting the wing he slid back the cockpit hood and climbed in, sitting in the parachute well of the seat, the metal cold and hard against his buttocks. Her odour of fuel and glycol and rubber was, next to a woman's scent, something that stirred and excited him most. He rubbed condensation from the windshield so that he could look through it at the long nose and the motionless propeller pointing to the clear starlit sky. The brooding quietness in the air made it difficult for him to imagine a countryside teeming with men and guns, armoured vehicles and artillery, dark harbours thick with troop transports and landing barges, the thousands of men waiting unknowingly, if not unsuspecting, of the death that awaited them on whatever killing ground had been selected for the invasion. And he was a part of it. That he could be one of those destined to die was a thought he blocked before it could take real shape. Death, so far, was something that had happened to other people. That he was still alive proved it. At the moment, he was more concerned that that stupid bitch Morwenna had got herself fertilized, that Poxton was regarding him maliciously as a candidate for an LMF report.

Poxton – the arrogant bastard! – rankled with him most. Too unimaginative to see the utter stupidity of getting oneself killed for no significant purpose, a man filled with an insane obtuseness that would be called bravery. Swordsmen didn't impale themselves blindly on an opponent's rapier just to get inside a defence they could otherwise penetrate. No more would a fighter-pilot with a Messerschmitt or a Focke-Wulf pouring shells at him. He would fling his aircraft around to avoid the fire for his own advantage, to win and survive. Flak was no different. Even the bomber boys dodged it where they could, and why shouldn't they? It made sense, not cowardice. Kelham, Tunnard and the two Bomphoon pilots. Dead now and their aircraft destroyed. And what had they achieved by it? Nothing but some ineffectual holes in a Frog château and probably a few flak gunners. Whereas he was alive and three Kraut pilots were not. He scowled in the darkness of the cockpit. The same thing was going to happen again until they had all been clobbered. If Poxton bought it first it would be no more than he deserved. He wanted the bastard to buy it. A picture of him came into his mind with his rufous hair and the pukka-wallah's grey eyes that had looked at him with such corrosive contempt. He had never hated a man with so much venom. The thought that he doubted his courage, believed him pusillanimous, was a shrivelling one and not to be lived with.

Holding the spade-grip of the stick in his hand, feeling the non-resistance of the cables pulling against the missing tailplane, his thumb resting on the firing button, he closed his eyes ... *he turned the Typhoon smoothly on its wing, keeping the aircraft approaching below him within his view, seeing clearly the roundels on the dark green and grey camouflaging of the wings, the black shape of Poxton's head and shoulders beneath the translucent hood. Pushing the stick forward and easing the nose down he held the other Typhoon steady in the red ring of his sight, watching it expand as it grew closer until he could see Poxton's face, the eyes behind the goggles no longer contemptuous but staring up at him in fear as he recognized the force of his hatred and his intent. When he was almost on him, drawing out and prolonging the period of Poxton's terror, he pressed the gun button with his thumb, feeling the aircraft shudder in the recoil as the streams of cannon shells converged in a hail of flying metal and shattered hood. He saw goggles and mask torn from Poxton's face to show a red and pink shambles of spouting blood and shattered bone as the Typhoon fell sideways in its long plunge to the earth ...*

He opened his eyes, frightened at the intensity of his imagery. He had never wanted to kill a man so much before. Not a man who was of his own tribe. But he had done it in his mind and, like his mental fornication with women unconscious of the ferment behind the unrevealing features, knew it to be wishful thinking.

He switched his thoughts to Laura. The remainder of the evening had been unrewarding in terms of getting closer to her. To know that she was willing to take him as a lover and not to be able to further it before a possible feminine change of mind was a torment to him. The supper had been long on silver and bone-china and short on food; the conversation civilized and impersonal and mainly about the progress of the war. Woollgar had been genial and affable, Lady Woollgar aristocratically gracious, her calm eyes keeping him in view without apparent interest. She had the mannerism of holding poised her heavy silver fork when she spoke to him as if weighing it against the reply he would have to make, and it made him feel uncomfortable. The eating of the food and the pouring of the wine into crystal goblets had been as ritualistic as that at a Mess Guest Night. He had suffered rather than enjoyed it, conscious of Laura seated opposite him, quiet and content apparently to listen and joining the conversation only when she had to. He considered that he had survived the evening reasonably well, holding in check the garrulity induced by the gin he had shared earlier with Laura in the conservatory, being modest and unassuming and unwilling to discuss his own operational sorties. It had been difficult to keep his gaze away from Laura, but wondering how she could be so bloody casual and impassive in her regard of him while his own imagination projected them forward to the following night when they would lie naked together in her flat. Between them, he felt, was more than the prospect of an animal coupling, although he needed the sensuality of flesh against flesh as the essence and expression of it. A woman was a woman and man the instrument to satisfy her need. Until now it had not mattered if one had held herself unentered against his intention to penetrate for there was always another and, subject to the qualifications of having a clean and unwrinkled body, white teeth and an uncomplicated generosity in her giving, that had been enough. Now there was Laura and it did matter. None before had so indifferently, yet so deeply, pierced the skin of his dispassionate sexuality to bleed the emotions behind. If this was infatuation, then he was infatuated. Even if it meant the virtual exclusion of everything else, he had to possess her. The 'everything else' included, very definitely, the threat posed by Morwenna and her pregnancy.

He climbed from the cockpit and slid from the wing to the ground. The moon was rising, a papery silver disc silhouetting distant trees and, from high above in the paling sky, he could hear the pulsating rhythm of the engines of bomber aircraft, see the thin lines of their contrails as they headed towards their target. He wished that he could be with them, riding herd in his Typhoon. It was a Hunter's Moon more than a Bombers' Moon and the Luftwaffe night fighters would be waiting like sharks to decimate them, sharks who in their concentration on the kill could be exposed in their turn to his cannon.

Standing in the shadows at the rear of the manor house he waited, listening for sounds of movement from Morwenna's room. The blackout curtains had been drawn back and he could see her in the darkness, a dim shape in the bed, her face a paler oval turned towards him. Feeling for the tiny gap she would have left for him between the window and its frame, he tapped warningly on the glass with his fingernails, then opened it and climbed through. He closed the curtains over the window and stooped over her, kissing her because that was what he had always done, turning his mouth away to her cheek when she sought to prolong the contact. She smelled fragrantly of scent and talcum powder and of the indefinable odour of a woman in bed. He knew that she was expecting him to make love to her.

"I've missed you," he whispered, moving from her and sitting on the bed at her side.

"I've missed you too, darling. I looked for you. You weren't in the Mess." She reached out and in the near total darkness found his hand and held it, her own moist and hot.

"No." He waited a few moments and then added, "I've had a bad day."

"I worried a lot. You were hit. I saw the damage."

He shrugged. "It was sod-all. I'm still in one piece."

"What was the bad day about?" There was a gentle insistent pull on his hand that he resisted.

"About you. About what you were doing." He wasn't looking in her direction. 'Did you speak to that quack of yours?'

There was a short silence. "I'm sorry, darling. It's quite definite, I'm afraid."

"He's going to do something about it?"

"I didn't ask him."

There was a leaden lump in his chest, a feeling that he never wanted to make love to a woman ever again. He could almost envy men who had only to worry about being killed or mutilated. He compressed his lips, holding back the anger he felt rising. "And now that you know for sure, are you going to do something yourself?"

She withdrew her hand from his. "I wrote to James this afternoon, telling him. It's gone now, Oliver."

"Gone! That was premature, wasn't it?" He wanted to snarl at her bloody-minded obstinacy, but kept his voice low and under control.

"I've thought about it a lot, honestly I have. It's the only way I can feel clean."

He heard footfalls in the passage outside and he waited until they died away with the banging of a closed door. Near him, he could feel the heat from her body, a furnace of white flesh in the black nightdress she wore to please him, eager to envelop his own in its soft pulpy embrace.

"You asked me why I'd had a bad day," he said. "All right, I'll tell you. I suppose it's only right that I should. I've had the most bloody depression. A dark night of the soul. I still have. Not wholly about your pregnancy, although that hasn't helped ..."

She reached again and clutched at his hand. "Darling ..."

"No," he said, "let me finish. You'll probably think I'm weak, neurotic ... anything you like." He made himself sound defeated.

"I've got this feeling of impending ... a premonition that I'm due for the chop. I nearly got clobbered this morning on that hare-brained von Rundstedt op and the odds are that I shall be before I've finished my tour." He squeezed her hand hard. "I'm not snivelling, Wenna, because I suppose I'm not really frightened about being dead. I have to go sometime anyway. Some German bastard is eventually going to have my name and number on his scoreboard. But the thought isn't exactly a cheerful one.'

"Darling, please." She was trying to pull him to her. "I'm sure that you're imagining it. You're tired. You've done too many."

He shook his head. "No. Christ Almighty, it's not unknown! People do get it. It's inside me. A dead certainty." He laughed incredulously, shakily. "Do you know what I was doing this evening? Driving around the bloody countryside in the dark with a bottle of whisky, not quite knowing where I was going or what I was doing. In a daze, trying to make up my mind ... God! It's stupid! The last thing I believed I would ever think of doing, but I'd got myself in a state. I took my revolver with me. I thought the best thing for me, for you, would be to blow my bloody stupid brains out. That's what this depression thing does for you. I was thinking about you, worrying, cursing myself for getting you into this godawful trouble. I thought ... I thought that if I took off before it was too late for you to do something about it, at least I wouldn't be dying with the responsibility of having fathered a bastard on you ... of knowing that you'd been humiliated. What stopped me was the thought of leaving you ... not seeing you again. Even though it might only be for a short time. And if I'm being honest, the disgrace to me came into it too."

He watched the dark hollows of her eyes, waiting for her reaction, wondering whether or not he had laid it on too thick.

"I don't know what to say." Her voice was sad. "This ... this isn't like you. You're frightening me. I don't feel humiliated about having your baby. I want it."

Christ! She was clinging to him like a sticky white slug, not getting the bloody message at all. Why had he let himself be used by her? She was a fat, sentimentally maudlin cow made revolting by pregnancy and he wasn't going to allow her to stand between him and Laura. He wanted to reach inside her and scrape out with his fingernails the tiny monster barnacled to the wall of the uterus that had betrayed him with its fecundity.

"I love you so much, Wenna," he whispered. "Too much to let this thing in you come between us. Not now. Please God if I'm wrong about this premonition business and I do get through, then when we're married we can have a child who isn't going to suffer from being a bastard."

Her hand squirmed in his in the anguish of her emotion, a small white mouse being strangled in his fingers. "Don't, please don't, Oliver. You don't know what you're asking. Even if I wanted to it's wrong, a crime. I could go to prison for life. And it's dangerous. I might die. You're not a woman, Oliver, and you don't know what could happen. And the baby. Now that it's started it's entitled to live. Killing it would be murder."

"For God's sake, Wenna, be sensible. Don't bloody well dramatize it. None of those things are likely to happen." He knew now why women like her got themselves throttled and buried in unfrequented woods. 'It's nothing at the moment but a bit of jelly. And if it's half mine, surely I've a right to decide that it isn't fair to allow it to be born into this shambles of a world."

"I'm sorry, I honestly am." She was softly obdurate. "But I can't kill it. Please don't ask me again. I know it's wrong that I should be having it and I know that if we can't get married it will be a ... that it will be illegitimate. I love you and that's the only reason I've got for having been unfaithful to James. I've hurt him too and I don't know what he will do when he hears about it." Although he couldn't see, he knew that her eyes must be soggy with tears intended to unman him, a woman's ultimate weapon he was determined to resist.

"You're quite set on it then? Despite whatever might happen to me?"

"Yes. But don't worry, Oliver," she said with a quiet dignity, "I shan't involve you. I won't bring you into it. Give me a cigarette, will you?"

He opened his case and passed her one, taking one for himself. The flare of his lighter, dazzling for a moment, allowed him to read her face. There were no tears, only an expression of calm acceptance. Then there was darkness again in which only the cigarettes glowed as small red coals.

"You know I love you," she said sombrely. "God only knows I've told you often enough. It's something I can't help, but it doesn't blind me to the fact that you don't love me. Not in the same way."

"Dammit, sweetheart," he protested, unable to keep his irritation with her from his voice, "you know I do."

"No. I'm not that much of a ninny. A woman can tell." She was bitter. "All you have for me are just words; all you are now concerned about is being involved. I'm sorry, but I can't believe anything you've said to me. You just aren't the man to shoot yourself because of a woman and it was a vile thing to tell me that you could."

"That's a bloody nasty thing to say to me." The bitch, he thought, after all I've been to her, done for her, and the risks I've taken.

"You've no intention that we shall get married," she said quietly. It was a statement, not a question.

He stood, his anger back with him. "Obviously not, if that's the way you feel about me." He had difficulty in stopping himself from shouting, aware that the rooms on either side could be occupied. "So why the hell are you so bloody obstinate about getting rid of it, so anxious to leave your husband!"

"Oh, God," she wailed. "You won't understand, will you. I knew when we first made love that I would have to tell James."

"You could have told me, damn you. You must have known I'd have no intention of breaking up a marriage."

"You only wanted my body? Is that what it amounted to?" There was the sound of movement as she lifted the bedclothing. Against the white sheet she was a dark bulkiness with pallid arms, her flesh showing opalescent through the thin chiffon of her nightdress. "It's still here and it's my misfortune that it still needs you."

He looked down at her without desire, hating her and the tiny malignant fœtus growing in her womb; watching him, he thought, through the flesh of her belly. He could not put any part of himself within its reach. In his imagination she was visibly and grossly swollen with expectant motherhood, a gravid possessive female alien to his needs and repugnant to him. He stubbed his cigarette in the ashtray on the table at her side and moved to the window, putting on his cap and pulling the curtains open.

"I'm sorry that you feel this way about me," he said coldly. "In view of what you've said, perhaps you'll think differently about getting rid of your ... of that thing inside you."

Without waiting for an answer he pushed the window open and

lifted his leg over the sill, stepping out into the moonlit night. He closed the window and turned to be dazzled by the beam of a torch directed at him from the shadow of the garden wall. His heart jumped and the breath caught in his throat as he held a hand up to his face to shield his eyes from the blinding glare.

"Damn you!" he called out fiercely. "Whoever you are, put that bloody light out!"

The beam snapped off and the figure of a uniformed man stepped from the black square of shadow. Below the two chevrons of a corporal on his arm he wore the brassard of a service policeman. A rifle hung slung over one shoulder and he saluted Oliver awkwardly. "I'm sorry, sir," he said, "I'm only carrying out my instructions."

Oliver took in the man's face, clear now in the moonlight, searching it for signs of his knowing. So much as he could see, it was disciplined stolidness centred around the big nose of a lumpish yokel dragged away from his horses and plough. He prayed that Morwenna would not blunder to the window to see what was happening, that she would remain in her bed and not flap in female panic.

"Now that you're satisfied who I am, Corporal," he said, "I'll say goodnight and leave you to whatever it is you're supposed to be doing." He turned and started to move away.

"Sir!" The corporal switched on his torch again, this time directing the beam on to a wooden notice board pushed into the soil of the border. It read OUT OF BOUNDS TO ALL RANKS. "With respect, sir, I saw you climbing out of the window." His voice in the quiet darkness was too loud for Oliver's comfort.

He halted and turned back to him. "You are mistaken, Corporal." He put a superior rank's hardness in his words. "You saw me walking past it, taking a short cut to my quarters. And stand to attention when you speak to an officer."

The corporal stiffened, his expression suddenly wooden. "Beg pardon, sir, but I saw you climb out. May I ask whose room, sir?" He swivelled the beam of the torch to throw a disc of light over the window.

"You are being insolent, *Corporal.* I said you saw me walking past it. Are you doubting my word?"

"No, sir. But I saw you climbing out. Those are Waaf officers' quarters, sir, and out of bounds. To all ranks, sir." He spoke in a loud voice as if giving evidence at a court martial and Oliver knew it wouldn't be long before this uncouth blabbermouth attracted the attention of the occupants of the other rooms.

He was as mortified as he was angry, realizing that he had antagonized the man into bloody-minded obstinacy. He softened his words. "All right, Corporal. You are doing your job and I'm not blaming you for that. It's dark and if you've made a mistake, that's understandable. Let's leave it at that, shall we? I won't take the matter of your attitude towards an officer any further."

He had left it too late. While the man's expression remained superficially respectful, his eyes had hostility in them. "Sir, may I have your name, please."

He pulled the peak of his cap further down over his eyes, feeling grittiness at the NCO's intractability, wanting to hit him in his stupid bovine face. Once he had his name, he knew that he would be for the chop. He felt cheapened, the situation in which he found himself sordid; called to account by a bloody general duties erk who did little more than walk round the airfield in the dark with a rifle it was unlikely he had fired at anything more dangerous than a canvas target. And questioning a man who risked his life daily for someone like him who probably spent as much time at the NAAFI tea wagon as he did hounding airmen for unfastened buttons. His predicament fed his anger, making him speak distinctly in measured tones as though to a half-wit.

"Corporal," he said, "you are an NCO and your authority is with those of your own rank and below it; with any matter concerning the security of this airfield. It is not with operational aircrew. It is not – particularly not – with a commissioned officer."

"It says 'all ranks' on that board, sir," he said stubbornly, "and I'm only asking for your name to give to the Duty Officer. Them's my instructions. Specially, sir, when anybody's found trespassing in the Waaf quarters." There was the slightest suggestion of a sneer in the way he said it. As if he were savouring the thought of his having caught an officer in so plebeian an activity as unlawful fornication. "Your name, please, sir."

"Damn you, Corporal," Oliver ground out furiously, "it's Lloyd. Flying Officer Lloyd."

He turned then and left him standing there, pulling a book from his pocket to write the name down. When Lloyd – who was shorter than Oliver by a head and clean-shaven – had been seen in the morning and inevitably not identified, they would detail the corporal to seek out the remaining officer pilots until he was recognized. And it was that stupid bitch Morwenna who had got him into this trouble. Her room would be identified and she would be interviewed, her association with him deemed as improper as his with her. Whatever she said to keep him out of it, sooner or later she would have to disclose her pregnancy and compound the trouble he was already in. Poxton would love that and be implacable in his efforts to see that Oliver suffered for every breach of every regulation to which he could fit him. Suddenly he felt that everything was going wrong for him, his problems becoming insurmountable. He was in a rage of frustration, hating too many people; people who were getting in his way and whom he wanted to smash into a mess of splintered bone and bloody flesh.

Fifteen

The countryside to which Philip found himself bound in the curious limbo of his mind retained its aspect of unreality, its twilit dimness and muted colours. A wind he could not feel, and which did not disturb his hair, fluttered silent leaves on trees. Occasionally, as if seeing it astigmatically from the corners of his eyes, he thought he could discern another landscape, dark and purplish, underlying and conforming in shape and configuration to that he travelled. Weird and strange, he sometimes saw in it moving figures that were vague and indeterminate in outline. The shapes and colours faded and vanished when he tried to concentrate on them.

He recalled a story by H. G. Wells about a character called Plattner who, after an explosion in a school laboratory, found himself seeing a different landscape while still living physically in his own surroundings. He had been invisible to the boys of his form although he could see them, hazy and unreal. Nor had he been able to communicate with them. There were parallels and his own crash could have been the catalyst for a similar happening. No, he told himself, that was fiction and an improbability in fact. He had to keep his feet on the ground, be a realist.

He discovered that he could keep his mind from falling into directionless confusion and despair only by the confirmation of the solid reality of his physical self; by a sustained awareness of the familiar such as by fingering the buttons and zips of his leather jacket and flying suit, the identity bracelet on his wrist and the feel of his feet in his boots. These were the only tangibles, trivial enough in the nightmare of his hallucinations. That he would emerge from this disorder between reality and dream he had no doubt. He knew himself to be a sick man with a mind given over to dreams and fantasies, but that it would soon be clear of whatever was causing it. Each time he prepared to sleep, which was often, he forced himself into the conviction that when he woke he would find himself back to daylight sanity and an awareness of where he was. It surprised him that he could think of his condition objectively, trying with his small knowledge of disorders of the brain to identify it. He considered that schizophrenia might be what he suffered; a split mind with himself living a distorted awareness in one part of it, hallucinating the phantasmagoric countryside and its inhabitants from his compulsion to return to Laura, the wish impelling the mind to this tortuous response. That he was alive and physically aware he had no doubts. That he was actually making his way through France was impossible to equate with his being no part of it but a moving observer, apparently unseen and undetectable by the wraiths of people he had encountered. Nevertheless, undetectable as he appeared to be, the thought of entering a town with its hundreds of people he would be unable to avoid frightened him. When he came to the outskirts of one he took to the fields, unable to face again the proof of his non-being to them. Where he could he kept to the more easily negotiable roads and hid from the occasional passers-by, silent and semi-opaque in their own world. Objects that had been solid to him took on a different dimension.

He discovered that the trunk of a tree, a fence post, the stones of a wall, had become as insubstantial as the twilight into which they merged, possessing a dream-like tenuity incapable of resistance to his touch. Yet, as he walked, the ground beneath his feet was solid and unyielding. In passing through a village around which he was unable to go, he passed close to a shop window and, looking into it, saw that there was no reflection of himself in the glass. That had shocked him, stopping him in mid-stride where he had been hurrying to peer unbelievingly among the reflections of the opposite buildings for his mirror image. Its absence reinforced more firmly his belief in his dream state, that he was wandering in this nightmare world within his own skull.

To his shame, he had frequent outbursts of weeping that accompanied his more acute periods of depression. He no longer tried to orientate himself in a landscape that was strange to him, where the name of a town or the signposts he saw meant nothing other than that they were French, but walked steadily, drawn compellingly to an unknown destination by the same unthinking instinct possessed by a migrating bird. Nights were now barely distinguishable from days, only the nearly deserted roads and village streets allowing him to guess which was which. And neither made any difference to the insistent compulsion in him.

During one of his periods of sleep, when he had again dreamed within his dreaming, he heard Laura's voice, clear although remote and thin as if reaching him through the airlessness of space. It had taken him to her, suspended above her as she lay in bed. Her head was deep in the pillow, only part of her face visible in the shadowed room. He saw the smudge of eyelash over the one visible closed eye, dark against the pallor of her cheek, the familiar sweet curve of her mouth and the gentle rhythm of her breathing. An arm rested on the pillow that had been his. Although her lips remained unmoving, he heard her voice. "Philip, Philip, my love. Come back to me ... please come back." The haunting sadness in her words brought tears to his eyes.

"I'm coming, darling," he wept. "Wait for me." He felt choked with the anguish of his love for her.

"I can't see you, Philip. Where are you?" She lay unmoving in her sleep, although he could hear her sobbing. "I don't know where you are."

"I'm here, sweetheart. Here with you."

"Remember me, Philip ... remember me ..."

Then horribly, as though picturing it with her, he saw himself in the cockpit of his Lancaster, a rudimentary cockpit imagined by a mind that had never been in one. There was darkness outside it and a sensation of falling and there was his unmasked face distorted with terror, the mouth opened grotesquely in a silent scream of terror. Yellow flames curled around the phantom figure, its clothing smouldering and Laura sitting up in a convulsion, her eyes staring and her mouth shaking in her fear. Then he lost his vision of her in the awakening reality of the half-light of his surroundings.

The intensity of her grief and the horror of her dreaming had remained with him, strengthening his desire to return to her, to assure her of the needlessness of her mourning his supposed death.

When he could find them, he slept in barns or sheds away from where he might be seen. He was still free from physical tiredness, but his mind needed frequently a shutting down, a resting period from the emotional confusion of his thoughts, a cessation from the repetitive recall of his being shot down. He had found a barn on the periphery of an untidy huddle of farm buildings surrounding a paved courtyard and out of sight of the road he had been walking.

The large horse, tethered in its stall inside and steaming quietly, was as unaware of his presence as he was of the means by which he had entered, for the door was closed and he had not opened it. A ladder rested against the floor of a hay loft in the roof space. When he attempted to climb it, it confirmed once more that for him objects had no more substance than the ungraspable surrounding air. He laid himself on the dirty cement floor in a shadowed corner and closed his eyes.

I am in bed somewhere, he told himself. When I wake I shall be myself, although I don't know where. It doesn't matter, not even if I have to feel pain. I won't care. Just so long as my mind is back in my body. "Please, Lord," he whispered, "please help me. I don't know what's happening to me." He forced his thinking to canalize on touch, to an awareness of bed sheets touching his skin, the soft pressure of blankets, the sounds of people moving around him. It had to happen. There had to be an ending to every dream.

In the gradual merging of awareness into sleep, he saw the door open and through it a man entering, followed by a woman. The man, middle-aged with a wind-weathered sun-dried face, was heavily moustached and wore soiled blue overalls and muddied boots. The woman, younger by several years, her face flushed as if she had come from a hot kitchen, closed the door and stood with her shoulders against the wooden slats of the wall, her arms flaccid against her sides. She waited, her heavily built body palpitating with her breathing. She spoke unheard words to the man and laughed, showing white teeth and a shiny pink tongue between her pulpy lips. He approached her, pushing himself against her belly, his mouth open and engulfing hers within his moustache as his big hands lifted her dress to her waist. Her own hands slid down between his thighs, her fingers moving like feeding white worms as they manipulated him into her. She pulled her mouth away from his and it gaped in an O of pleasure, her arms now around him, her hands clutched on his buttocks as he jerked into her with a metronomic regularity while he gazed unseeing at the wooden slats over the top of her head.

Philip stared, hypnotized by the grossness of this hallucinatory copulation taking place before him and drawn from God only knew what dirty part of his mind. It nauseated him and as he watched their panting culmination he realized that the act, wholly animal and sensual, an excitement of the physical senses with nothing of the higher love for another in it, was something he could not again imagine doing. It was as if this revolting animality of man and woman had no further part in his being, that this putting an extension of himself into a woman's body was a perversion he had left behind in the wreckage of his aircraft. Sensuality and eroticism had left him, the man he had been a shrunken shadow inside the hollow husk of his masculinity. His unwitting voyeurism should have stirred the chemistry of his sex, moved him to something approaching tumescence. Yet he felt only a comparable depletion of *post coitus*, a disgust with himself for the remembered prurience of his sexual greed. Lust had drained from his veins like a tainted liquid and left his body bland, purged of its animality. Never, he was convinced, could he again subject Laura to this debasement of the flesh. "God in heaven," he whispered. "What's come over me?" He put his hand to his loins, his fingers feeling for his genitals, surprised that they were still there, that he hadn't been gelded in the crash.

He never saw the withdrawal of the man and woman from their copulating for he had dropped into a sleep, his last vision of them forced from his awareness by the closing of his eyelids. When he awoke the barn was empty, the horse gone and the man and woman remembered only as shadowy phantoms from a dream, leaving only the impact of their grossness with him like the mound of manure left by the horse on the floor of its stall.

Leaving the farm and regaining the road, he walked between the rows of poplars that stretched in front of him in straight lines until they dwindled and dissolved in the half-light. As he walked, so there came to him a gradual recollection of incidents in his life from childhood to the time of his falling to earth in the Lancaster, pictures flickering like a coloured film behind his eyes. The air was full of voices he remembered from the past and he felt as though he was newly dead and come to judgement, a melancholy and guilt-ridden flagellation of his conscience as he judged himself, seeing dispassionately and subjectively his faults and vices and how they had affected those against whom they had been directed. It was a naked stripping and an exposure of all he had done and not done and, for the first time, he knew. It was a shaking experience to which he wished his mind had not given room and it left him with an inner emptiness.

He saw the large stone blank-faced building on the outskirts of the town around which he intended to go, having come on it unexpectedly. A lorry stood outside with its tailboard down. Coming from the building was an emanation of terror and pain, a suffocating sense of suffering as tangible to him as a cry of unbearable agony and to which he was drawn against his shrinking will. He knew that he had to go in and, although he fought against it, there came the familiar dreamlike shifting of location and he was there. It expanded slowly into focus, resolving itself into stark bare whitewashed walls and a metal rail from which hung three pinkish-white headless bodies on steel hooks. A small heap of wet black-and-white skins lay on the cement floor and a large pool of blood ran sluggishly into a drain. A planked pen held four calves huddled against its rear wall, their eyes rolling in fear and distress. There were two men in bloodied overalls and rubber boots. One opened the gate to the pen and grasped a calf by its ears, dragging it out with its hooves slipping and sliding as it resisted with stiff slender legs. Philip watched, paralysed with the most violent horror he had ever experienced as the calf was gripped tight between the knees of its captor, its head forced upwards to expose the windpipe and tendons of the throat while its mouth, running ropes of saliva, opened in a young thing's unheard bawling, the bulging eyes staring at the second man approaching with a knife in his hand.

Philip shouted then and was outside before the calf died its bloody death, sinking to his knees near the lorry and vomiting, beating his fists on the ground, shaken by the utter pitifulness of what he had seen. As he stumbled away he cursed the slaughtermen for their merciless brutality, shouting angrily to God that they should be sent to the worst hell of his imagining. It came to him slowly and by degrees that he was inescapably brother to the butcher, different only in the manner of his killing. With none of the feelings of horror or pity he had felt over the approaching deaths of the calves, he had slaughtered with an unthinking barbarity by dropping his bombs on cities and towns like an unselective and vengeful god. That he had done it in the name of patriotism, for the defence and love of his country, to defeat the inhumanities of an enemy, was now no vindication of his killing hundreds, if not thousands, of non-combatant men, women and children who could have had no conceivable part in causing or fighting the war. He thought he could see them waiting for him, silent accusing figures in the dark and purplish landscape that was a part of his hallucinating, their bodies torn redly and mutilated by his explosives, charred black and liquefied by fire. It was a newly awakened enormity of guilt that he had to rationalize, a realization that if it were wrong and cruel to kill defenceless and innocent animals then, equally, it was so to kill human beings, approved and encouraged though it might be as a necessity of war. There was an alternative, one that would be judged cowardly and unmanly, even traitorous, which he could no more face than the fact presented to him by his awakened conscience.

As he struggled with his confusion, a quiet part of his mind was telling him that there was a connection between the obscenity of the man and woman in the barn and the slaughter of the calves for which he had felt such an anguish of compassion; not anything he could understand, but he knew that inevitably he would.

Sixteen

Breakfast in the Mess was an exposure of himself that Oliver would sooner have avoided. He ate his porridge, sausage and scrambled egg as calmly externally as a man would with no nagging fears, but feeling them as a large rock suspended by a frail cord above his head. He was expecting the Duty Officer or the Adjutant to enter and order him summarily to the CO's office.

When Lloyd came in and sat near to him he searched his features for signs that he had been interrogated and accused of fornicating with a WAAF Officer. If he had, he was acting no differently from his normal amiability on any other morning at breakfast. When Lloyd mentioned the routine shoot-up of locomotives he had been on during the night, Oliver realized that he could not be suspected anyway, that he might not even be questioned. Giving his name had been a stupid and reckless lie made on the spur of the moment in his efforts to get out from under the questioning of an officious and over-zealous NCO who was probably now in his bed snoring off his night's mooching about looking for trouble. At least, he wasn't yet skulking around the Mess peering with his respectful insolence at the faces of the officers. The thought of it, that he might be subjected to the indignity and humiliation of an identification by an NCO, stirred anger in him. On the other hand, he may have thought better of it, deciding that he wanted no trouble involving an operational pilot. It wasn't a lot of comfort but he hung on to it while not allowing it to interfere with the assertions and denials of the defence he was already framing in his mind.

Morwenna sat with another WAAF Officer at her customary table and, when she met his eyes, shook her head almost imperceptibly. He felt nothing for her but resentment. She was the cause of his present troubles; no longer a soft pillow into which he wished to spend his recurring lust and anaesthetize his fears, but a distasteful blubberiness of smothering flesh that threatened him with its gravidness.

Poxton and the CO breakfasted together at the top table. Poxton had given him his pukka-wallah's grey-eyed stare with no friendliness in it, no acknowledging nod of the head, resuming his conversation as if Oliver had not been seen or, had he been, that he was numbered among the untouchables. Had Oliver any doubts about his being *persona non grata*, they were resolved. It gave him a sick feeling in his stomach and he fed his anger with the man's bloody-minded contempt for him. There came again an urge to smash it from him.

His bile gave him a sense of isolation from the others who were, he imagined, talking and eating to his deliberate exclusion. Apart from Lloyd who had not, anyway, been over-communicative. He left the Mess without taking a cigarette with his coffee or looking again in the direction of Morwenna.

In the Crew Room, he saw that the U/S chalked against his Typhoon identification number on the Squadron Formation Board had been rubbed off, indicating that it was once more serviceable and needing his checking out. There was also a notice, signed by Poxton, ordering a briefing for elements of A and B Flights at 10.30 hours for an escort mission at 12.00, listing the names of the pilots detailed for it. His was among them and it lightened his feeling of being treated like a pariah-dog.

Situated in the battered and neglected main building vacated early in the war by the flying club, the Briefing Room doubled up for use as an office for Flight Lieutenant Summerbee, the Intelligence Officer. Its ceiling was fly-specked and stained saffron with cigarette smoke. Duplicating the Crew Room, a wall was given over to the front, plan and side view silhouettes of Allied and enemy aircraft, of armoured vehicles and a miscellany of warships, mine-layers and flak-boats. Pinned to a notice board were Air Ministry information sheets advising of enemy aircraft and defence developments and the IO's collection of camera-gun photographs of rocket strikes against rail rolling stock, coastal batteries and radar installations. On the wall behind his desk was a montage of maps of Northern France, Belgium, Holland and West Germany covered with mica. Through the single window which looked directly at the black side of the hangar, looming over it like a cliff of basalt, came the rarely absent roar of 24-cylinder engines being tested and the sounds of petrol bowsers refuelling.

Oliver and the other officer and sergeant pilots of the two Flights occupied hard wooden chairs in front of the desk. They stubbed out cigarettes and stood when Gowersby, the CO, entered. He was followed by Summerbee and Poxton.

"Sit down, chaps," Gowersby said, "and smoke if you wish."

Most did and there was a sharing out of cigarettes as the three officers took their places behind the desk. Gowersby remained standing. Short and squat with big square teeth beneath a bristly ginger moustache, he walked with the limp he had earned flying a Hurricane in the Battle of Britain. On his sleeves were the two and a half rings of a Squadron Leader, beneath his pilot's brevet the ribbons of the DSO, DFC and bar and AFM, the latter indicating that he had been commissioned from the ranks. He was a ferocious killer of Germans who had been ordered not to indulge his aggressiveness further in operational flying and was now deskbound against his wishes.

Oliver was almost as fearful of earning his displeasure and contempt as he was of flying into flak. Gowersby would look upon an officer's sexual consorting with another officer not only as a grave breach of discipline but, equally, as a serious dereliction of duty when his every effort and waking thought should be concentrated on a singleminded determination to take death and destruction to the enemy. Oliver's mind baulked at imagining how he would view a report of a pilot's breaking off a rocket attack because of flak. At his mildest he would call it being flak-happy and that was a euphemism for being frightened enough of it to show cowardice which, in its turn, would certainly result in an LMF report.

Poxton, who had taken his seat with Summerbee, let his eyes check on the appearance of each man of his Flight. For officers and NCOs alike he demanded a strict discipline with no scruffiness of uniform, no deliberately misshapen and crumpled caps, no unauthorized embellishments such as silk scarves or the unfastened top button of a tunic to denote fighter-pilot status. The wearing of white roll-top pullovers, hitherto held to be an operational pilot's privilege, had been forbidden them, adding to the resentment they already held against their role as airborne artillery. Himself an exemplar of precise and well-polished neatness, he held that sloppiness in dress and deportment led to sloppiness in combat.

If he found anything not to his taste now he would save it for later, not letting it go.

Gowersby held a stubby pipe in one hand and he rapped it on the desk for their attention. "A relatively cushy number today, chaps," he started when there was a momentary lull in the noise of the engines from outside. "You're going to be nannies to a flock of Flying Fortresses engaged on a secondary raid on the synthetic petrol works at Mainz. There are three hundred of 'em and the 8th Air Force can't raise enough Mustangs to fully cover that and the primary mission to another target. So they've asked Second TAF for a fill-up for their bomber-escort squadrons. The bombers will be flying in three boxes and we shall be responsible for the rear end of the third. They've sufficient elements of their own to cover the other two." He smiled as though he were promoting them *en masse*, giving them something they wanted above all else. "You're there to ride tail-end Charlies on them and all you've to do is to chop down any Jerry kite before it gets in shooting range. The Met forecast is bags of cloud and the Forts'll be spread pretty thin, so there's a certainty of their being jumped from cover. Keep to your own box and for Christ's sake don't lose contact with them. Your primary purpose is to get them and their bomb loads safely over Mainz where you'll be relieved by a withdrawal support group of more Mustangs." He lowered his ginger eyebrows. "Don't go tear-arsing off after Jerry for a kill if he's been clobbered enough to break off combat. It'll leave your part of the box unprotected for others who haven't been clobbered. Bagging a confirmed Jerry for your log book is less important than getting those bombers through. The same goes for any Fort that gets wounded and drops out. Even if it's still under attack. Sorry, but it gets no more cover and will have to fight its own way back."

He paused for a moment as if expecting one of them to question this, then continued when nobody did. "Watch your fuel, you won't have too much to spare. The bomber stream will be moving at 250 Indicated Air Speed so you'll use more of it keeping down to theirs. I don't want any of my Typhoons finishing arse-up in a Dutch farmyard or in the drink on the way back. Your rocket rails will have been removed so you shouldn't have any trouble in meeting Jerry on equal terms. And don't worry about the flak they'll certainly send up. It isn't meant for you, anyway."

Oliver thought he saw Gowersby's eyes rest briefly on him. He wasn't sure, but the words made him uneasy. That bastard Poxton could have mentioned something to him. And he could have been making a point for his benefit.

Gowersby showed his teeth in a smile. "It'll give some of you chaps who are browned off with train-busting – and don't fool yourselves I haven't heard about it – a chance to mix it with the Luftwaffe boys again. But don't think it's too much of a piece of cake. Don't underestimate them. They must know that they're up shit creek and they're getting pretty desperate. They won't let you through without a fight. One of their cities is going to get plastered in the process, some of their women and kids killed, and they'll go full throttle to clobber the bombers. Don't forget, desperate men do desperate deeds." He was genial with them, his smile wide. "If you miss out on a dog-fight, don't fret that we might be short of ammunition back here. You don't have to bring it home with you. Split into sections on the way back and give it to anything you might see with a swastika on it. Your Flight Commander will have words with you about that." He stuck his pipe into his mouth and put a match to it. "I'll leave you with Flight Lieutenant Summerbee for the details. Jolly good huntin'," and that was something he always said. He turned smartly on his sound leg and limped towards the door, gone while they were still getting to their feet.

Summerbee, as Briefing Officer, was more precise. Although he was a "penguin", never having flown other than as a passenger, he probably knew more of the tactical theory of operational flying than most of them. He was, as Intelligence Officer, certainly the recipient of more technical and logistic information. He held a short cane in his hand and looked like a schoolmaster about to lecture the sixth form.

He pointed the cane to red lines crayoned on the mica over the maps that joined Deal to Breda in Holland and from it to Mainz. "This is the required track," he said, "and you need no more information about it than you'll get sitting on a bomber's tail. The Fortresses and escorting fighters will rendezvous at the assembly area over Deal. You will be joining up with the third box at 12.20 hours at 24,000 feet, maintaining your height at 1000 feet above them and covering their rear. You will be joining an escort of forty-six Mustangs which will cover the middle and front of the box. Five miles short of the target area you will, unless engaged with an intercepting force, hand over to the American withdrawal support group. Now, your likely opposition. The track will take you south of most of Luftfloton 2 Group fighter stations, but don't anticipate that they won't intercept in strength." He referred to a sheet of paper he picked up from the desk. "You'll certainly be within interception distance of the 26th and 2nd Fighter Wings equipped with Focke-Wulf 190s and the 3rd Fighter Wing with Messerschmitt 109s, possibly with some 110 Destroyers as well. And for those of you who haven't done a daylight bombing escort before, allow me to tell you that they now concentrate anything from twenty aircraft upwards on one bomber, finish it off and then turn back for the next. They'll obviously avoid the escorting fighters if they can because there's no great profit in shooting you down. If you do get into a brawl, for God's sake don't make it a fratricidal one. Remember that Typhoons have been shot at by the Yanks in mistake for Focke-Wulfs and, conversely, that it wouldn't be the first time that a Mustang has been downed because it looked very much like a Messerschmitt 109."

That, as Oliver knew almost to his cost, was true. An unexpected split-second view of a fast-moving aircraft with the thumb already on the firing button didn't lend itself to immediate recognition when hesitation might mean the difference between a bellyful of armour-piercing incendiaries and survival. Being shot down by a friendly aircraft could be just as fatal and only a degree or two less mortifying than its being shot down by the same error. And Oliver, doing a test flight over Canterbury, had had a wingtip shot off by an American Thunderbolt diving from cloud cover to prove it. That the pilot had almost immediately recognized his Allied status and escorted his limping Typhoon back to the airfield hadn't lessened his mortification about having been jumped so easily.

Summerbee unrolled a meteorological synoptic chart and pinned it to the wall. "Expect some dirty weather *en route*," he said. "Stratocumulus to the Dutch coast topping at 4000 feet, then breaking up into cumulonimbus up to 30,000 feet. Quite well spaced out, but there could be squalls and turbulence if you get too near them." His cane traced a circle midway along the chart. "After that it's broken cumulus until it clears well before the target. That won't give you any bother, but it will, of course, provide cover for intercepting aircraft attacking from below." He turned away from the chart. "Are there any questions?"

Poxton came in then. "Before there are," he said, "let me repeat what the CO told you." He regarded them all sternly from under the peak of his cap. To Oliver, he was making clear his own leadership. "Tempting as it might be to some of you, there will be no haring off after trouble in another box." His eyes met Oliver's briefly. "Or leaving the formation for any other reason. Such as a concentration of flak," he added with deliberation. "And that's an order. The Yanks won't thank you. Certainly the bomber crews won't who get jumped because we aren't where we should be to protect them." He twisted his mouth in a sour grimace. "And let me be quite definite that neither will I."

It was a threat that Oliver accepted as being aimed directly at him, that it must be clear to the other pilots sitting with him. He felt his face flushing. For him now the level of his involvement in fighting the enemy was no higher than his hostility towards Poxton. He sat through the remainder of the briefing hoping that something fatal and painful would happen to Poxton before his own animus spilled over and caused him more trouble.

Seventeen

Oliver had drunk two whiskies and swallowed a benzedrine tablet before attending the briefing, knowing that there would be no time afterwards to return to his room. Their effects were wearing thin and his nerve-ends felt raw. His mind was orientated towards his preparations for the forthcoming operation and needed no extraneous problems to distract it from them.

Outside, the few small clouds in a blue sky glided their shadows over the flat green fields with no sign of the overcast Summerbee had promised. The familiar smells of exhaust gases and petrol fumes tainted the mild air, not yet fully warmed by the sun. Typhoons were being hauled tail-first from their parking bays to the taxiing strip by small tractors. Others were still being worked on by airmen mechanics and armourers. Oliver's Typhoon stood ready for take-off, the cockpit hood open and waiting for him. He wanted to go over and stroke her on her sleek nose as a man would his favourite horse.

Walking with the others to the Crew Room, he was overtaken by a corporal. He held a folded piece of paper in his hand. "Mr Missen, sir?"

"Yes, what is it?" He thought he knew. A summons to the CO's office. There was nothing that fed pessimism so fully as a guilty conscience.

"A telephone call for you, sir." The corporal held out the paper. "A Lady Woollgar who asks you to call her at this number. It's urgent, sir, she insisted."

"Thank you, Corporal." The sun shone a little brighter at his reprieve, although not by so much that he was happy about her trying to contact him. It boded nothing, he guessed, for his pleasure. And had she been anybody but Lady Woollgar he doubted that the message would have been taken.

The Signals Section hut lay on his route, although the private use of the telephone there would be unauthorized. But nothing, he considered, about which to get hot flushes. Nor was Morwenna, whose Section it was and whom he had no wish to meet anyway, likely to be present.

The Waaf stood from her blanket-covered table when he entered. He gave her his most ingratiating grin. "May I use the phone?" he said. "An emergency and I'm due for take-off. No time for nipping back to the Mess."

She hesitated a moment, then said, "Of course, sir. I can't go away, though."

"And I wouldn't wish you to." He moved the handset nearer the window and stood where he could look out of it. While he waited for the operator to connect him, he studied the Waaf's body in its thick blue serge, peeling her down to her skin in his imagination and deciding that she had possibilities. She was a peroxided yellow-blonde with coarse good looks and a mouth like a trodden-on strawberry; hefty enough, he thought to break a stevedore's spine. He knew from her first reaction to him that he wouldn't have to twist her arm very hard to get it, although the reality of any intimacy with an Other Rank Waaf would pale his involvement with Morwenna to a triviality. But it seemed a long time since he had relieved his sexual tensions and he could no more turn off the recurrent urging of his loins than stop his stomach being hungry for food.

"Lady Woollgar? Oliver Missen here," he said when he heard her voice at the other end of the wire.

"Good morning, Mr Missen." The telephone exaggerated her cool patrician accent. "Thank you for calling back so quickly."

"I'm afraid it'll have to be brief. I'm about to ... well, I'm on flying duties."

"I've no intention of keeping you, but I must see you today." It was in the tone of a voice unused to being refused.

Damn and blast the bloody woman! Did she know? Suspect that he was to visit Laura? With the Waaf watching him, he kept his features impassive. "That's difficult," he temporized. "I don't expect to be back until late this afternoon." If I get back at all, he qualified to himself.

"Please, Mr Missen. It is important."

He would have liked to have said that he was confined to camp, but that wasn't on with his seeing Laura and she possibly knowing. "What is it about, Lady Woollgar?"

"Nothing that I care to discuss over a telephone."

"I see. Anyway, I couldn't possibly be with you until after six. Not with debriefing, changing and all that stuff." The Waaf caught his eye and he let her see his interest in her.

"That will do perfectly well." The articulation was elegant and beautifully modulated. "I will expect you."

He saw Morwenna walking briskly towards the signals office and it pushed him into hasty agreement.

"If nothing stops me," he said. Whatever it was she considered so important, she sounded a woman prepared to enforce it on him and he was certain now that it would be nothing to his advantage.

As he replaced the receiver, Morwenna came in through the door and, seeing him, looked surprised. "Sorry about this," he said. "A most important call. I threw my rank at your airwoman, so don't blame her."

She didn't answer that, but said, "I'm glad you're here. I wanted to speak to you." She returned through the door and he followed, giving the Waaf a smiling nod and a brief lifting of his hand to the peak of his cap behind Morwenna's back. It did no harm to keep the contact alive.

Once outside with the door closed, Morwenna halted and stood close to the wooden side of the hut that smelled strongly of creosote in the growing warmth of the sun. She wore her working battledress which emphasized her plumpness, the trousers showing bulging haunches and fat thighs, and he wondered why he had not before been repelled by them. He knew it to be too soon for her pregnancy to show but, for all that, imagined he could see a thickening waist and the beginning of a fecund pod beneath the belt of her tunic.

Where they stood he felt exposed, their association flaunted. There was a constant movement of uniformed bodies along the cement path a few yards away from them. It wanted only Poxton or the CO to see them together and later to remember when it became significant. Knowing that only thin wood interposed between his words and the blonde inside who would undoubtedly be straining her ears to listen, he kept his voice low.

"For God's sake," he said, "why don't we broadcast it over the Tannoy!"

A shadow crossed her face at his displeasure and she bit at her lower lip. "I had to speak to you, Oliver ... please."

He saw that she was going to be humble and forgiving and it irritated him. "You heard that bloody corporal last night?"

"Yes. I'm so sorry. Has anything been said?"

"Not yet, but it will be. I'm going to deny it, of course. With you to back me up it'll only be an SP corporal's word against the two of us. You can show a fair bit of righteous indignation about it, too."

She looked surprised and shocked. "I'm not very good at telling lies, Oliver, and I wouldn't wish to make the corporal out to be a liar. He could get into serious trouble."

"Dammit! Not a liar. Mistaken in saying he saw me climbing out of your window."

"I think that if we're asked we should be honest about it. Surely it isn't all that serious? We weren't doing anything but talking. We can be truthful about that."

Her female naïvety staggered him. "Do you think for one moment that anybody's going to be bloody simple enough to believe I wasn't in bed with you! That it's only a coincidence that you happen to be pregnant?' He felt his lips trembling with his rising anger. 'What were we supposed to be doing? Having a cosy chat about today's call sign in your bedroom? *Out of Bounds*," he snarled at her savagely, "that's what it says outside your billet. Out of bounds to all ranks. You personally might not give a damn about being hauled up in front of the CO, probably finishing up with a court martial, but I do."

"I don't want to cause you any trouble, Oliver," she said in a small voice. "You know that."

He stared at her, trying to read what lay behind the hurt look she had on her face. "Like hell I do. You've caused me enough already." He was curt. "If that corporal's reported it, as he probably has, they'll send a female down here from the DAPM's office to interview you. You're surely to God able to cope with another woman? She can only ask you questions and all you have to do is to deny that I was ever in your room, that you don't even know me other than as somebody you've spoken to in the Mess. And stick to it. If you're determined to make a martyr of yourself over this pregnancy of yours, for Christ's sake wait until it begins to show." He let his gaze travel down her heavy body and was brutal. "And with your figure that shouldn't be for some time."

She was close to tears and there was a quiet dignity about her. "You forget, Oliver, that I happen to be in love with you."

"Then I wish you'd act as if you were. Bloody-minded obstinacy in refusing to do what I ask isn't what I call love."

He turned and walked rapidly away, leaving her standing there, knowing that her wounded cow-ish eyes would be following him with the love in them that was now as unwanted by him as it was dangerous.

Eighteen

Four and a half miles above the shrinking patch of just discernible streets and houses that was Deal, the sea resembled blue glass set in rigid corrugations edged by the sand flats reaching to the jutting protuberance of the North Foreland, the landscape a mosaic of green and brown threaded with the veins and capillaries of rivers and roads. The fourteen Typhoons flew in a wide orbit behind circling Mustang fighters. Below them, the air filled with the battering thunder of their engines, the stream of Flying Fortresses rumbled in formation towards distant Holland, an enormous stretched-out school of red-tailed, aluminium-plated leviathans reflecting small explosions of sunlight from their polished wings and turrets bristling with guns, their bellies pregnant with destructive eggs to spawn over Mainz. The escorting quicksilver Mustangs, stepped above them in clusters, weaved and darted like tiny fry protecting their monstrous mothers. The leading bombers of the stream were already dark midges strung out over the sea towards the quilt of cloud reaching out to them.

When the last formation entered the tail of the stream from their orbiting, Poxton led the flight in station behind and above them with Oliver as Red Two on his wing and, to his own rear, Pilot Officer Rogers as Red Three. The other Sections, riding on their tails, rose and sank in relation to the leading aircraft as their pilots maintained position on each side in echelon. Thin plumes of contrails stretched behind them, scoring straight lines through the coldness of thin air.

Oliver, encapsuled in his cramped cockpit and shielded from the buffeting airstream by the teardrop-shaped perspex hood, felt less raw-nerved and tense, his anger left behind with Morwenna. The high reaches of rarefied air was a world in which he moved as near heaven as he thought he was ever likely to get and in which, when it was possible to ignore its dangers, he could feel euphoric. He switched on his gun-sight and turned the firing button to "live", activating the four stubby snouts of his cannon to fire their lethal 20-millimetre shells at forty-four rounds a minute. From his position behind, he looked down into the cockpit of Poxton's Typhoon, seeing only the back of his leather helmet and goggles strap over the top of the armour-plated seat back. His head, as were those of the other pilots, moved with clockwork regularity as his eyes quartered the sky above and below for ambushing aircraft.

Away from land and over the sea, tracer began to come in short bursts from the turrets of the Fortresses as the gunners readied their Brownings for action. Oliver didn't envy them their huge aircraft, doubting that he possessed the phlegmatic courage needed by a bomber pilot, the will to maintain under attack by cannon fire and flak a steady course in an aerial bus heavy with its cargo of sensitive explosives. It wouldn't be a survivor's choice of occupation.

He had been trained in Arizona by the USAAF, had been awarded his wings there, and he knew men like these who flew the Fortresses. For them, the giant aircraft were the queens of the Air Force and it was a faith with them that when queens died they died proudly. Which they did and in large numbers in the German skies.

With Holland remote beneath them they were now above the ledge of stratocumulus, cottonwool white in the sun, the shadows of the aircraft sliding undulating over the hummocks of cloud. Occasionally, Oliver lifted a hand to blot out the sun's dazzle, a quarter from which any attack by enemy aircraft having altitude on them could come. The bomber stream would already have been detected by the German radar stations and somewhere along the track there would be fighter aircraft gaining height at full boost to intercept them. Despite the mechanization of their chargers, the sophistication of their weaponry, they were in essentials no different from squadrons of cavalry galloping headlong towards each other with lances couched, narrowing the gap between those airmen, alive now with their minds intent on destruction and killing, who were destined to die and those who were destined to kill them.

Heavy flak reaching up through the cloud floor burst its flying metal fragments around the bombers from dirty puff-balls that shredded into tatters and drifted behind them. A Fortress in the middle of the box turned in a downward spiral with black smoke boiling from its port engine nacelles and, as it headed back in the direction of the sea, the bay doors in its belly opened and a column of bombs tumbled out. No escort fighters followed and if it died it would die alone.

For Oliver the flak was impersonally distant and not being directed at his own destruction, the bursts being fused to explode at the level of the bombers below. Occasionally, mistimed, they burst higher but he felt none of the cold fear that filled his chest with banging heart when light flak was hosed at him in a ground attack.

When they reached the ravines and canyons of the cumulonimbus cloud that towered above them in bulbous ramparts of glaring white, the leading bombers and their escorts were no longer in view. With the clouds on either side as points of reference, Oliver's feeling of being motionless in space gave way to one of racing like a thundering missile between the mountains of mist, his Typhoon rumbling through the rough air over cobblestones of turbulence. Occasionally its wings shivered as it lurched and dropped, needing a constant adjustment of its altitude and a care not to overtake and collide with Poxton, or to have Rogers climb up his own back. They were over Germany now and there were craters in the cloud floor through which could be seen momentarily, as if looking down into an abyss, the patchwork of tiny fields and the huddled-together masses of villages and towns.

Any attack on them must be imminent and Oliver checked his instrument panel, the radiator temperature, oil pressure and heating, feeding himself more oxygen to clear his brain and inflate his lungs with well-being. Doing this, he saw a Tortoiseshell butterfly resting on the radio controller box, its vibrating wings closed over its back. Despite its being over four miles high with the minimum of oxygen and the always present toxic leakage of carbon monoxide from the exhaust gases, it was still alive and Oliver was concerned that it would survive its accidental imprisonment in his cockpit. Oddly, he was glad of its company. He recognized it as an incongruity that while he could be anxious about the tiny creature's survival, he had no such concern for the Germans he was expecting to kill.

Poxton's voice came over the R/T, level and unemotional. "Phoenix Leader to Flight. Attack on box formation from ten o'clock high. Hold positions. I repeat, hold positions."

Oliver located the swarm of aircraft curving in on the leading bombers of the box, far enough away to appear as silhouettes against the white ramparts of the cloud from behind which they had come, at least twenty-five in number and moving fast. He identified them as Messerschmitt 109s supporting a core of three twin-engined Messerschmitt 110 Destroyers. Lines of orange tracer poured at them in converging arcs from the Fortresses under attack and the escorting Mustangs, gleaming silver in the sun as they turned, broke towards them, firing as they closed the distance. With no return fire coming from the Germans a 109 staggered and fell away abruptly, its rudder and tailplanes fluttering loose, attached only by its control cables.

At what must have been a command from the flight leader, long streaks of rocket trails left the 110 Destroyers, slowly at first then gathering speed, followed by green tracer from the 109s that curved in a concentrated cone of cannon shells into the leading group of bombers. A Fortress, its wings and fuselage suddenly pockmarked with gashed metal, bloomed into flame, flying on in formation until it abruptly disintegrated with a brilliant flash into burning fuel and shattered particles. The shock waves from the exploded bombs flung the two Fortresses keeping station on its flanks in ponderous cartwheels, their pilots fighting to control them from smashing into other aircraft.

Another Fortress, one wing sliced open in a spangle of sparkling lights to expose spars and stringers, the pilot's cabin an open black hole of ruptured metal and perspex, swung away from its formation, the wing folding upwards with inexorable slowness. Small crouched figures of the crew jumped from hatches, snapping open their parachutes as they fell towards the cloud floor. One of the crewmen, accidentally jerked free from his harness, dropped unchecked with his arms waving, the now useless nylon canopy floating after him. A 109, its cockpit hood shot off and the pilot lolling unresponsive in his seat, climbed vertically on its propeller until it flicked over crazily and fell spinning to smash nose first into the upper fuselage of a Fortress. Locked together, they tumbled earthwards in a clumsy spiral, a thick streamer of flame and smoke following them down.

Then the Messerschmitts were gone, undershooting the bombers and diving at full throttle into the cloud below, the escort Mustangs closing on them and firing their cannon after their vanishing tails.

The attack had been measurable in seconds, leaving behind the noise and smoke of the destruction of three bombers. Men had died and Oliver thought of the crewman who had lost his parachute, still falling his four and a half miles and yet to die his terrible death.

The turret guns of the Fortresses fell silent, but angling the sky as the survivors of the attack closed the gaps in the formation. It was Oliver who saw the cluster of aircraft appear on his starboard quarter from a cloud canyon: Focke-Wulf 190s already commencing an approach on the Fortresses below him. He shouted then, urgency making his voice a croak in the microphone.

"Phœnix Leader! Bandits at four o'clock low! Four o'clock and attacking!" Without waiting for orders from Poxton, he heeled his Typhoon over in a half-roll and split-essed to aim his nose at the Focke-Wulfs now less than two thousand yards from the rearmost bombers, the black crosses becoming visible on the upper surfaces of their wings, the dark shapes hunched in the cockpits as goggled pilots. They were attacking in a pack on a narrow front for a first devastating punch with their concentrated fire power, ignoring the escorting fighters for a desperate killing of the bombers.

Oliver's earphones crackled with Poxton's voice. "Break right! Break right!" and he thought he could read into it his anger that Oliver had anticipated him. He was, he told himself, going to get there first and, with Poxton on his tail and able to see him doing it, down a bastard or two and shove the Flight Commander's contempt up his bloody backside. He was supremely confident of the capability of his four cannon to hurl explosives in an accurate pattern of bloody destruction at his mind's will, the power of death resting in the pressure of the pad of his thumb.

When the blunt nose of the Focke-Wulf he had singled out for his first attack grew larger and began to enter the annulus of his gun-sight, he applied the first pressure of his thumb to the firing button. Before he could depress it fully, his engine cut dead and he was powerless. Immediate stupefaction and panic took over as he instinctively pushed his nose further down, lurching against his harness as he slammed the stick sideways in a violent twisting roll away from the Focke-Wulf, his mind incapable of doing more than activate a response for survival. He had a momentary glimpse of the Typhoons of his Flight diving steeply on to the enemy aircraft and tracer coming from the Fortresses before he was into the cloud and everything blotted out in grey mist.

With the roar of his engine silenced, its ton of dead weight dragging his nose down in an unpowered fall through space, he heard the whistling of the airstream over the wings and fuselage, the muffled banging of distant cannon fire and the sounds of somebody shouting incoherent words in his earphones. The propeller had slowed to a speed where he could distinguish the individual blades. As he pulled back cautiously on the stick to ease out of the dive and into an angle of glide that would hold the heavy mass of aircraft from falling into the ground, his eyes frantically hunted the instrument panel. The fuel pressure light was showing its warning red eye.

"Oh, Christ! Christ Almighty!" he breathed, the words in him without blasphemy. He was trembling and felt sick. In his intent to get in first and with Poxton on his mind, he had omitted with unbelievable stupidity to release his wing drop tanks, his throttling into a power dive on the Focke-Wulfs draining the last of the fuel. He snatched at the jettison lever, feeling a jerk and a decrease in drag as the tanks fell away and then he was breaking through the cloud base to a water-sodden landscape tilting through a rain-spattered windscreen.

With the fuel switched over to the main tanks, the windmilling propeller should have restarted the engine, but she was going bloody-minded on him just when he was in danger of running out of sky. The re-starting of a refractory engine in the air was nothing about which he could be happy. Unintended flooding with petrol of the hot cylinders and air intake could cause a fire that would mean baling out over enemy territory and the recollection of the American crewman falling to his death was still with him. The thought of it made him sweat. He said, "Please God, if you're ever going to do anything for me" into his mask, angrily and without servility, and pulled at the toggle that fed the remaining cartridge into the starter breech, opening the throttle lever to its stop and pumping the cylinder primer. Holding his breath he pressed the booster-coil and starter push buttons, hearing the bang of the cartridge exploding and seeing smoke belching from the exhaust ports as the engine fired and caught.

With the cylinders drinking greedily from the fuel tanks he pushed the throttle through the notch into boost and held back on the stick, spiralling her into a steep climb up and back into the clouds on a thrashing propeller. He was uncaring of the strain he was putting on her, savage with her as the most convenient cause of his humiliation. Part of his destructive rage wanted to shake the engine from its mountings and he saw the needle of the oil temperature gauge rising with a perverse satisfaction. She was a pig-headed bitch, another Morwenna who had failed him and promised only trouble. Had there been a way of leaving her to fall out of the sky to smash herself to death on the earth he was in the mood to have done it.

"Phœnix Leader! Phœnix Leader!" he called, needing urgently and early to make good his unsought defection from the scene of combat. There was no reply. The shouting had ceased although he could hear voices, tiny like distant newsprint and remote in his ears, telling him nothing beneath the racketing of the engine.

Incredibly, the butterfly was still clinging to the radio controller box and although its wings were no longer vibrating it had to be alive. He identified himself with it in his determination to go on living. The cloud thinned and then he was above it into the glare of sunlight reflecting from the towered and turreted flocculence of cumulonimbus and the white cloud floor. Screwing his eyes against it he saw that it was empty of aircraft, that he was solitary in a sky from which friend and enemy and the noise of their conflict had passed. Sweat ran into his eyes and from beneath the edges of his mask, his spine damp and sticky where it pressed hard against the back of his seat. Overriding the oxygen he was breathing he smelled exhaust gases, tasting its acridness in his mouth. His anger remained with him and with it a kind of despair. He was already thinking out the answers he would need to give. By anyone but Poxton he would be judged only as a bloody idiot who needed to pull his finger out, a stupid clot who had made an elementary error in airmanship. Poxton, on the evidence of his own eyes, would have to believe that on sighting the Focke-Wulfs he had immediately turned away and run for it, funking out again. Poxton would reject any explanation about forgetting to jettison his drop tanks with the scathing contempt that Oliver feared.

When his altimeter needle pointed to 24,000 feet he levelled out and turned on to the compass course taken by the bomber stream. In his dive he had moved miles away from the ground track and, apart from their being as far or more on their way to the target, the bombers and the escorting fighters could be hidden from him by intervening cloud masses. If he followed, the most he could expect would be to meet the escort group on their return route. And only that if they had not dropped altitude to attack ground targets. It wasn't much, but preferable to turning back to base and arriving before the rest of the Flight as if he had indeed fled from the scene of combat.

He looked at his watch. It was fifteen minutes past one. Estimated time of arrival over the target for the leading bombers had been given as 13.05 hours. If he was anywhere near the correct track he should be meeting the Flight on its return in ... his mind lost the figures as he tried to relate them to his own increased airspeed, his probable position and the Flight's turn back five miles short of the target. There were too many unknowns and unpredictabilities for him to expect to find them in this vast expanse of clouded space. When he had some evidence that he was somewhere over Mainz and that he had seen nothing of the Flight, he would head back. To be able to say that he had been there would be better than nothing.

He flew exposed and without deviating his course between the clouds, his eyes searching a target for the restoration of his self-esteem, wanting a repeat of his earlier salvation, praying for the appearance of a Focke-Wulf or a Messerschmitt he could put on record in his camera-gun and on which he was able to vent his frustrated anger. He was bloody-minded enough to take on several of them. A Typhoon could overhaul a Focke-Wulf, if not a Messerschmitt, like a runaway express train and he had no fear of them.

When the cumulonimbus gave way to scattered cumulus, he searched the landscape below for Mainz. He saw the smoke rising at what he judged to be fifteen miles beyond his port wing and he turned towards it. Nearer, he saw the smoke as ugly columns that slanted in the wind in writhing billows of dirty brown with the red glow of fires at their bases. There were no signs of the bombers that had created this inferno or their fighter escorts, no defending aircraft or flak over the smoking shambles. It was incredible that so many aircraft could vanish so completely in so short a time. Separate smaller fires sending up black oily smoke from the outskirts of the city showed where at least three of the Fortresses were not on their way back. He looked for the white patches that would indicate parachutes on the ground, but could see none. Dropping his nose and lining up the smoke columns in his gun-sight, he took a few frames with his camera. It was a useless exercise, but a necessary one if he was ever going to get out from under Poxton.

He checked his fuel gauge, seeing that he had little to spare for much more than getting back to base, and turned to lose height slowly as he flew on a 280-degree course towards where he hoped Holland to be.

He was alone in an empty sky, feeling himself to be the only living man in the world and being in the mood to wish he were; a speck of flesh, blood and bone in a metal capsule hanging suspended midway between heaven and earth and belonging to neither. He called Phœnix Leader again on his R/T and thought he could hear a remote phantom voice answering behind the static, but unable to make out the words.

"Phœnix Leader," he repeated, his own voice sounding loud in his ears. "Red Two leaving target area with no contact. Am proceeding independent ground attack and returning to base. Acknowledge." His only answer was the crackle of static and he switched off with an irritated abruptness.

Breaking through the cloud layer, he continued to descend until the landscape took on detailed form; trees and hedgerows and wooded hillocks, roads and streams and moving vehicles and figures in the complex of streets in towns over which he passed. The airfield first appeared in the distance as a foreshortened rectangle of flat green. It could have been a large meadow but, nearer, he saw camouflaged blocks of buildings and a broad strip where the grass had been worn to the earth by wheels. Taking off in the same direction as he was approaching, leaving behind a plume of dust, was a black twin-engined aircraft he recognized as a Junkers 88. Its colour and the radar aerials projecting from its nose made it a night-fighter. The pilot, his mind occupied with the mechanics of lifting it into the air, would never know what hit him. It was a sitter for Oliver and he pushed his nose down until he had centred the Junkers' fuselage in the red filament of his sight, fighting the shaking and swaying of the Typhoon with rudder and stick as the ground, now only two hundred feet below, streaked beneath his belly.

Then, with terrifying suddenness, luminous balls arched towards him from near the buildings, slowly at first and gathering speed, each seeming to be aimed to hit him between the eyes but curving away to one side with tearing noises he heard above the bellowing of his engine. His mouth was dry with his leaping fear and his first instinct was to pull away but knowing that in doing so he would present an even larger target. His fear choked his breathing and sent pain in his heart like an angina pectoris. It was too late, he was committed with no time for hesitation. He thumbed at the firing button and shouted obscenities, unaware that he was doing so, the Typhoon shuddering from the recoil of his cannon. Explosions erupted in a line on the runway behind the Junkers and, as its wheels lifted from the ground and it became airborne, catching up with it in flashes of light that chewed debris from the tail and fuselage. There was a whoof of flame and the Junkers plunged nose-first back to the ground, skidding in a flaming ball of wreckage and Oliver was over and past before its final disintegration, pouring on full throttle and jinking away from the flak that was overtaking him and passing over the cockpit in orange streams.

He had done it and proved himself. A German pilot and his crew had died as burnt offerings in order that Poxton would swallow his contemptuous words and choke on them. The flak would show on the film. Oh, Christ Almighty! He groaned his utter dismay as realization came to him. Unbelievably, he had done it again. In his singleness of purpose he had overlooked activating the camera. He was left with nothing but his own assertions and they could only make his defence against Poxton's accusations seem less probable. God! What a bloody stupid sod he was! He felt belittled, a blundering half-wit smothered in his own incompetence. He was tempted to turn back and make another run over the airfield to take his pictures, but facing the barrage of flak again, already alerted, would make him even more stupid. But another chance. He needed a second chance.

When, far in front of him, he saw the column of grey-green vehicles crawling like an articulated snake along a narrow road between hedgerows, he turned away in a wide sweep before he could be identified as a hostile. There were about ten seconds of fire left in his magazines and that should be enough. Coming in from the rear at tree-top height, the Typhoon buffeting, he turned on the camera switch and held the rearmost vehicle of the column in his gun-sight. Unconsciously, he had bared his teeth behind his mask. Leaping towards him, the column resolved itself into a unit of trucks and personnel carriers and if there were defensive flak guns he couldn't see them. But his fear of them was with him.

His cannon shells hit in a series of stuttering explosions that threw debris into the air and the column vanished beneath him as he banked steeply for another pass. On the second approach, holding back his speed for accuracy, he saw uniformed men running from the burning vehicles. Some were kneeling in the road and firing at him with rifles. He raked the column again with a sustained burst until he heard the banging of empty breech blocks in the wings, then turned back on course and looked back over his shoulder at the smoke and flames rising from the shattered column. Bodies lay scattered along its length, some writhing and flopping as if still striving to find concealment from his fire.

The action had left him unarmed and vulnerable and he held his Typhoon at ground level, skimming over the fields, following the contours of the countryside to avoid detection by radar. All he wanted now was to reach the airfield and crawl into a dark corner with enough whisky to anaesthetize what he accepted as being an ignominious failure to prove himself in Poxton's eyes.

That he had a film of Mainz as a funeral pyre and of his ground attack on the column would mean as little to Poxton as had his previous record. It would infuriate him, give him the opportunity of pointing out that the column was self-evidently undefended and, by implication, needing no particular courage or skill to blast it out of existence. Whichever way he considered it, Oliver knew that he was on a loser unless Poxton had, by an act of the beneficent fate he had wished on him before, been chopped fatally in the Flight's attack on the Focke-Wulfs. It was a warming hope that he nursed all the way back.

Nineteen

When he had received a clearance from the Control Tower, Oliver turned into the approach path, his undercarriage and flaps down, his airspeed held at a fraction over 100 miles an hour as the Typhoon's seven tons of metal sank to the earth. The rubber tyres left small puffs of white smoke behind them on their first impact and the aircraft rolled and bumped along the steel mesh runway, the tail dropping as it lost flying speed with Oliver's finger pulling gently on the brake lever. He raised the flaps and taxied towards the parking apron, pulling off his mask and raising the goggles from his eyes. On the cement apron, he idled the engine for a few moments then cleared it with a burst of throttle before cutting it dead. The propeller hesitated, slowed and jerked to a standstill.

He slid open the hood of his cockpit and let in the outside world, dazed with the abrupt silencing of the engine, feeling the familiar burring of his nerves and sweat cold on his body. Released from the tight leather helmet, his head felt swollen and thumped achingly. He badly needed a drink and a cigarette in the quiet of his room to help in the sorting out of the problems to which he had returned.

With the ground crew arriving to refuel and re-arm his machine, he unbuckled his harness and released himself from the parachute straps. Before climbing from the cockpit he looked for the butterfly, but it had vanished from its perch. Walking to Summerbee's office for his debriefing he checked the parked Typhoons for Poxton's squadron number PQ-A, not seeing it and feeling a momentary twinge of guilt that he had wished him chopped. But there was also a sense of relief and a reprieve from his problems. That, too, vanished when he saw it standing outside the workshop hangar, a line of holes rimmed with bright metal cutting diagonally across the fuselage mid-section. The fox-faced bastard was either phenomenally lucky or indestructible and, whichever it was, his troubles were returned to him.

Waiting outside the debriefing room he recognized the SP corporal he had encountered the previous night. Gooch, the Duty Officer, a non-flying type, stood with him. As he moved to pass them, not looking at either, Gooch said, "A good do, Oliver?"

Oliver shrugged. "I've had better." Seeing the corporal there had shaken him but he forced himself to stare coldly at the man's expressionless face until he dropped his eyes from him.

"All right, Corporal," Gooch ordered, "you can buzz off now." To Oliver, he said, "Flight Lieutenant Poxton wants you in his office after you've been debriefed."

"Why the corporal?" He tried to control his anger at being spied on, but Gooch saw it.

"Sorry, Oliver. I'm only following orders."

"So I hope you've both got what you want," he said curtly, brushing by him and entering the hut.

Summerbee, after giving Oliver one of his cigarettes, listened to him and took his notes, interrogating him about the location of the night-fighter airfield and the composition of the column. He smiled sympathetically in his schoolmasterish fashion about Oliver's boob with the drop tanks. If he thought it an unusually stupid boob for an experienced pilot to make he didn't show it. And Oliver, on edge and looking for signs of disbelief, felt some of his confidence creeping back. If Summerbee, why not Poxton? And Summerbee, having extracted all he could from Oliver's recollection, said that subject to the camera-gun's confirmation he was prepared to credit him with a partial destruction of the column, but the unwitnessed death of the Junkers 88 only as an unconfirmed probable.

Oliver chose to return to his room before reporting to Poxton, changing from his flying kit and showering, taking before he did a generous undiluted whisky with which to wash down a benzedrine tablet. It got rid of the burring and muffled the ache in his head, but did nothing about the truculence and rebelliousness he felt as a man who was going to be misunderstood, a man about to be accused of something he had not, this time, done. Poxton could wait. Whatever Oliver now did would not buy him anything. He could create in his mind the lines the interview would follow and it was nothing he wished to anticipate. But if Poxton thought he was going to treat him like an erk up on the carpet for dirty buttons or for being absent without leave, he was due for a surprise. He was no more than a rank above himself, not even entitled to a courtesy "sir". Deliberately he took his time, rubbing after-shave lotion into his skin to camouflage the odour of whisky and adjusting his dress cap at an acute angle he knew would irritate Poxton. He spent more minutes bringing his Flying Log Book up to date.

Knocking on the door of the Flight Commander's office, he stepped inside. Poxton was alone and sitting at his desk, still in his flying kit, his helmet and goggles in a filing tray at his side. His rufous hair was ruffled from their removal and he looked as though he had been building up a smouldering anger. Patently, Oliver could see, in a mood to be savage and to make unjustifiable accusations. He saluted with a definite casualness and stood in front of the desk. He wouldn't be invited to sit. "You wanted to see me," he said.

Poxton pushed back his sleeve cuff with a finger that shook and looked at his wristwatch. Then he stared grim-faced at Oliver. "You were ordered to report to me after debriefing. I've been waiting."

"I needed a shower." He made it sound as if he thought Poxton should have had one also. "Gooch didn't say I had to gallop here at the double."

Poxton breathed deeply. "This is official, Missen, not a social call. As your Flight Commander, I want an explanation of why you chose to break off from the Flight on the approach of enemy aircraft. Again," he emphasized. "And where you've been to since. I warn you that I intend to make your conduct the subject of a report to the CO." He picked a pencil up from the desk and held it poised over a pad of paper.

Although expecting it, Oliver's stomach tightened and he felt the pulses pounding in his neck. "It's all down on my debriefing sheet," he said stiffly. "As you were so obviously keeping tabs on me you must have seen I hadn't jettisoned my drop tanks. In the dive on the 190s I ran out of fuel and had to break off and release them, lucky that they didn't take my tailplanes with them. If you wish to report me for being stupid, do so and I'll plead guilty." He hardened his voice. "But be bloody careful about accusing me of what you did last time."

Poxton glared at him from under his sandy eyebrows. "That's just what I am doing. I didn't see your drop tanks, I didn't see you jettison them. What I did see was your breaking away from the

Flight on the appearance of enemy aircraft and diving into cover. And Rogers saw you too, being right behind you."

Oliver's face flushed and he clenched his hands into fists. "You've been doing a bloody survey on me again. Isn't your own opinion good enough?"

"I'm not going to let you goad me, Missen, and please don't swear in my office. Just answer my questions."

"I haven't heard any yet, only accusations."

"Did you or did you not break away on sighting the Focke-Wulfs?"

"Yes. For the reason I've already told you." He glared back at Poxton, loathing his contemptuous guts.

"You ran dry while still in formation?"

"No. I said, on the way down."

"Why did you break away before I'd given the order?" There was disbelief in every word.

"I saw them first and gave you warning over the R/T. I didn't anticipate you'd need to do any thinking about going into the attack."

"My interpretation is different and it's one I prefer. You funked out as soon as you saw them."

He knew that he must be pale with his anger and it was with difficulty that he held back spluttering furious words, feeling an atavistic desire to smash him. It wasn't the man who stopped him, but the extra ring of his rank.

"I can't stop you reporting what you want to. But be bloody careful about putting down what you can't prove."

"Don't threaten me, Missen. Do you think I like doing this with an officer of my Flight? Knowing that I have one in whom I've lost confidence?" He stabbed a finger at Oliver, raising his voice. "We lost two Fortresses shot down and another crippled in that attack! How does that make you feel!"

"It makes me feel that you're blaming me for your own failure to clobber them before they got there."

There was quietness in the office. Poxton sucked in his cheeks and his face blotched with pink. "That's unforgivable insolence, Missen," he said at last in a choked voice. He scribbled words down with a pencil, his hand shaking. "In fact, we shot down five. You'll apologize for that remark."

"Like hell I will. Do you think because of your rank that you've a monopoly on making accusations? Such as accusing me of cowardice on no evidence at all?"

Poxton spoke quietly and evenly, his effort at controlling himself showing in his face. "You're trying to provoke me into saying things I've no wish to. I have to ask you these questions and you know I do. Please act in a disciplined manner. You are an officer and this attitude of yours does you no good. Where did you go after you broke away from the Flight?"

"I'll answer questions, yes. I've no intention of not doing so. But unjustified and prejudiced accusations which you aren't competent to make are a different matter."

"I'm asking you a question."

"And I'm answering it." He felt that he was getting on top of Poxton. "I couldn't start the engine on the prop and I had to use ground starter procedure. You can check that I've used an extra cartridge if you don't believe me. This lost me about fifteen thousand feet and by the time I'd got back my altitude you'd all gone. I may have been off track, I don't know. It's not surprising that I could be. All I know is that I'd an empty sky. I couldn't raise you on the R/T and I tried to catch up. When I made the target area you'd been and gone and so had the bombers." Seeing no softening in Poxton's expression, he put more emphasis in his words. "I took a few frames of Mainz and that's something else you can shove in your report. Does that sound as if I was dodging trouble?"

Poxton raised his eyebrows and made notes on his pad, but said nothing.

Oliver continued. "I tried to raise you again, telling you that I'd lost contact and was proceeding on independent ground attack. Which I did. I clobbered a Junkers 88 night-fighter on take-off from an airfield. I saw its squadron number when I pulled away; 3D HH. Don't ask where the airfield was because I don't know. But I ran into a hell of a lot of flak."

He held Poxton's eyes. His back was aching, his head renewing its thumping. He felt gritty and raw-nerved. "I forgot the camera so you can please yourself whether you take my word for it. Frankly, after what you've already said, I don't give a damn."

"You're telling me, Missen, and I'm writing it down."

"So I see." He waited until the pencil stopped writing. The bastard was making him feel like a criminal being interrogated by the police. "Almost immediately I picked up a Wehrmacht column heading west which I clobbered in two passes until I ran out of ammo." He paused, waiting for him to trip over his own assumption.

"And you forgot your camera again," he sneered, as he did.

"I'm sorry to disappoint you, but I didn't. It's on record and the IO has the details. Are you satisfied?"

"It doesn't matter at the moment whether I am or not. That's for the CO."

"But on your report." It was obvious to him that Poxton was going to do everything he could to make it stick that Oliver was LMF.

"On my report," he agreed. "And on how he accepts your own version. In the meantime, you'll consider yourself confined to the airfield until I get the CO's instructions."

"Are you putting me under open arrest?" His anger was rising again.

"No. Making certain that you're about should the CO wish to see you."

"You can't do that. Not unless you're giving me a specific duty."

"I'm doing it," Poxton said flatly, "and that's an order."

"When is the next Flight commitment?" He thought of Laura waiting for him, of Lady Woollgar's peremptory demand for words with him.

"Tomorrow morning. Briefing at 08.00 hours. And you'll be on it." The Poxton contempt was all there. "Don't think that you'll be scrubbed from it because of this."

Oliver's mouth shook and he pushed his chin forward. "Are you suggesting that I'm trying to get out of it?"

"I'm saying that you'll be on it."

Oliver made a noise in his throat expressive of his own contempt. Poxton studied him with narrowed eyes, leaning back in his chair and thinking. "Unless, of course," he said, "you're prepared to take certain steps. I'm seriously concerned about your attitude – that goes without saying – so I'm asking you officially whether you wish to make an application to be relieved of flying duties. If you do, it'll mean you'll have to see the Medical Officer at Group. I want you to think about it before you answer. It'll be your choice."

"No, I bloody well don't!" He ground the words out, feeling swollen with his anger. "You're as good as saying that I'm a candidate for LMF!"

Poxton shook his head. "No, I'm not. I'm not qualified to do so. As your Flight Commander I can only express an opinion, make a recommendation."

"Damn you, Poxton, I've had enough! Can I go?"

"No, there's another matter." He reached for a thin sheaf of papers, the top one of which was a typewritten form.

Oliver's heart thumped and the floor felt unsteady beneath him.

Poxton's mouth grimaced as if it was tasting something nauseous. "The Adjutant's passed me a report from Corporal Huthwaite of the Service Police. He alleges that at 11.58 hours last night he was on airfield patrol when he saw an officer climbing from a window of the WAAF Officers' Quarters." Again the twisting of the mouth in distaste. "The officer gave his name as Flying Officer Lloyd. Corporal Huthwaite has since identified the room to the Duty Officer as that of Section Officer Howis and you, whom he thought he recognized at the time and has since confirmed it, as the officer concerned ..."

With his expression showing utter incredulity, Oliver made his anger obvious. "That's the second most outrageous thing that's been told me in this office today," he said furiously. "A load of lying rubbish!"

The other man slapped his open hand on the papers. "Will you control that temper of yours! I won't warn you again. Are you denying that you are the officer?"

"I'm not denying that the corporal spoke to me. Why should I? But I deny – and damned strongly – what he says about me. I'd been over to workshops to check whether my Tiffy was going to be serviceable for this morning's op. I spoke to Flight Sergeant James about it. So check that, too. It was about eleven-thirty. I sat in the cockpit for a while and then decided to return to my room. So what time had I got for climbing in and out of a Waaf's bedroom? Even if I'd wanted to, which I damned well didn't." He pushed his chin out aggressively again. "On the way back this clown of a corporal put his torch on me to check, I imagine, who I was. I was passing the Waaf billets, yes. *Passing*, not doing anything else. I'm bloody furious that he should take it into his thick head that I was climbing out of a window. And Mrs Howis's at that, a married woman. Or that I gave him Lloyd's name. I never gave him any name at all. Why should I have? He seemed to be satisfied who I was and I assumed – rightly apparently – that he knew me by sight. So why didn't he say anything to me about climbing out of a window?"

Poxton ran his finger down the report. "He says that he did and that you denied it, suggesting that he was mistaken. He seems quite certain that you said you were Flying Officer Lloyd."

"The man's either an incompetent fool or a bloody liar. Probably one with a grudge against officers. And though I wouldn't have said it under any other circumstances, I was certain at the time that he'd been drinking. Why don't you speak to Mrs Howis? Isn't that the obvious thing to do?"

She'll have to support me, he told himself. I've made it plain enough to the silly bitch. As an officer and a married woman she can't admit we've been screwing together. She couldn't be that soft.

"And the obvious thing to me," Poxton said drily, looking down his nose, "is that if Section Officer Howis *is* involved – and I hope to God that she's not – then she will almost certainly deny it. We shall see, shan't we? No doubt the CO will instruct the DAPM's department to send along a WAAF Investigating Officer to ask her."

"Does this mean that you don't believe me? That you prefer the say-so of an NCO?" He was truculent. The thought of Poxton's not accepting his story against a corporal's report was an affront to him.

"Apart from your insolence, Missen, these are serious charges that have to be investigated. You've been in the service for how long? Two and a half years? You know the drill as well as I do. There'll have to be a Court of Enquiry at the least."

"A Court of Enquiry!" he echoed. "Christ! The Krauts *will* be happy. There's a bloody war on, any of us could be chopped on the next do and you're wasting your time and mine on muck-raking, on deciding whether I was seen coming from a WAAF billet by a corporal I've told you doesn't know what he's talking about." He wanted to get the triviality of it through this man's obduracy. "Look," he urged. "Imagine – only just imagine – that I *had* been with Section Officer Howis. So what? I mean, she's a grown woman and of my own rank. What does the RAF expect from us? To live like a lot of emasculated monks? You could probably drag in half the Mess who've really been there. I won't go down on this thing on my own," he threatened, "believe me.

Nobody would thank you for being such a bloody prig. Least of all the CO. And as for your saying that I funked out this morning, you're going to make yourself look a damned fool. All you have is an unsupported, unjustified opinion that I'm not afraid to make you take a sight higher than the CO if I'm forced."

Poxton was unmoved and laid his pencil down. "Is that all you wish to say?"

Oliver glowered at him for long seconds then turned and, without saluting, strode from the office, not bothering to close the door behind him. He heard Poxton call out words which he ignored. Had he stayed any longer he would have boiled over and disregarded the Flight Commander's seniority, done something violent to release the bitterness of his fury at Poxton's stubborn refusal to believe him.

Twenty

With his legs moving mechanically along the road that was an endless monotony, Philip felt no tiredness, no fatigue to his muscles. Only his mind was weary and wretched. The grey half-light of his world remained unchanged, the road before him vanishing into its seeming endlessness. He walked the floor of a dismal silent ocean that covered a sunken landscape. He had been travelling for interminable years in this condition of mental confusion, yet he felt that the total of what he had done and seen could be held within the compass of a single dream. When not forced from it by the phantasmagoria of his condition he thought only of Laura, reliving in imagination every detail of their being together in the past, forcing his thoughts forward to when they would be together again. It was as though she filled the larger mass of his brain, leaving only its periphery to take in visual and tactile impressions. He talked to her to shut out the hallucinations his mind conjured up in his sickness. He would have closed his eyes against them, but he retained his fear of falling or of walking into something that might prove to be solid or horrifying.

Every so often, a sickly purplish discoloration would resolve itself in the twilight and deepen to foreshadow the landscape, alien and desolate, in which he would see – or imagine he saw – the sad dark figures that held for him an air of menace. As he approached, driven by the compulsion he could not resist, so the shadows would thicken and obliterate the vision, leaving him only the road that stretched before him. He remained conscious of the landscape and the figures in it even when he could not see them. They meant something to him, their haunting of him significant. Although he saw them only as dark shapes, entities without detail, he knew them to be German. Of that he was certain.

Imperceptibly, his eyesight was failing him. When he encountered isolated buildings and villages he saw them as blurred shadowy shapes without solidness, the people and animals moving about them attenuated and gauzy, wraithlike in their insubstantiality, their colours bleached from them like photographs exposed to the sun. And still with him was his deadening deafness.

His mind was in the grip of a melancholic depression and but for Laura whom he loved with every beat of his heart, with each breath from his body, he knew that he would have surrendered to the apathetic inertia of a sick animal and died in this hallucinatory nightmare he was suffering. Occasionally he wept, angrily wiping the tears from his cheeks and feeling ashamed of his unmanliness. Men cried only in their dreams, he told himself. He would put his fingers to his face and read the contours of his nose, his chin and eyes, feel the smoothness of his hair, prodding firmnesses to reassure himself of his physical reality. He repeated his examination of the familiar hands he had used all his life, looking down at the twill-trousered legs and flying boots striding below him, feeling the solid ground jarring the soles of his feet. He was real enough and with nothing in him that could be a part of the dream landscape in which he seemed to be trapped.

He moved openly through the villages now, stepping aside from the people he met, having a horror of their walking unknowingly through him as though he was a thing of invisible gossamer. Once he had been overtaken by a car he neither heard nor saw until suddenly its bonnet and headlamps were protruding through his belly from the rear, the body of it following as it was driven through him with no more effect than had he been in fusion with the shadows. It had given him a particular kind of terror.

And even as he was dissembling the terror, the feeling of being enclosed sent his mind back to see with a vivid clarity the instrument panel of his stricken Lancaster and, as though it was happening to him at that moment, the dark ground sliding beneath as he struggled at the controls with the body of Davies lolling bloodily at his side, the formless masses of trees rising to meet him and then the huge wing with its silent engines tilting in slow motion and digging into the ground; felt again the terror as he heard the shocking thunderclap of suddenly-arrested metal impacting into explosive confusion. He was standing where he had been thrown in the yellow light of the burning bomber, shaking from the anguish of his fall from the sky. And then in his vision the light changed imperceptibly until the sun was high in the sky, showing the upper structure of the wreck in shadowless detail. The nose and engine nacelles were crumpled shapelessly into the soft ground, the tail section and its gun turret impacted into the forward fuselage and wings. The huge oval rudders had broken off and were lying among the burnt trees ahead of the aircraft. On the one undamaged, the squadron letter over the red, white and blue of its identification strip was still visible. The main wreckage of the Lancaster had been carbonized to soot-covered ruptured metal, the grass around it grey with fine ash. An army truck stood at its rear and men in boiler suits and grey-green forage caps worked at the front of it with long hooked poles. An NCO in a dark-blue uniform with red patches, seated on the running-board of the truck, watched them. Side by side on the ground lay two grey cocoons of charred fabric showing crisped flesh peeled away from white bone. As the men with the poles pulled at something in the tangle of metal so a puff of fine ash and a mist of smoke rose to obscure what they were doing and the scene faded.

In spite of the detail in what he had seen, he knew that what had followed his escape from the Lancaster had been wholly of his imagination. It had to be because he was certain that he hadn't waited at the scene for daylight, certain he would never have put himself so close to the possibility of being seen and captured. That he could visualize with such extraordinary vividness a happening in which he could have had no part convinced him of the reality of his mental sickness. It put terror back in his mind and he started to run as though to leave the tormenting vision behind him.

Twenty-one

It was in the indeterminate period between afternoon and evening that Oliver was freed from Availability State to return to his room. At first he had intended to use Poxton's prohibition on his leaving the airfield as a good reason for not visiting Lady Woollgar, but his resentment against it decided him otherwise. It would be twenty-odd miles from Dunsham St Michael to Hyde Park Corner and if she didn't detain him too long with her arrogances he might arrive in time for Laura to give him something to eat. One danger in leaving before dining was being missed in the Mess. Eating in wasn't obligatory, but it depended on whether Poxton was there, whether he would notice his absence and check on it. If he did, it was a misfortune he would worry about when he returned. The other danger was in changing into No 1 dress, his best tunic and trousers. If he were seen in it by Poxton, he would know he was leaving the airfield.

After drinking a large whisky he left by the Lodge road, unguarded because the gates had long been removed for melting down, rumoured on the Station for cast-iron Spitfires. His not booking out at the main entrance would be a disciplinary offence in itself.

He drove the MG as fast as he dared in the narrow roads leading to Dunsham and by the time he drew up before the porticoed door of Saxinge Hall he had convinced himself that he was about to face some pretty lethal verbal flak. There could be no other reason for Lady Woollgar demanding his presence.

She answered the door to his tugging at the bell-pull. Neither her dogs nor the housekeeper – or whatever she was – were in evidence. She wore a tunic heavily embroidered with blue Chinese dragons and a gold-coloured skirt. Her pale-blonde hair had been drawn back in a pony-tail and a necklet of lapis-lazuli circled her throat. Seen in the shadow of the doorway, she looked not too much older than her stepdaughter.

He put his hand to the peak of his cap and showed his teeth. "A little later than I had hoped," he said.

As he had anticipated, there was no discernible friendliness in her expression, no brief social smile of greeting. Her green eyes gave him the feeling of being a tradesman calling at the wrong door.

"Please come in, Mr Missen." She turned, leaving him to close the door as he took off his cap and followed her. Behind her, he smelled the fragrance of a musky scent.

She led him into a small room off the hall; a woman's room, he decided as he entered it. The walls were panelled to shoulder height in blond wood and one held a white fireplace surrounded by an elaborately-carved centrepiece. An escritoire stood near the single large window that overlooked grass and trees and lengthening shadows. There were massed flower paintings above the panelling and, in a corner, a black and gold lacquered cabinet. Two delicately-legged chairs with pink seats stood on either side of a small matching table holding a parchment-shaded lamp and a silver box. It was a less intimidating room than that in which he had been previously examined and assessed.

She stood at the cabinet and said, "There are Virginian cigarettes in the box on the table. What would you prefer to drink?"

"Whisky, please. Nothing in it." He took the cigarettes to her and she shook her head.

"I have my own," she said. "Please sit down."

He lit a cigarette and watched her pouring the drinks. There was about her a precise symmetry, her movements smooth and feline; an aristocratic cat who made him feel crude and gauche, that his flesh was a coarser material than hers, his blood a common and proletarian red.

She handed him his whisky, the crystal tumbler generously filled, and sat in the chair at his side, only the small table separating them. Her own drink was a pale sherry in a very small glass.

He said "Cheers" and when he sipped his whisky she inclined her head without joining him. It was a good whisky, strong and warming to the stomach.

She took a cigarette from a pink packet and waited for him to light it, staring disconcertingly at him as he did so. The green arrogance of her eyes unsettled him and he dropped his gaze from them. The whisky, he considered, could have been given to him to numb the impact of what she was about to say.

Her first words put him on the defensive. "Have you made arrangements to meet my stepdaughter, Mr Missen?"

The unexpectedness of it made him hesitate in his indecision whether to deny or admit it, knowing immediately that his hesitation had already given her the answer. "I was hoping to," he temporized.

"At Kensington?"

"I don't know. It has to be arranged." He cursed the flabby deflation to which this woman could reduce him.

"You must know," she said crisply. "Were you expecting to see her this evening?"

"I was going to telephone. It depended on whether or not I was flying."

"And are you?"

"No. I mean, I'm not flying. Not tonight, that is." The scented smoke from her Turkish cigarette drifted to his nostrils.

"Then you *were* intending to see her?"

He was nettled and, to his mortification, felt colour rising from behind his collar. "I was hoping to. Are you objecting?"

"I will tell you. Is there something wrong with the whisky?"

"No, of course not." He took a large swallow. The woman's words were buzzing around him like wasps, keeping him off-balance.

"I am going to be blunt, Mr Missen, because I don't believe I have any alternative. You had proposed to visit my stepdaughter this evening at my flat?" There was distaste in her expression, the tone of her voice making it a squalid and vulgar intention.

"I was going to telephone her there, yes."

"Which is a quibble. You were hoping, or expecting, to stay there. I am not a schoolgirl, Mr Missen," she said tartly.

"No," he agreed. She was pushing him to retaliation. "Neither is Laura. We've a perfectly normal arrangement to meet while she is in London. No doubt we shall go to a show or a night club. Something like that," he ended lamely.

She drank her sherry and stood. "Let me give you another drink," she said. He emptied his tumbler and handed it to her. She baffled him with her alternating hard words and generous hospitality. "And please help yourself to cigarettes."

If only she didn't keep him off balance and tottering in uncertainty. He couldn't be sure whether she was guessing about his intended visit to the flat or that Laura had told her. No, it wouldn't be anything she would confide in her stepmother, even by implication. The bloody woman was femalely intuitive. He looked glumly around the room while she did things at the cabinet, wanting nothing more than to be out and away from it and her.

She gave him his whisky – another generous tumblerful – and sat.

"My stepdaughter," she said, and he noticed that she had never familiarized her to him by name, "is very vulnerable and her father and I are naturally concerned for her. She has not yet recovered from the shock of her husband's death and your unfortunate resemblance to him does nothing to help her. There is no bringing him back by her substituting you for him. You mustn't for one moment think there is. Your seeing her can do nothing but stir up memories which should be left where they are. That you should be thinking of her in terms of ... of whatever your intentions are, is something we will not countenance." She held his eyes calmly. "And, Mr Missen, if I may be blunt again, my stepdaughter's future is a matter of closely associated families ... you understand?"

The flak was beginning to come up thick and fast and, with it, a stirring of his anger. "Thank you very much," he choked. "I'm sorry I don't come up to your expectations." He pushed himself from his chair. "If that's all you have to say, I'll go. I'll do what I damned well choose to. Laura's a grown woman and it'll be for her to decide whether she sees me or not."

She hadn't moved although she raised her eyebrows fractionally. "Sit down," she said sharply. "I haven't finished what I wish to say."

"Lady Woollgar," he said with deliberation, "at the risk of my being rude, you've said enough already. If you'll excuse me ..."

"Please sit down," she reiterated, "unless you wish to stand there like a servant. I shan't be long." Her eyes, steady and unblinking, were willing him and he sat.

"I don't believe you understand what I mean, Mr Missen," she continued. "My stepdaughter is attracted to you – if she *is* attracted – only because your physical appearance, your wearing the same uniform, reminds her of her husband. You need not think that there is any other reason. This might not be obvious to you, but it is to me. It would be to her were she not so emotionally vulnerable."

"It's still a matter for her, however she feels." He was stubborn, for he now had nothing to lose by fighting her. "I shall telephone her and if she still wishes to see me, so she shall."

"I suppose I shouldn't be surprised, Mr Missen. It was no more than I had expected from you. For you, it's not enough that her father and I disapprove?" There was in her voice the barely concealed contempt of a woman speaking down to a social inferior.

"No. I'm sorry, but it doesn't. I happen to be extremely fond of Laura. Enough, I'm afraid, not to be warned off by you or anybody else."

There was a long silence as she sipped at her sherry, studying him over the glass with calculation as though he were a horse in a sale ring. Then she smiled, transforming her face into friendliness, astonishing him with her sudden change of mood. "It's my turn to apologize," she said, her voice softer, less arrogant. "I honestly didn't realize that she meant so much to you. There are certain kinds of men who would ..." She pouted her mouth ruefully. "I thought that you were one of them. In my anxiety to protect her, perhaps I did you an injustice." She reached her arm across the table. "Yes, I can see that I did. Please forgive the things I said."

He took her hand and felt the warm fingers alive in his. "It's quite all right, Lady Woollgar," he said, forcing a smile back at her. "I can see your point of view."

She wrinkled her nose girlishly. There was an incongruity about it, like an archbishop winking at a very junior curate. "I rather think we're going to like each other. It is Oliver, isn't it?"

"Yes." He began to warm to her. Behind the patrician coldness she had shown that she could be a woman capable of responding to his masculinity. There were going to be no problems now, no disagreeable objections. It had taken his frankness, his refusal to be intimidated by her, to thaw out her opposition. And, hell, he was personable by any standards. She had been testing him, seeing how far his spine would bend with the Are-your-intentions-honourable inquisition usually left to the father.

"Shall we have another drink, Oliver?" she said. "And then, I imagine, you'd wish to be off."

"Allow me to get them." He had almost called her Cynthia, but dared not. His tumbler was empty – he couldn't remember finishing it – and he felt a velvety smoothness of well-being. At any other time he could have relaxed in his chair for the rest of the evening, putting away the beautiful stuff as fast as she supplied it. A rose-coloured glow seemed to be leaking in through the top of his skull.

"No." She stood from her chair with her lithe elegance. "You stay there. It is my pleasure."

He watched her from beneath eyelids that were unaccountably heavy. What a woman she was. Wasted on the old bugger who was her husband. Christ! He swallowed and licked his lips. If he ever dared ... He reached for another cigarette, fumbling clumsily with the lid of the box. Manual coordination minus five, he told himself. He would have to watch it. The whisky was strong and he was on the edge of being fuddled. And that wouldn't do. Not with Laura waiting for him on her back.

As she poured out the drinks – and with her back to him he couldn't see what she was pouring – she said, "Will you be free tomorrow evening? I would like you to dine with us. I'm quite sure Laura would, too." She turned her head and smiled gently. "I must make amends, mustn't I?"

"That would be pleasant. Provided there isn't a night do on the board."

Her mouth made a moue of self-reproach. "I'm always forgetting there's a war still on," she said. "If you find that you can't, another time, perhaps."

She put his whisky on the table. It was as large as the others had been. She lifted her glass. "Death to the enemy." That, too, sounded incongruous said with her accent.

"And d-damnation." He tipped his tumbler and let the fiery stuff pour down his throat, blinking his eyes against their watering, imagining he felt the chair seat squirm beneath his buttocks. He frowned. He had certainly drunk more in his time without turning a hair. Fumbling at his sleeve cuff, he peered at his watch. "Mus' go, I s'ppose." Dammit! He had slurred the words and she must have noticed. His tongue felt stiff and wooden, the thumping of his pulse loud in his ears.

"I wonder ..." She looked doubtful, then shook her head. "No, perhaps not."

"What, Lady W-Woollgar?" That was better, his words articulated more clearly around his tongue although the bloody stammer was there.

"I wouldn't wish to trouble you, but if you are calling on Laura

I have a small chair I intended having taken to the flat." She creased her forehead. "It might fit in the spare seat of the car."

"No trouble," he said. "Be glad to do it."

"Well ... if you wouldn't mind." She still sounded doubtful. "It would certainly be a great help." She gave him a grateful smile with lips that were, he noticed, beautifully smooth for an older woman. "It's upstairs. Could I persuade you to help me carry it down?"

"Of course. Your humble servant, ma'am." He drained his whisky and stubbed out the cigarette, levering himself cautiously from the chair. His mouth felt numb and bloodless, the floor shifting under his feet, but he could cope. Just slightly uncoordinated, that was all. Jesus! Those had been strong whiskies. Oddly tasting, too, as if mixed with brandy. He needed fresh air to clear his head before meeting Laura.

He followed her from the room and up the wide stairs, carefully lifting his feet to negotiate the shallow risers to avoid tripping, holding on to the handrail. As they climbed, she was telling him things about how tiresome it was not to be able to keep servants because of the quite stupid and arbitrary Emergency Powers Act and having to manage on her own with no man to help. There was a friendly intimacy in her confidences that made him realize how much he had misjudged her.

She led him along a corridor, its wine-red carpeting muffling the sound of their footfalls. There were closed doors along its length and, between each, a large potted plant. She halted at one and he nearly cannoned into her. As she opened it by its huge brass knob she glanced at him doubtfully before entering it. It was a bedroom; not hers, that he could see by the absence of cosmetics on the dressing-table which held only two lamps and a glass ashtray. The single bed with its orange plush-covered headboard was surrounded by paintings of racehorses and their jockeys against a gold fleurs-de-lis wallpaper. A mahogany straight-backed chair stood by the bed. Through the windows, the setting sun bathed the room in a reddish glow.

She pointed at the chair with her thumb. "Is it going to be too big?"

He went to it and lifted it, dropping it back again with a thud as he lurched to recover his balance. It was heavy enough and he doubted that it would fit into the seat of the MG. He swore at himself for his clumsiness, muttering silently that he was acting like a pimply schoolboy who'd been sniffing the barmaid's apron. Lifting it again, he was aware of her at his side, not showing the signs he expected that she had noticed his drunkenness, her shoulder and hip momentarily pressed against his as she pushed down at the chair.

"No," she said, "it doesn't matter. Put it down."

He turned his head. Her green eyes were close to his, her mouth unsmiling. The smell of her perfume sent a frisson of sudden desire through him. They stood like it for long moments until he heard her whisper, "You may, if you wish," moving her body so that she was facing him.

She could have been talking about the chair, but even in his fuddled confusion he didn't think so. He took his hands from it, turning as she moved the few inches that separated them and they were touching, the protruberances of her pelvis, the long thighs and the soft rubberiness of her breasts against him as though there was no intervening clothing. The flesh of her face seemed looser, her eyes a darker green that stared at him with her expression still serious. A strand of hair had come loose and hung across her forehead. He put his hands on her shoulderblades and pulled her closer, lowering his head and searching for her mouth.

"No," she said, tightening her lips and twisting her face from him. For a nasty sinking moment he thought that he had misunderstood her intent until her hands slid between them, her fingers undoing the top buttons of his jacket. Then she brushed a hand lightly over his thigh and pushed away from him, going to the windows and pulling at cords that drew the curtains.

In the dim twilight she stood by the side of the bed and unfastened the front of her tunic, shrugging herself from it as though unaware of his presence.

With his legs apart to hold himself from staggering he began to remove his jacket and trousers, never taking his eyes from her body as she stepped out of her skirt. He couldn't believe his incredible good luck. The chair! That was a laugh. Two women so close together and both wanting him. That was it. It explained everything. She had been jealous and now he was going to take the place of the dead Philip with her also. What a lucky bastard he'd been to have had both of them. And now they were competing against each other to keep the hairy animal of him busy and happy.

And he had allowed the arrogant bitch to talk to him like a bloody mangy dog. She didn't give a curse for Laura just so long as she had what she wanted from him. And, drunk as he might be, he would be man enough for the two of them.

When she unhooked her brassière to reveal her breasts he drew in his breath as though vouchsafed a view of the sanctum sanctorum itself. He could already feel them in his fingers, under his mouth. Down to his underwear his fingers were trembling, his chest full of pumping heart. He felt red-eyed with a burning fever in his loins. He was naked but for his watch and the identity tags around his neck when she slid her panties down over her thighs and stood lean and palely elegant with no pretence of modesty, regarding him expressionlessly.

He laughed inside his mind. Panties. Women like her didn't call them panties. Or knickers. What the hell *did* they call them? Passion-killers, like the Waaf? And he thought of Morwenna's blubberiness, the hanging breasts, against this woman's exciting slimness.

He wanted to take her in the held-back violence of the shaking desire she had aroused in him with her cool and blue-blooded whorishness but sensed that, despite it, she would demand a courtly and deferential love-making. He wasn't intending to spoil their future loving for the sake of a little restraint. As he moved towards her, lurching slightly, she sat on the bed and lifted her legs on to it, lying back and closing her eyes. Climbing on to it, his head swimming, he knelt astride her, pinning the flesh of her thigh with his knee as he did so. She winced and opened her eyes and he saw annoyance in them.

"Sorry," he mumbled thickly, "Did I hurt you?"

"You're drunk," she said brusquely and closed her eyes.

With a part of his mind he knew that he was acting like a goat in rut and he cursed the whisky she had pushed at him so freely. When he kissed her mouth she did not repeat her objection, but her lips remained closed and unresponsive. When his desire could be held back no longer he took her clumsily, her body flaccid and undemanding under his until the moment when she convulsed against him and then lay still.

Twenty-two

The light being switched on woke him to a formless and shifting shimmer of gold that resolved itself into the magnified pattern of interwoven threads in the silk stuff of the bedspread close to his eyes. He was alone in the bed, his body damp with cooling sweat, his head full of thumping hammers. His stomach felt nauseatingly bloated with curdled whisky and he was at the nadir of wretchedness.

He raised his head and saw her standing at the side of the bed, his eyes at the level of the blue dragon on her tunic, lifting them to her face looking down at him. He gave her a weak smile, blinking his eyelids against the light. "Sorry," he mumbled, "I must have gone to sleep."

"You did," she said. "Can you hear me?" Her eyes were cold and she regarded him as she might a mess left on the bed by one of her dogs.

"Yes." He was suddenly chilled by her manner. "What's the matter?"

She was at her most patrician and contemptuous. "I shall, if I have to, tell my husband that you came to this house uninvited; that you took advantage of his absence to attempt to make love to me. Attempt, Mr Missen," she emphasized. "Nothing more but, I promise you, bad enough."

He goggled at her, his mouth open. She wasn't being straight-faced humorous; she was actually serious. "I don't understand."

"Then I'll explain. What you did was against my wish, in spite of my objections. You tried to force yourself on me. I believe the police would call it attempted rape. However anybody may choose to regard it there can be, of course, no more question of your seeing my stepdaughter."

"You couldn't!" He pushed himself up to a sitting position, dazed and confounded by her monstrous perversion of what had happened, conscious now of his nakedness. "You wouldn't dare!"

"Dare? You tell me that I wouldn't dare? Who is my husband going to believe? Who will the police believe?"

He stared at her incredulously and shook his aching head. Poxton was one who would believe her, disbelieve him. It would be all of a piece with what he must now know about his visit to Morwenna's room. And it would be the word of Lady Woollgar, wife of Lieutenant-Colonel Sir Clive Woollgar, DSO and MC of Saxinge Hall, against the already doubted word of Flying Officer bloody-ordinary Missen, O.

"You can't mean it," he said, knowing that she did before she even answered him.

"But I do mean it. I mean it most definitely. And what would you say? That I went to bed with you willingly?" There was distaste in her expression as she looked down the length of his body. "Me? With you? Is my stepdaughter going to believe that? Or approve of it even if she did?"

"You bloody bitch!" he said in a strangled voice. "You meant this to happen."

"Did I?" Her lip twisted in scorn. "Would it have happened had you been a man suitable to associate with my stepdaughter? Haven't you rather proved to be the sort of person who isn't?"

"You telephoned me. I can prove you asked me here."

"Can you? No doubt I could find an adequate reason were I forced to."

"You cow!" he said shakily. "I could smash your bloody face in."

"So you could," she agreed calmly, not visibly disturbed by his threat. "It would help. I believe violence *is* associated with attempted rape." She put scorn in her words. "Now listen to me and don't be stupid. For the time being I shall not complain of being abused and threatened by you – it would be understandable that I should not wish to make public the humiliation of it. Not unless I have to. Which is what I shall do if you force me, if you make even the slightest attempt to contact my stepdaughter. Do you understand?"

He wanted to vomit, tasting the bile in his throat. "You put something in my whisky."

"You're a fool, Mr Missen, and a tiresome boor. Get your clothes on and go. Don't ever come here again. You disgust me."

There was a gleam of triumphant derision in her eyes as she turned and left him, leaving the door open, the soft padding of her footfalls dying to silence along the corridor.

Climbing from the bed he staggered to one of the windows, fumbling for the catch he couldn't unfasten and vomiting over the inner sill and on to the wall and carpet beneath. He trembled with rage and mortification at his humiliation. Picking up one of the lamps from the dressing-table, he pulled it by the cable from its socket and hurled it hard at the mirror reflecting the loathsome body that had made him the oafish dupe of the scheming woman he now hated as much as he did Poxton.

There was no sound of her returning and he dressed, pulling himself together sufficiently to walk along the corridor and down the stairs with as much dignity as he could retrieve from the wreckage of his self-esteem. From another part of the house, he thought he could hear water being run into a bath.

His cap lay on the table in the hall, a piece of white paper propped against it. When he saw that it was a five-pound note his almost unbearable fury at the insult made him rip it savagely into small pieces, scattering them on the floor and scuffing them with his shoe.

On his way out through the gates he could see only dimly in his masked headlights he turned more sharply than he intended, the side of the car scraping against the stone pillar and throwing it momentarily out of control as he fought to keep it on a straight line. The sky was clouded and the moon not yet risen, the night black and pressing in on his unhappiness. The fresh air had done nothing for his drunkenness and he drove with his nearside wheels close enough to the verge for him to see it and give him direction. At each junction, the signposts having been removed in the early days of the war, he stopped to orientate himself.

When he saw the blacked-out shape of the Crown Inn, he pulled on to the forecourt. The hair of the dog that had bitten him, he decided, a snifter of his favourite glycol. One more would steady him, would anaesthetize the horrible thumping in his head. The bloody woman had poisoned him with whatever she had put in his whisky. He climbed from the car and waited for a few seconds until the dizziness of standing passed, then walked carefully into the bar. He knew none of the men in there and was glad he didn't. A smile would be the hardest thing he could produce. He was in the mood to resent the interest of another man's stare and to do something destructive about it. He nodded at the landlord and supported himself on the bar counter with his elbows. "A whisky, please," he said.

Because the landlord's version of a single whisky was hardly worth the effort of drinking it, he had two. Neither did anything to clear his brain that he felt was swirling around in his skull, nor to numb its throbbing.

It was raining hard when he came outside and fell into the car, fumbling blindly with the key for the ignition he couldn't find. His cap was a tight band around his aching forehead and he pulled it off, throwing it on to the passenger's seat. "Mus' get back," he mumbled aloud. "Bloody Pox'on … bast'd out to get me."

On the road and belatedly switching on his lights and windscreen wipers, he trod hard on the accelerator pedal, his head pushed forward to the glass screen as he strained to see through the watery distortion into the darkness ahead. He was travelling fast when he took the bend and saw the red warning lights of a check point barrier across the road. Standing in a cone of light from the blockhouse were a military policeman and a uniformed constable, his cape glistening wetly in the rain. The constable stepped into the road as he approached and flashed his torch.

Oliver took his foot from the accelerator pedal, realizing as he did so that he could never stop in time and that when he did he would inevitably be recognized as a drunken driver. He had a vision of his arrest and a police cell, of the humiliation of being handed over to an RAF escort in the sobered-up morning, dishevelled and unshaven and stinking of stale alcohol. Panic seized him and he accelerated. He heard a shout and then a momentary glimpse of the red-and-white barrier in the pool of his lights, the constable falling away to one side with his helmet falling off and a squashy thud against the door of the car just before he smashed the tripods flying and was through. He kept going, expecting the sound of the MP's pistol being fired, but hearing only his own laboured breathing as if he had been running. Bent metal scraped on one of the front tyres, but he dared not stop to do anything about it. *Dear God*, he prayed, *let it be all right*. The panic had sobered him. Not physically, for he still felt wretchedly sick, but his brain was not swirling around in his head so confusingly.

The stupid, stupid bastards! Putting up a barrier so near a bend in the road. And that fool of a policeman jumping into his path so unexpectedly, waving his ridiculous torch that he hadn't seen until it was too late. He couldn't have been hurt. Just pushed to one side and serve the silly bastard right. What the hell was he supposed to have done? Jam on everything and finish upside-down in a ditch? If he had stopped and been arrested he would have missed the op tomorrow morning and that was a damned sight more important than a twopenny-ha'penny civil charge that did nothing for nobody.

Turning into the Lodge gateway, he reduced his speed to a crawl with the engine making the least possible noise. He parked at the side of the house with the damaged mudguard close against the wall. In trying to straighten it, he saw that the front number plate had been torn off and was missing. That was all he needed to finish a disastrous evening. When they traced the car to the Woollgars, he would have had it. He thought about it, racking his brain that wanted only to sleep and forget. Coming to a decision, he replaced the key in the ignition and left it there, then wiped the rim of the steering wheel and the gear lever knob with his handkerchief. That was it. Unknown to him and while he had been in his room, one of the other pilots had borrowed the car. It was done often enough. He would have to take a chance on that Woollgar arch-bitch saying that he had been there. She wasn't likely to were she satisfied that he wasn't going to see Laura and knowing what he could say about their evening together. She was as vulnerable as he was, despite what she had said she would do. He would deny everything. All he had to do now was to get to his room undetected and swear by all that was holy that he had never left it. Everything was going to be all right.

He entered the house by what had been the servants' door and made his way through the dark passages to the main hall. It was empty and he climbed the stairs, thankful that Poxton hadn't been waiting for him. When he opened the door to his room the light was on and Gooch, the Duty Officer, was lying on his bed, his cap on and holding a book he had been reading.

Gooch grinned when he saw him. "It's me again, old son," he said amiably. "I thought you were never coming back."

Oliver closed the door. He felt as though the sky had fallen on him. "I've been out walking. What the hell's the matter now?"

"I wouldn't know. But the Adj wants words with you." He

looked at his watch. "I'm to give you fifteen minutes while he prepares himself and then it's on the double to his office. If I were you I'd take my parachute, old son. He didn't sound too happy about something."

"You must know what about." If Gooch didn't, Oliver did. He had been checked on by Poxton and missed and he was sunk. In every way that could be imagined.

"Honour bright and cross my heart I don't. I was ordered to camp out in your room until you returned and it's spoiled my evening." His face showed concern. "Are you all right, old son? You look as though you're going to drop dead on me."

Oliver managed a feeble smile. "The way I feel at this moment I wish to God I was."

Gooch rolled from the bed and stood. "Better dunk your head in some cold water before you leave," he said. "Don't forget, fifteen minutes from now on the dot."

Twenty-three

Laura sat with her legs up on the settee and her eyes half-closed, a glass of pink gin in her hand. It was her third that evening. She felt depressed and melancholic, her mind occupied by the remembered images of Philip, the memories of whom not even alcohol could soften into nostalgia. His death was an open bleeding wound in her and always would be.

She had drawn the curtains against the night and, apart from the muffled sounds of passing traffic and the footfalls of the few pedestrians, London was quiet in its shroud of darkness. The bombing raids had all but ceased and the sirens rarely sounded. When she had served with the Red Cross at Stepney earlier in the war, she had cared very much that she should survive the almost daily devastation and death caused by the bombing. Now that she would prefer to be dead with Philip than alive with anyone else, she felt that she was doomed to live for ever in a bleak and arid emptiness.

She had bathed and perfumed her body, dressing it in preparation for the satisfying of its need, an impersonal ritual to which her emotions were indifferent. If there was anything, it was a resentment against its continuing need to be sexually pacified. This Missen man, the brash and conceited image of her dead Philip, was coming to do what the gins she drank to excess had so miserably failed. There would be no happy affection in it, no sweet conjoining with a love that had in it more of an inner spiritual emotion than a body's animal satisfaction. All she could hope for in pandering to her sexual need was a self-induced deception that she held at least the simulacrum of Philip in her arms to deaden for a few moments the ache of his going from her, to fill something of the emptiness of her loss. At the least, this image of him might palliate the emotional aloneness which neither her father nor her stepmother had been able to fill.

Despite her belief that death was almost certainly the final closing of a door, she began to accept that she could be wrong, that she could give room in her mind to the possibility of Philip's continued existence on another level, to give a temporary reality of his presence on those occasions when she sensed that he was near her. Her mind, its inhibitions of unbelief loosened by the alcohol she had drunk, imagined him as occupying another dimension, a graveless ghost of a man who could see her from the plane of his own invisibility. It could, she thought, explain the often intense sensation of his presence.

Thinking of him, she became aware that he was in the room as though in response to the opening of her mind, a distinct presence as strong and compelling as she had sensed before in her bedroom, the essence of his personality seeming to fill her with his love. Her eyes brimmed with tears and she looked around her at the empty room, willing herself to see him. Was it all in her imagination, her mind's projection of an anguished yearning to bring him back? She refused to believe that. God – if there was a God – could never be that cruel; to allow him to die and then to mock her with it. It needed a step in the direction of the unknowable for her to accept unequivocably Philip's presence, a putting aside the feeling that she was being maudlin. She put her glass down and stood, holding out her arms as though to embrace him. "Philip," she whispered. "My dearest love. You've come back."

For a brief moment there was in her an exhilaration of ecstasy and then, as though the sound of her words had snapped the thread of their rapport, there was nothing and what she had felt of his presence had gone, leaving her alone and weeping. But she no longer doubted; she was convinced. He had died only as a physical being. He had been with her from wherever he was, telling her of his continuing love and this she would accept unquestioningly and with a belief that he would be waiting for her.

Now that she knew, she recognized for what it was the shabby carnality into which she was allowing her body to lead her. When she went to him it would be as she had been and was, not tainted with the sexuality of another man that would keep her from him, poison his love for her. She could no more do it now than to have considered it when he was alive. She must have been mad, looking through the bottom of a gin glass at a man who could never take Philip's place even in a lifetime of sexual need.

With a new lightness of spirit in her, she went to the telephone and lifted it from its cradle. When she had been given the number she asked for, she ordered a taxi. If there was no delay she could catch the last train that would stop at Dunsham.

While she waited for it she retrieved her glass and poured the gin from it into the wash-basin in the bathroom and then, as an afterthought, disconnected the telephone.

Twenty-four

The Adjutant's office smelled of waiting trouble. Flight Lieutenant Ashmole, sitting at his desk with Poxton standing behind him, nodded as Oliver saluted him. Chubby and balding, with deceptively mild brown eyes behind steel-rimmed spectacles, he was the Commanding Officer's guardian, his watchman against trivial intrusions, his disciplinary sieve. He had Poxton's sheaf of papers in front of him.

"Flying Officer Missen?" he said. That was a formality, for he knew him as well as he knew every pilot in the squadron.

"Sir." Oliver felt a twitch starting in the corner of his mouth. The unshaded bulb over the Adjutant's desk hurt his eyes and he felt exposed to the two men watching him, bone-brittle and raw-edged. Although he had swallowed a benzedrine tablet and splashed cold water on his face, his head still ached, his stomach churning its nausea. He never wanted to drink another whisky as long as he lived.

"This afternoon, Flight Lieutenant Poxton ordered you not to leave the Station. Did you leave in defiance of his order?" Behind his words was all the authority of Air Force Law and Air Council Instructions.

Poxton's eyes were on him and, although he answered the Adjutant, his own stare challenged Poxton with his enmity. "I don't agree he had the authority to do it. I didn't accept what he said was an order as I'd committed no disciplinary offence." He was only staving off the inevitable, but he wasn't going down without firing back.

"You left the Station?"

"Yes, sir."

"What time?"

"I can't remember. Not precisely. Eight o'clock at least, possibly later."

"You dined in Mess?" Which, Oliver was certain, he knew he hadn't.

"I wasn't hungry and I was browned off. I went out for some air. Walking," he added.

"In your Number One dress?" Ashmole frowned his disbelief.

"Yes. I thought I might drop in for a drink somewhere."

"And did you?"

"No."

"You haven't been drinking?" The disbelief was there again.

"No, sir."

"Your car was missing from the park."

Although that shook him, he shrugged as if it was no surprise and of no importance. "It was? I didn't know. It's been borrowed before without my knowing it and I haven't used it since yesterday."

"Give me the key." Ashmole held out his hand.

"I don't have it. I left it in the ignition. Is the car still not there?"

Ashmole's spectacles glinted, disconcertingly shielding his eyes, but his mild contempt showed in his expression. "Who should know better than yourself? Pending the collection of the key you will not, of course, use it. A further matter arising from this: when you left the Station you failed to book out at the Guardroom."

"I went out by the Lodge Gate. I didn't think of it." For God's sake why didn't he get it over with and let him get back to his room and be allowed to die in peace. It was taking all his will-power to stand without swaying. And standing, he felt, under a black cloud that was growing bigger, that would soon be raining on him.

Ashmole was obviously restraining himself against being angry. "That's a Standing Order, Mr Missen. It isn't a thing you don't think about." He stared at him bleakly for several seconds. "I've listened to what you've had to say and perhaps fortunately for you it's not for me to decide on the truth or otherwise of it, but you'll now consider yourself under open arrest. That means that you will return forthwith to your room and stay there. You will not use the Mess for any purpose. Your meals will be brought to your room. You will not talk to or communicate with any other member of the Mess." His expression became stern. "Should there be any disobedience of my orders you will be placed under close arrest. Is that clearly understood?"

"Does that mean I'm relieved of my flying duties?"

"No, it does not. You will report for briefing on Flight Lieutenant Poxton's orders. Do you wish to say anything further?"

"Yes, I do." He looked directly at Poxton, letting him see his hatred. "Those papers you have on your desk. Is there a report from Flight Lieutenant Poxton on my operational flying?"

Ashmole hesitated. "There is. For the CO's information, of course, and not yours."

Poxton, the buttoned-up bastard, was really out to clobber him. It wasn't enough that he should go out and kill Germans. If it wasn't done Poxton's way, it had to be wrong. And now he was putting him up for lacking moral fibre.

"If he has had his say, I should, too. I want it put on record that he has made totally unjustified accusations to me about my last two missions. Accusations that I can prove to be false and due to personal spite and malice."

Poxton, his eyes shadowed beneath the peak of his cap, glared at him as though he could have killed him, his expression promising no mercy.

Ashmole frowned. "I'm not taking evidence, Mr Missen. You'll have an opportunity to make your defence to the CO." He looked down at the papers, tapping them with his fingers and thinking. Then he spoke to Poxton. "Would you mind leaving us. This particular matter doesn't concern you."

As Poxton passed close to him on his way out, Oliver felt the current of an antagonism that raised the hairs on the nape of his neck. Whatever he felt about his Flight Commander was returned, a male atavistic hostility that needed a resolving by violence on one side and submission on the other.

When they were alone, Ashmole said, "Where, otherwise, this would be no concern of yours, there is a further possible charge against you involving Section Officer Howis and I ..."

"That's something else I strongly deny," Oliver cut him short. "It's more evidence of Flight Lieutenant Poxton's vindictiveness."

Ashmole straightened in his chair. "Please don't interrupt me," he said coldly, "and be very careful what you say about Mr Poxton. I repeat. In view of a possible future charge against you, I feel obliged to tell you that Section Officer Howis was admitted to hospital earlier this evening."

Oliver felt chilled. There was going to be no end to what the woman was doing to him. "Why should that concern me?" He had difficulty in getting the words out. "What's happened to her?"

"I find this distasteful and embarrassing," Ashmole said, visibly reluctant to say anything further, "and I'm not wholly certain that I should tell you. She was found unconscious in her room. It appears from what the doctor at the hospital reports that she is in a, ah, certain condition and that she unwisely attempted to do something about it. She is dangerously ill and I understand that what she did will be a matter for the civil police to investigate." His expression was an accusation, an affirmation that he had no doubts about who was to blame.

"I deny that this is anything to do with me." Inside his chest was full of suffocating apprehension. The stupid bitch! She couldn't do anything right. She had been nothing but trouble for him. And, now, having changed her mind about getting rid of the thing, she had botched it and dragged him into what was essentially her own problem. There couldn't be anything more that could happen to him.

"Is that all you wish to say?"

"It's all I can say."

Ashmole shrugged his scepticism. "If," he said harshly, "I find that you mention anything about Section Officer Howis outside this office, directly or by implication, I shall personally see to it that you are court-martialled. You understand me?"

"Yes, sir."

He waved a dismissive hand at him. "You can go. Report to me here at 14.00 hours tomorrow for your interview with the CO." He turned his attention to his papers, looking down and not acknowledging Oliver's salute as he left.

Outside, he was almost expecting Poxton to be waiting for him, but there was nothing but the unfriendly darkness of night and the isolation from his fellow officers that now awaited him. There was a resentment in him that none of this was of his own making, that he had been used in different ways by Morwenna and Lady Woollgar, crucified by Poxton because of his dislike for him. But if any of them thought that he was going to snivel, to apologize for things for which he wasn't solely responsible, they were mistaken. He shut out from his mind the possible consequences of his drunken driving after satisfying himself that there could be no real proof that he had been driving the car. Not even were it connected with the scene of the accident – and it had been an accident, the direct responsibility of Lady Woollgar who had spiked his whisky – by the missing number plate. He had enough bleeding to do for himself without having to bleed for others as well.

Twenty-five

In the soundless half-light that surrounded him, Philip's encounters with units of the Wehrmacht were becoming a more frequent occurrence. Walking through a village, a presence invisible to its inhabitants, he had seen two German officers leaving a *boulangerie* with long loaves of bread in their hands. A camouflaged car with its driver at the wheel waited further along the street. He had frozen, then stepped into a doorway, still not confident enough of his invisibility to face the enemy. The encounter had frightened him, forcing him to retrace his steps and wait at the entrance to the village until he judged them to have gone. They were the first Germans he had seen at close quarters since he had crossed the Rhine and he had come so suddenly on them that it had given him no opportunity of adjusting his mind to their presence.

More frightening was his meeting with a column of Panzers and half-track flak gun carriers under attack from aircraft. When he came upon it first, he had thrown himself into a depression in the verge beneath a hedge as the grey monsters rumbled silently past. No sooner had he concealed himself than the spidery barrels of the flak guns began to spout soundless orange streamers upwards as explosions of flame and smoke burst on and around the tanks. He caught a brief glimpse of a blunt-nosed silver aircraft with white stars and blue bands on its wings that emerged from the twilight and streaked low over the column to vanish again, followed by three more, recognizable as American Thunderbolts, in rapid succession.

A sudden flash of brilliant light at his side startled him, erupting in a shower of earth and debris and leaving him unharmed, although flying metal fragments lashed the leaves of the hedge above his head and his body felt the shock waves convulsing the ground under him. A tank, a towering metal monster he thought was going to crush him, skidded with a wheel-track flailing loose into the verge only feet from where he lay, smashing through the hedge as flames licked out from the furnace inside the cracked and buckled turret. A charred body, burning brightly and swelling into greasy bubbles, hung folded over its edge, helmet and earphones dangling from a blackened head crisped of its hair. Fear had given him a magnified acuity of vision and he saw in minute detail the rivet heads in the heavy metal plates of the hull, the overlapping treads of the damaged track and the rubber-tyred bogie wheels left spinning without traction. A red gryphon Divisional insignia stood out from its grey and khaki background, beginning now to seethe and ripple into blisters from the inferno inside. The realism of detail and the utter soundlessness of the tank's destruction gave it a special horror to him.

The two crew members appeared by the side of the tank as though metamorphosed from the oily smoke belching from it. They wore hard leather helmets and oil-stained brown overalls tucked into calf-length boots. One, an officer and apparently the tank commander, carried a holstered pistol at his hip. Patently having escaped from the burning shambles, they stood dazed, their faces showing their shock and disbelief. Then they looked around and threw themselves down in the gully like men seeking the safety of a trench.

Fully within their vision should they look in his direction, Philip held himself motionless, his shakily held belief that he could not be seen giving him no confidence. An armed enemy only feet away gave him an unsettling fear. Oddly, he saw both men more clearly, as having more solidness and form than the tank from which they had escaped, three-dimensional figures superimposed on the unwinding of the silent pale-coloured film he had been watching.

The officer, lying on his stomach and propped on his elbows, spoke to his companion in hard rasping German syllables that Philip could not understand. With his non-comprehension came the realization that he had heard the words with his ears, that they had come from outside his mind, breaking the silence of his deafness to the sound of the brewed-up tank and the explosions of its ammunition. It was uncanny. Two men talking in what had otherwise been a void of soundlessness. He found himself staring at them, their flesh and blood reality confusing him, an inconsistency in a world that he had come to accept as amorphous and insubstantial.

Both men must have felt the force of his stare for each simultaneously turned his head and met his eyes. He saw that he was visible to them, their awareness showing in the sudden change of expression and the tensing of their bodies. Neither could be any older than himself and their features looked absurdly small and boyish beneath their padded helmets. They both appeared to be as frightened as he himself felt. Recognized as an enemy as he surely must be, he saw the officer's hand moving jerkily down to his pistol, his fingers hooking at the holster flap. His mind, seemingly incapable of dealing with the situation, formed the word "*Kamerad*" for his tongue to articulate, at the same time urging him to lift his arms in surrender. He did neither, panic and an instinct for survival driving him to leap to his feet, turning in a mad scramble and running through the hedge and across a ploughed field, expecting to hear the crack of the pistol and feel the shocking blow of a bullet in his back. But there were no sounds of pursuit and he was again back in the solitary silence of his deafness.

What he had seen had been undreamlike in its clarity, in the nuts and bolts of its detail, like his vision of the removal of the bodies from the burned-out Lancaster and outside the limit of his remembered experiences. No hallucination could account for it and he was convinced that he had seen an actual event, that he was here where his mind and eyes told him he was, no matter how inexplicable was his physical detachment from the violence of it. And if that were so, then his belief that he was lying injured in a bed, dreaming or hallucinating, was born only of a need to explain to himself what was happening. If that was a fantasy, then what was this other-world in which he found himself? Despite the pervasive twilight and the insubstantiality of its inhabitants and artefacts, despite its silence, it was a physical world familiar to him with all the factual stuff of human living, with all the bloody evidence of the war being fought. While not of it, he was indubitably solid flesh and tissue and, he had no reason to doubt, with blood running through his veins and arteries as it had always done.

The flying kit he wore. That was essentially material and he could feel it touching his body, could read inverted his squadron identification *F/O GRAHAM P.* on the breast pocket, could undo the zip fastener if he doubted and see the RAF pilot's wings stitched to his battledress tunic. Patently it was the clothing he had worn on his last flight. His mind was his own; Philip Graham's mind with its remembered memories of his past life. It reacted to circumstances, if not with its accustomed coherence, at least in its usual channels and with its habitual attitudes. He had been real enough to have been seen by the two surviving tank crew and recognized for what he was, enough for the officer to reach for his pistol. And, had he not run for it, he would undoubtedly have been taken prisoner or shot. That incident, above all, puzzled him. Why had they been able to see him when others he had met on his wanderings had not? And his hearing the officer speaking, externally through his ears and not in his mind; definitely not an hallucinatory voice.

He was a sadly perplexed man walking a lonely road with the demon fear dogging his heels, sensed as if it were a flickering shape that might be seen peripherally from the corners of his eyes, yet never resolving itself into identification. He was a fugitive from what he knew not, drawn irresistibly towards an unknown destination he had neither the resolution nor the energy to resist.

When he grew conscious of a drowsy weariness in his mind he entered a field and lay beneath a hedge, closing his eyes and allowing sleep to wash over him. The room in the flat was as he remembered from the occasional visits he had made to it with Laura and he saw it indistinctly through an iridescent veil. She was lying on the settee, illuminated in the cone of light from the lamp behind her, not in sharp-edged relief but blurred and diffused. Her face was drawn and dejected and the sadness that emanated from her reached him in his dreaming. He felt an overwhelming longing for her, a compulsion to let her know he was there. Too, there was the foreboding of impending danger to her which he had experienced before; that she should remain where she was, that whatever the reason it involved, in some indefinable way, himself. It was nothing that he could understand, nothing for which he had a reason, for he could think of no danger to which she could be subject. But it was there, intruding on his love for her, a sickening premonition of disaster. "Laura! Laura!" he cried, but it was as though his words, spoken against a muffling wall of unawareness, fell dead to the floor. He cried her name again, willing that she should hear him, desperate to communicate his warning.

To his distress he saw her eyes running tears on to her cheeks and she straightened herself from the cushions, looking around her as though searching for him. He stood in front of her and she stared straight at him, her arms outstretched welcoming him, her mouth saying words he could not hear but which he knew were spoken to him. He moved forward to take her in his arms and saw that her eyes were focused past where he was standing, that she could not see him. Despair made him drop his arms and then there was darkness into which she receded and vanished and he opened his eyes to the grey suffusion of the twilight and an awareness of the contact of his body on the hard ground. He was alone again in the anguish of his parting and he realized that he was whimpering like a lost pup.

That he had seen her he had no doubt. There had been a definite feeling that it had been as and where she now was. His need to return to her, to warn her of whatever it was that threatened her, was more compelling than before and he lifted himself from the ground. Walking, there came an inner conviction that his journey was nearing its end but, with it, no sense of achievement, only the foreboding of tragedy that was haunting his thinking.

Twenty-six

The batman that Oliver shared with two other officers carried in his breakfast on a tray and shook him awake at five o'clock. The tray was not a concession but an humiliation, a reminder that he was considered unworthy to eat with his fellow pilots. The batman would know this and Oliver looked for signs of it in his expression, finding none against which he could vent his resentment.

He drank the tea, leaving the bacon and dried egg untouched to show his opposition to the injustice of his open arrest. He washed, not bothering to shower or shave, and put on his battledress and flying suit. The foulard scarf he knotted around his throat was intended to attract Poxton's disapproval, a small show of defiance.

Dressed, he opened his Flying Log Book and wrote the day's date in it, his talismanic ritual against not coming back and having the book finish up somewhere inside the Air Ministry, uncompleted and endorsed "Killed in Action". The pages in his writing recorded every minute he had flown in training, on conversion courses and on operations, detailing the enemy aircraft he had shot down or damaged; the miscellany of locomotives, bridges, tanks, flak-ships and assorted road transport he had attacked, all representing the unnumbered men who had died under his cannon and rocket fire.

He flung it back in the drawer. None of it would help him in the last resort. He could be the rawest, most milky-faced newcomer to the squadron for all his record would counter Poxton's allegations of LMF and the charges into which Morwenna had led him. Nor would it help with the police did they happen to suspect him of being the driver of the car the previous evening. God only knew what had happened to the stupid sod of a policeman who had literally flung himself in front of his car. Probably not anything serious and he was worrying his guts out about nothing. What had he done anyway to deserve all the shit that was coming his way? No more than any other normally orientated man with an uncertain future would do. He was just plain unlucky and that was no comfort to him either.

The nausea in his stomach had gone and he felt better, but not much better, certain that his brain was swimming in acid, his eyes scribbled with bristled red worms. He was at the nadir of his appetites, having had a bellyful of women and whisky. Had the blonde Waaf from the Signals Office been dancing naked in his room with a bottle of Johnny Walker in her hand, he knew he could not have been less interested. He swallowed a benzedrine tablet, washed down with water.

It was dark outside and raining from low overcast as he joined other men making their way to the Briefing Room. Apart from unsociable early-morning grunts, he ignored them as they did him. They would know that he was under open arrest and it made him surly and uncommunicative even in that.

Briefing was finished in the length of time it took to smoke a final cigarette. The objective was the ground strafing of opportunist targets at the Section Leaders' discretion. Red Section, detailed to a triangular area bounded by Le Mans, Orleans and Chartres, would be led by Poxton with Oliver and Rogers as his wingmen. Air combat was only to be engaged in if attacked. Poxton had not spoken to Oliver during the briefing and if he noticed the neck scarf and the unshaved chin he ignored them. But each of them was very much aware of the other.

There was a sheen of water on the fuselage and wings of his Typhoon when he came to it, the engine idling with the ground crew standing by. Made bulky by the Mae West he wore over his flying suit he was cramped in the tiny cold cockpit, not yet heated by the engine whose roaring would be with him until he returned. Taxiing to the take-off point he turned on the oxygen against the exhaust gases entering the cockpit and did his check, dropping flaps and racing the engine against the brakes. He had a tightness in his chest, an emptiness in his stomach that he would lose once he was airborne.

Poxton's voice, clipped and impersonal, sounded in his earphones. "Red Leader to Red Two; ready for take-off?"

"Red Two, Roger."

"Red Three?"

"Red Three, Roger."

Poxton's propeller blurred with increased speed and his Typhoon trundled to the runway, Oliver and Rogers behind him in Vee formation, following as the green light from the Control Tower gave them clearance and synchronizing their acceleration with his. The take-off was short and steep with only the tiny navigation lights on each side of Poxton's invisible rudder and the mauve flames from his exhaust ports to show where he rose in the darkness.

With his undercarriage thumped home in the belly of his Typhoon and the flaps raised, Oliver dropped behind and above in line astern, Rogers taking his position stepped above the turbulence of his wake. With the navigation lights now extinguished he was balanced in directionless space, holding his position only by reference to Poxton's exhaust.

On course and over the Channel, a suffusion of grey showing beyond the black mass of overcast above them, he switched on his gun-sight and set the cannons to 'fire'. When Poxton's Typhoon took on shape against the growing light he began to check his mirror and the port and starboard quarters for any enemy aircraft that might have been sent to intercept the routine dawn flights. Breathing oxygen on top of the benzedrine his mind was sharper, his movements mouse-quick, and he had to consciously slow himself down. He had, he tried to convince himself, left his troubles behind him at the airfield and would worry about them only when he got back.

Poxton's voice came over the R/T, softly as though cautious of being overheard. "Red Leader losing altitude to ground zero: formate at one thousand yards."

It was a necessary distance to be not to fly into the debris thrown up by the leader's rockets during an attack and Oliver let Poxton draw ahead. He was clearly visible now against the grey lustreless fields of France beneath, the growing light gleaming fish-silver on his fuselage. When Oliver levelled out behind him, his Typhoon bumping in the dying slipstream, the three planes were at tree-top height with the ground streaking in a blur beneath them. Poxton had slowed down their airspeed to 250 miles an hour with an arrogant disregard for any enemy fighters alerted to their presence by the radar towers over which they had passed. Laden with six hundredweight of rockets that spoiled the airflow over the wings, they could be outpaced and outmanœuvred. Oliver would feel happier when he had fired them.

Roads glistened in the rain like rivers and cattle stamped in the sodden fields as they thundered their way through the wet air. When a railway line bisected their track, Poxton turned sharply to follow its path. There were long minutes before a plume of steam appeared in the distance and as the locomotive became visible it was seen to be hauling a train of empty coal wagons. Poxton's 'No' over the R/T came as they swept towards it, flattening and dispersing the rising steam with their rush of air as they passed over.

Oliver was beginning to feel cramped and uncomfortable, his neck aching from the ceaseless turning of his head to watch the sky above and behind him, not so good now with the benzedrine wearing off and his emerging whiskers rough against the rubber of his face mask, damp from his breath condensing inside it.

The Panzer laager came into view on the starboard side of a rise in the ground and then they were over and past it. In the second or two in which he saw it through the side of his hood Oliver identified tanks, mobile guns and troop carriers, blotched with camouflaging and nose-to-tail. They were all stationary, the bulk of them in a sunken cutting, the remainder in a straight poplar-lined road. In a field adjacent to them were square stacks of fuel cannisters covered with broken-off tree branches. The small groups of men around each vehicle turned pink faces upwards as the Typhoons passed over. With luck, they could believe that they had not been seen.

"Red Section." Poxton's unhurried voice crackled static in his earphones. "Maintain course. You hear me, Red Two?"

It was a clear warning and Oliver's face burned with his sudden fury. There had been no similar message to Rogers and he would know why. He felt an overpowering urge to loose his rockets at Poxton and blow him to hell.

"I hear you," he said into his microphone, putting his hatred of the man in the words. *You vindictive bastard!* he added silently.

"Red Section, prepare to turn on reciprocal track, line astern." Poxton sounded as if he were smiling. "Leader will take cutting group; Red Two take the road; Red Three do a good job on the fuel dump. Acknowledge."

As they acknowledged, Poxton turned steeply on his wing and dropped to ground-scraping height where their approach would be unseen by the Germans until they were on them.

Oliver adjusted his elevator trim to tail-heavy. Should he lose control in the action his Typhoon would have the impetus to climb rather than to bury its nose into the ground. Turning his head to check his flanks, he saw four aircraft as lighter shapes against the dark overcast, banking with their noses down to converge on them. At that distance and in the bad light they looked like Mustangs, but he knew that they were not. They had to be the much faster Messerschmitt 109s manœuvring to get on their tails.

"Red Leader," he called urgently. "Four bandits at nine o'clock and coming in." Three Typhoons on a run-in, loaded with encumbering rockets, would be sitting ducks. They had to fire off their six hundredweight of metal and solid fuel and turn to meet their attackers. From the thousand yards that separated them he saw Poxton's head swivel in the direction of the Messerschmitts.

"Roger, Red Two." His voice was calm and unhurried. "We'll stay with it. All the time in the world."

As he said it, so the laagered column appeared in the fold of ground and Poxton's rockets left his wings in rapid sequence, thin smoke trails arcing downwards. Streams of flak in balls of orange fire began to rise and Oliver's heart thumped as they approached leisurely, seemingly aimed at him alone, and then accelerating past. He felt sick with his fear, but this time there was no option open to him. Poxton in front, without a doubt watching him, and Rogers on his tail. Expecting to feel the shock of cannon shells from the Messerschmitts racing up on them, he held the road between the poplars steady in the filament of his gun-sight, waiting until the tanks slid into it, squat green beetles with elongated proboscises that were their guns and men running from them, then let go his own rockets. Immediately he was above the explosions erupting from Poxton's attack, his Typhoon pitching wildly as he yanked back on the stick in a climbing shuddering turn towards the overcast, seeing spirals of black smoke rising from the column and a gigantic convulsion of red flame from the exploding fuel dump falling away beneath him.

He looked frantically for the Messerschmitts. Two were coming at him, winking flashes of light from their gun muzzles, green tracer criss-crossing the air in front of him. He did a diving barrel-roll, pushing hard at the throttle lever as they flashed by, he wasn't sure whether above or below him for the fields and clouds were revolving around his spiralling plane in a dizzying confusion.

"Red Two, break!" Rogers's voice and he slammed at his rudder pedal to skid sideways away from the cannon shells streaking past his wing tip, ducking his head below the armoured seat back, pulling back on the throttle and making the Messerschmitt intent on his death overshoot him; seeing the red spinner, pale-blue belly and underwings and the black crosses on them only feet above his hood, the battering of its engine adding an earsplitting clamour to his own.

The stick forward now and full throttle, dust and pieces of grass from the floor floating around him, his body strained painfully against his harness and the creeping pink suffusion of a red-out in his eyes as blood was forced into them. Behind the Messerschmitt and bouncing in his slipstream as they dived towards the earth he put the red spot of his sight on the German's tail and pressed his gun button, giving him a burst of fire that chewed debris from the fuselage. The Messerschmitt swelled and large pieces of metal came away, followed by a balloon of flame as the fuel tanks exploded, continuing its dive and plunging into the ground where it disintegrated with a blinding flash of light.

Oliver sweated, his flesh hot and greasy, but cold inside with his lust to kill. He climbed, searching for the column to reorientate himself, then seeing the smoke, coiling grey worms of it rising away to his right. He had to get back to where Poxton could see him. Although the killing of the German had taken less than a minute, he was three or four miles from the target and this time the bastard wasn't going to be able to say that he had taken himself off and funked it. He circled in a shallow bank around the column, far enough away not to attract flak and searching for the two Typhoons. When he saw the Messerschmitt climbing parallel to his own line of flight, he half-rolled on to its course and put on boost to get under its tail and to shoot his unsuspecting enemy in the back. It was going fast and he wasn't gaining on it. Nor would he unless he could gain altitude and dive on it. And that he couldn't do. It was just within range of his cannon, but far enough for him to miss horribly and to find himself on the receiving end of a diving attack by the Messerschmitt. He measured the deflection in the annules of his sight. Thumb on the button, keeping the Typhoon rock-steady, he held his breath behind his teeth with all his attention canalized, his eyes focused through the glowing ring on the threequarter view of the underside of the Messerschmitt.

Nothing existed but himself and the man he was going to kill. He put pressure into his thumb and felt the jolting of the cannons' recoil, saw the blur of smoke and the tracers burning upwards towards the target, missing it by yards. Saw, too, the nose and fuselage of a Typhoon sliding inexorably across his windscreen and then into the sight at an angle and filling it, recognizing the letters PQ-A and knowing it was Poxton's even as he maintained the pressure with his thumb his mind refused him to release as the plane flew into the stream of shells that splashed into its engine nacelle and shattered it to a tangle of wreckage. Only when the magazines emptied and he heard the clanging of the empty breeches was he able to release his thumb. Horrified, he saw Poxton's goggled face turned towards him as black oil from the crippled engine flowed over the hood and blotted him out, the plane falling away below him.

In his shaken confusion he was oblivious of the world outside his cockpit. His mind babbled with the frantic realization of what he had done. Oh, God! he groaned. He had as good as killed Poxton and Rogers could have seen it happen. He hadn't intended to, he was sure he hadn't. It had been Poxton's fault, the stupid bastard. Flying across his line of fire. How was he to know that Poxton had the Messerschmitt in his sight as well. He visualized the Typhoon flying into his path. Could he have released his pressure on the button in time? He didn't know. Could his hatred of Poxton have made him hold it there, the reflex of his bitter resentment against him stiffening a purpose already in his mind? It had all happened so fast and he couldn't be sure. The only certainty was that nobody would believe him. Not knowing of the charges Poxton had made against him. And certainly Poxton would not should he survive. He remembered Sandison's flying into the line of his rockets in the attack on the train. That had been an accident too. Like mid-air collisions, it was always a possibility in the confusion of combat.

He shook his head violently. He had been paralysed like a bloody rabbit. He had to see what had happened. Typhoons could take a lot of punishment and still get home. Christ! The thought struck him. If that happened, Poxton would surely charge him with trying to murder him. He searched the landscape below, straining to see through the rain-obscured hood into the wet murk. One minute it was all hell and confusion and, the next, the calm of an empty sky. Nothing but the distant smoke of the Panzer column burning. Then a flash of fire and smoke in a field caught his eye and high above it the white canopy of a parachute drifting in the wind with a figure hanging below it. It had to be Poxton. He hadn't gone in with his Typhoon. Oliver felt a deflation of his hatred for him. He couldn't nurse it for a man dangling helplessly in the harness of a falling parachute and lucky if he finished up only as a prisoner-of-war. And, if he did, even from there he could still …

A thunderclap of sound deafened him as the hood behind his head exploded and the blast and heat of a shock-wave knocked him sideways against the metal side of the cockpit. A thin shriek of air came through the shattered perspex. He shouted his fright and banged the stick sideways to split-ess away. There was a dead numbness in his shoulder and knee and he caught a glimpse of the Messerschmitt that had bounced him blind from behind pulling away to one side as a dark film shadowed his vision. Through the moonlight dimness he could see the landscape tilting drunkenly and he fought to bring the Typhoon into a falling dive. Fragments of shell had smashed his mirror and made havoc of the airspeed indicator and oil pressure dials. He couldn't turn his head enough to check the damage to the hood, but probably only the one shell had hit him. His left arm lacked strength and its manipulation of the throttle lever sent pain through his shoulder. A slit in the fabric of his Mae West showed where the shell splinter had entered. He could feel the warm stickiness of blood on the flesh of his chest and stomach. A red blotch on the knee of his trousers was beginning to spread and moving his leg on the rudder pedal made him groan. He wanted to vomit, felt the onset of faintness, his flesh cold behind the mask with the blood drained from his face. If he fainted now he would be a dead man when he hit the ground. Hell! He was going to die anyway. If the Messerschmitt didn't return and finish him off, the haemorrhaging in his shoulder would. This was it, the thing he had always feared. Yet, oddly, he felt none of it now. A little regret, nothing more. Morwenna's unhappy face came into his mind. She was part of his regret, the only woman who had loved him and he had been a shit to her, her Judas Iscariot. Too late now, for he had really ballsed things up for them both.

His instinct for survival was still with him and he breathed in deep draughts of oxygen, searching for a field in which to make his forced landing. Oh, Jesus! Even if he didn't die he would finish up with Poxton as a prisoner-of-war. Poxton, the bastard! His hatred returned full flood and black. If he hadn't had him on his mind he would never have been bounced so easily. And where was the Messerschmitt? It should have been coming in on its second attack to finish him off. He looked above and around him, straining his eyes against the shadows and seeing nothing but an empty sky, a sky that was darkening even as he looked at it. He would have to make his landing soon. Numbness was going and ragged pain creeping in. If his shoulder seized up he would be unable to lower the undercarriage and flaps. His faintness, the sick coldness in his belly, was draining him of vitality. He wanted to let go and sink into the welcoming darkness of non-feeling.

When he saw the field, long and narrow with trees at both ends, he turned towards it, thinking desperately of the forced landing procedure with a mind distracted by his pain. He tried to wind back the hood and, when his enfeebled arm couldn't manage it, pulled the jettison handle and cried out at the agony of it. The hood vanished backwards and he felt it hit the rudder as he was slammed back by the intensified inrush of air. Rain hit his exposed cheeks like sharp needles and spotted the glass of his goggles. He was guessing his airspeed, feeling the response of the elevators and rudders to the airstream. If he dropped below a hundred miles an hour he would stall and spin in. Undercarriage warning lights green, then back to red and green again as the legs locked into position. His thinking was sluggish and balanced on the edge of a deep black pit.

He saw sheep grazing at the far end of the field and it was suddenly important that he didn't run into them. He had a special repugnance against killing animals. The propeller control forward. It hurt his shoulder and he groaned again. Supercharger to moderate ... radiator shutter down ... flaps dropped and the nose rising with the increased lift. The airspeed was close to stalling, the Typhoon beginning to shudder and feel heavy, the ground coming up fast.

"Morwenna," he mumbled. "Sorry." He was going now, never making it, the light failing and the goggles buffeting against his forehead in the wind, his eyes staring white-rimmed through the rippling moonlight of his vision. The tip of a wing brushed a tree with a flurry of leaves as he misjudged the clearance and then the jolt of the wheels hitting too hard ... the throttle fully back and bouncing, bouncing, his body screaming its pain, the agony in his knee holding straight the rudder . . . brakes on and sheep scattering . . . wings flapping and the tail wheel banging on the ground . . . slowing . . . slowing . . . trees coming towards him . . . slower and stopping. A still world and the absence of rushing air on him as he felt blindly for the harness release pin . . . the pain and the black pit and falling . . .

Twenty-seven

Although the twilight circumscribed his vision of the field and it appeared no different from the thousands of others he had seen or passed through on his journey, it possessed a significance Philip sensed rather than understood. There was an air of expectancy about it. Rain fell on it in slanting veils. He could neither see the clouds from which it came nor feel its dampness, his clothing remaining unmarked. He stood on a bare patch of earth beneath a tree and waited, its hanging foliage dissipating green light around him. A dozen or so black-faced sheep, oblivious of his presence, browsed on the wet grass, the only living things in the inverted bowl of half-light surrounding him.

The echoes of his encounter with the Panzer column were still with him, the two Germans who had seen him, whom he had heard talking, an unresolved enigma. They had appeared suddenly, materializing from nowhere and not having, he was now certain, climbed from the tank that had been brewed into a sudden inferno, inconceivable that they could. The turret hatch had been blocked by a dead man and there were no other hatches visible by which they could have escaped. The body hanging from the turret was undoubtedly that of the tank's commander, an officer. There wouldn't be two officers in a tank, that much was certain. It left him with what should be unbelievable, unacceptable, but that which he was being forced to accept. The two men had been killed. What he had seen had been ghosts, apparitions of the dead, despite their apparent solidness; entities capable of seeing him in whatever condition he was, being self-evidently in a different dimension from that of the shattered metal hulk in which they had died, from the dead flesh they had left behind to incinerate in the fire. And, being of substance to him as he was to them, then they must share the same dimension.

The realization came abruptly, stunning him with its inescapable truth. He was dead. He had died in his Lancaster and it was his own body that had been one of those being raked from its ashes. It should have been obvious to him. He had been in a limbo he had made for himself. His disbelief, his resistance to any evidence that he was no longer of the world he had lived in, his mistaken conviction that his surroundings were the nebulous and unreal hallucinations of a dream-state had led him to this. What he had taken for dreams had been the visions of reality as it existed for him to see and understand. He was a ghost, a phantom of the material world he had left by death. He was earthbound, disorientated by the suddenness of his violent dying. What he had never considered was that a ghost would, to itself, be physically solid and real, that its former environment would become the insubstantial unreality. He felt that he should be horrified to the point of madness from what was an apocalyptic realization but, recovering from the initial shock, he felt only a numbing detachment from it.

"I'm dead," he told himself and then looked around to discover whether he would be able to see God. But there was nothing other than what had been there before. This was the feared extinction, the cessation of life. Instead of the long sleep and ultimate resurrection he had believed, there was a continuing on of his personality. It was as if he had fallen into a terrifying black abyss and found himself miraculously unharmed in strange yet soothingly familiar surroundings, still to discover where and what it was, not quite believing the fall had happened. He experienced the same emotions and knew that he held the same attitudes he had always held. His memory of his earth life remained with him. He was physically as he had been and that, he realized now, was because that was how his mind believed himself to be. The mind was the reality, the body only its shadow.

He unzipped his flying suit and put his hand inside, feeling for the beating of his heart, then putting a finger under his jawbone, searching for the pulsing of the carotid artery. It was something that he should have done before. There was nothing. He was no more than the form of his own imagining, impervious to the heat, cold, pain and fatigue of which he should have been conscious during his wanderings. It explained why that, during the supposed reality of his escape from Germany, driven by his compulsion to return to Laura, he had neither eaten nor drunk, why his bodily functions had been non-existent.

His recognition of his death did nothing to lessen the intense desire, the need he had, to rejoin Laura. He was committed to its fulfilment. He was as he had always been and dying had changed nothing of him. He couldn't see the whole of it and what was to come remained as closed to him as it had always been, the foreboding of impending tragedy still with him.

An aircraft, its wings and fuselage gleaming in the rain, materialized out of the twilight and startled him with its sudden appearance as it bumped silently over the uneven turf with the sheep scattering in panic before it. Slowing to a halt it stood facing Philip, the propeller windmilling and with no movement in the cockpit. The black and white striping and roundels on its wings, the underslung radiator and empty rocket rails, identified it to him immediately as a Typhoon fighter. He ran towards it shouting although he knew that he would not be heard, frantic that it would take off again before he reached it.

As he approached he saw that the hood had been jettisoned, that the pilot was slumped in the cockpit with his head hanging forward on his chest, dead or unconscious. Philip stood beneath looking up, convinced that this was to be the means of his returning to Laura, that this was what he had been waiting for, the destination to which his compulsion had driven him. He tried to climb on to the wing and found no resistance to his grasping hands, no substance in the metal surface to support him. In desperation he shouted again at the unconscious pilot, willing him to help, projecting his whole mind to get himself into the cockpit against the tenuous insubstantiality of the aircraft.

His eyes lost vision, a black tunnel opening up in his mind into which he was drawn, swept along helplessly until there was a dizziness followed by a stillness, a passage of unmeasurable time. Tiny glimmering discs resolved in his darkness, growing larger as the noise of an engine battered into ears long used to silence, his body vibrating to its rhythmic resonance. He smelt the familiar fumes of petrol, oil and hot metal, felt the constriction of an oxygen mask over his mouth and nose, its rubbery taste, conscious of ragged pain in his shoulder and knee and of sickness in his stomach. As his vision cleared, the glimmers of light sharpened into the dials of an instrument panel, the levers, aluminium tubes and cables of a cockpit in which he was strapped. He felt moistness on his cheeks, the glass of the goggles he was wearing wavery with spreading raindrops. The twilight had receded and over the wet nose of the Typhoon he could see trees and, through them, a dreary landscape merging into a grey sky.

He was alone in the cockpit, cramped and constricted by its fittings, with no sign of the man whose seat he had taken. For a moment of confusion he thought he might be sitting on his lap until he recognized beneath his buttocks the cushion of his parachute and felt the metal back of the seat against his shoulderblades. He was wearing a Mae West over his flying suit and on it was stencilled the name of MISSEN, evoking no recollection in him. Behind it was the bloody mess of a wounded shoulder, raw and painful. His legs terminated, not in his own canvas and leather flying boots, but in unfamiliar brown suede boots with, above them, an ugly staining of blood soaking through the fabric of the trousers.

Nothing was as he had known it. He didn't feel right. The hands passive on his thighs were not as he remembered them. Black hairs curled from inside the sleeves and his silver identification bracelet was no longer on his wrist. When his tongue licked his dry mouth the teeth were not of the familiar conformation he had known. The rear-view mirror above his head was broken, but he pulled down the oxygen mask and lifted the goggles to stare at his reflection in the windscreen. Fugitive as the image was, he could see in it a different man; superficially himself but with the black bar of a moustache emphasizing the sick pallor of the face. It was another nightmare of incomprehension as his mind struggled to understand it, uncertain of who he was and how he had found himself in a Typhoon fighter instead of a Lancaster bomber. How had he come to be in this field? If he had been shot down – and it appeared that he had – it had gone from his mind. His last clear recollection was of flying the Lancaster in a night sky of searching flak and probing lights and, after that, a phantasmagoria of closed-in mist and twilit darkness, of frightening visions of men with rifles hunting him, of three aircrew walking away from him on a lonely road; of a man and a woman making obscene love, a terrified calf being slaughtered and a burning tank. He was conscious also of a somebody, a separate personality, at the back of his mind, trying to enter it, intruding on his thinking with echoes of names and things he had never heard before.

The burning rawness of exhaust gases in his mouth returned

him to the present and he pulled the oxygen mask back over his face, concentrating on the instrument panel he would need to understand to fly this machine. While strange to him, the essential dials were arranged in the same pattern as those on the Lancaster. He noticed that the air speed indicator and oil pressure gauge had been smashed and that the temperature gauge showed an overheating of the engine that could lead to its seizing solid.

Movement behind the hedge at the far side of the field caught his eye, a plume of spray trailing behind it. When it passed a gap he recognized it as a motor-cycle and sidecar heading towards him, the rider and passenger manifestly German soldiers, their helmeted heads turned in his direction. The one in the sidecar cradled a machine-pistol in his arms. He had no time now for anything but a fast take-off irrespective of whatever condition the aircraft was in. With his heart thumping his alarm, he pushed the throttle lever forward and turned in a tight circle, not checking further on the instruments but pouring on acceleration as the propellor bit into the air and she ran across the grass. He heard himself whimpering at the pain in his shoulder as he maltreated it with the movements of his arm. There was a swing to the right and he corrected it awkwardly with rudder, for a heart-stopping moment the wingtip dropping close to the ground. He had a glimpse of sheep scattering from his path. Against the thirty tons of a loaded four-engined Lancaster the Typhoon felt thistledown light and twitchy on the controls, needing all his concentration to keep her from ground-looping to disaster. Dirty smoke poured from the exhaust ports where he wasn't doing something correctly, but there was no dissonance or faltering in the thundering of the engine. When she felt light-footed he eased the stick forward and lifted the tail. He was travelling fast now, the airstream buffeting him in the open cockpit, almost as solid as rushing water. He didn't know what the take-off speed was and, even had he, the needle of the damaged indicator could not tell him when he had reached it.

The trees at the end of the field were racing towards him, the plane feeling unstable, the bounces beginning to lengthen, the stick and rudder pedals stiffening under his control. He aimed her at a gap in the trees and there came, as if he were being ordered, an imperative urge to pull back on the stick. It was suddenly firm in his grasp and he felt it moving back as the nose lifted and the trees fell away abruptly beneath him. He pulled at the levers marked

Undercarriage and Flaps and felt them slam home in the wings and belly, continuing to climb until the overcast blanketed him in its wet grey cottonwool invisibility.

Throttling back to what felt like a safe cruising speed, he turned until the compass indicated north, on which course he knew that he must hit the Channel. The fuel tank dials showed that they were less than half-full which, not knowing where he was or what it represented in flying time, meant nothing very much. Without too much pulling at the wrong levers he managed to trim the Typhoon to a stabilized level flight and had little more to do than to lower her down gingerly through the belly of the cloud every few minutes for a visual check on the landscape below. His clothing was soaked by the rain through to his flesh and he was one spreading dull ache with sharp spasms of pain biting at the torn muscles of his wounds when he used an arm or a leg. The loss of blood from his shoulder must have been considerable for he could feel it seeping through to his parachute. What blood he had left pulsed thinly in his ears and his finger-ends tingled. He felt cold and feverish shivering shook his body at frequent intervals.

The other mind was back with him and it was like sharing his bed with a stranger who had entered it uninvited, separate but together. He was involuntarily a party to intruding emotions which were not his; a tortured despair, a hopelessness and fear. Poxton. The name was shadowed with a strong sense of guilt and a hatred. He saw arrogance and contempt in cold grey eyes and that had been Poxton. Who was Poxton? He had never heard of him. Then a woman's face with a sad pleading look and love in her expression. Morwenna. Not her either. She was saying, '*You forget, Oliver, that I happen to be in love with you.* Was the other mind Oliver's? Someone who had done terrible things to her and made her so unhappy? These thoughts, disconnected and showing as small pictures in his mind, came with names. Strange names that meant nothing to him. And then there rose through his bewilderment a black and sexual hatred that made him feel sick with its intensity, a mental image of Cynthia as he had never seen her and, please God, that he never would; naked on a bed and flaunting her breasts and opened thighs, smiling sharp-toothed as the something in him went towards her to smash her face with angry fists. He closed his eyes and shook his head to blot it from his mind. Where in God's name had that come from? He had defiled Cynthia and himself by even thinking of her in sexual terms. His own mother-in-law. He groaned, filled with revulsion and disgust for the vileness to which his mind had given room. "No," he whispered, "I am Philip Graham ... Philip Graham." His name was the only reality to which he could cling. All else was a nightmare of dissociation from his selfhood, a schizophrenic madness.

When he lowered the Typhoon from the overcast the next time, it was to see the green haze of the Channel tilted before him and an easily recognizable Le Havre on the estuary of the Seine. He stayed down, losing height slowly under the cloud layer that was breaking up and letting the sun throw patches of brilliant blue on the shadowed sea towards which he dropped. The brightness, the shadow, the rain which had stopped, were all one to him, all a hardly noticed backdrop to the misery of feverish pain, to the sickness which had soaked into his bowels. He wasn't certain what was happening now, his control of the aircraft seeming to be the reaction to another's will, his own flaccid and submissive. It was as much as he could do to hold himself upright in the seat without sagging against the safety harness and letting the Typhoon take him where it would. The stick and rudder pedals moved with a volition seemingly of their own, his muscles guiding them in response to a purpose other than his. He had the distinct impression that he was not alone in the cockpit, that there was a strongly male presence forcing itself to superimpose its determination on him.

Laura. She came into his thinking; Laura in the conservatory and looking subtly different, seeing her with another's eyes, thinking of her as he would never himself think, a lewd travesty of his own love. Her mouth moving, speaking to somebody who was not himself and promising herself to him. Regret for her was there as her image faded. Then there was Cynthia, again in her whorish nakedness, and this time he felt her withering contempt and scorn and, with it, a hatred for her that flooded in bitter and harsh; an unendurable humiliation and a lust for revenge that he could not relate to his own affection for her as the stepmother of Laura. The changes of emotion, the words whispered in the back of his mind and the images projected that he could only half-see against the brightness of the clearing sky, were constant now.

He was over land and flying on a course parallel to the coastline, gradually losing height. The landscape which should have warmed him to his return did nothing to rouse him from the stupor into which he was sinking. The Typhoon was responding to the controls with a volition he felt to be entirely its own, being flown with an instinct that he could not have acquired in his own experience. A Spitfire, a slim green-and-brown fish in the sea of clear air, stationed itself on his wing, the pilot looking at him and obviously questioning the absence of the cockpit hood. If he was trying to reach him on the R/T his words were not getting through the humming of static which was all Philip could hear. He waved a feeble hand at the pilot who pulled ahead and slid smoothly in front of him, waggling his wings as a signal for him to follow and to be nursemaided into the landing circuit of the airfield he could see coming into view.

He wanted that. There would be an end to his nightmare, an end to the confusion and doubts, a release from the hatred and fear that shared the cockpit with him. He would be back with the familiar with which he could cope. A distinct 'No' came from the mind that dominated his actions and he felt the resistance in the arm that he was willing to put the Typhoon into a bank to follow the Spitfire. His hand was forced at the throttle lever and the Spitfire dropped below and behind as the airspeed increased. The controls moved as the aircraft chose its own course and the implacability of its apparent purpose frightened him.

There was only muted recognition when he saw the white horse cut into the chalk of the downland hill and, from it, being able to orientate himself to identify remembered roads, the golf course on which he had played and the avenue of beech trees leading to Dunsham along which he had travelled often to reach it and Laura. There was the darker scar of a runway diagonally across a field and a scattering of parked Typhoons near a camouflaged hangar which he knew must be Wallisham airfield.

He was low enough to see the figures of the two men through the tinted glass of the window in the control tower, one of them speaking into a hand microphone, without doubt at him. As though by association, the name Morwenna entered his mind again together with the unhappiness shown in the gentle face that was strange to him. He repeated the assertion of his identity to the confusion in his mind. "I am Flying Officer Philip Graham," he said into his oxygen mask, "Philip Geoffrey Graham," although he could not hear it above the singing of blood in his ears.

Intuitively, he sensed that he was approaching his journey's end, seeing from under eyelids he struggled to keep from shutting, his perception sluggish. He was dying, his breathing rapid and shallow, the body in which he had so inexplicably found himself lax with his increasing weakness. He had to get down before the little vitality he had remaining drained from him, before the vomit he was holding back rose in his throat and choked him.

He checked his landing direction with the orange windsock and forced his body's unwillingness to turn the Typhoon in a wide and shallow bank away from the airfield, looking down the wing at the slanting landscape to line up on the approach path. Deciding to leave the undercarriage up and to risk a belly landing rather than invite disaster in an aircraft he had not flown before, he felt blindly for the flap selector lever and pulled it home, the effort grating fresh pain into his shoulder. The flaps dropped with a thud and the aircraft shuddered, the nose lifting sharply. Alarmed, he pushed the stick forward to force it back until the runway was again visible through the blur of the propeller.

With a segment of sunshine crawling across the windscreen, he saw reflected in it, distorted by the curvature of its surface, the goggled paper-white face of the man in whose body he had found himself. The eyes were different now, seeming to show his own familiar personality and he was no longer conscious of the other mind's control, now no more than an insubstantial shadow, an amorphous ghost of a remembrance which was leaving him. He knew that the body he occupied was within a few heartbeats of death, that for all his striving, for all the suffering he had endured under the compulsion of his need to return to Laura, there was now only the bitterness of failure, the knowledge that what he had done was wrong.

His head was lolling, wanting to fall forward on a neck that felt a boneless stalk and he recognized the onset of faintness which would drain blood from his brain and blot out his vision. He forced his attention to the runway rising towards him through the veil of mist obscuring his vision. A red light winked frantically at him from the control tower, the klaxon horn behind his headrest, thin and remote in his ears, warning him that the undercarriage was retracted. The Typhoon felt unstable, wallowing clumsily at the point of stalling as he edged the throttle lever fully back. He was conscious only of the cramped-in cockpit and the instrument panel of vibrating dials, of the numbing pain in his shoulder and the smell of hot oil and petrol fumes. He was frightened and could hear himself panting.

The ground rose languidly as though seen in a slow-running film and, for a last brief moment, he saw dimly with an aching sense of loss the small white clouds in the blue sky, the clumps of trees and hedgerows flowing past him, the green grass moving sluggishly under the slowing propeller. He screamed as the Typhoon hit the ground, feeling the shattering jolt of sliding impact and hearing the shrieking of torn metal as the air scoop dug into the ground, jerking his body violently against the harness and snapping his head forward. He saw the propeller blades spinning up a shower of earth clods then twisting back and bending, stopping dead as the tail lifted with a dreamlike deliberation, the Typhoon cartwheeling and dropping with a thunderous crash on to its back.

He was upside-down and hanging helplessly in his harness, the mass of metal pressing down on him, his head jammed crookedly on the grass, the goggles tight over his mouth. There was no longer any pain, nor could he feel the warmth of the patch of sunlight that touched his face through the narrow gap between the cockpit's edge and the ground. The engine had died with the stopping of the propeller and only the bleeding of petrol from broken pipes and the creaking of settling metal reached his ears. Through the gap of dimming sunlight he saw moving boots and blue trouser ends in a thickening mist, heard the distant shouting of excited words he could not understand. It seemed important to him that they knew who he was and he mumbled through the blood filling his mouth, "Flying Officer Graham, Flying Off...", feeling the thin thread of pulse in his neck falter and stop as he fell into the darkness gathering around him, unconscious of the brilliant flash of light from the exploding petrol tanks.

With a starless night sky above him, Flying Officer Philip Graham stood unsteadily in the yellow light of the burning Lancaster, an almost unrecognizable mass of crumpled flaring metal, its skin already melting in curling black flakes and writhing as if in sentient torment. He could hear nothing of the explosions that shook the fuselage and threw out flaming debris in uncanny silence.

He was dazed and confused, his mind a chaos of vivid impressions of the destruction of his Lancaster by the Messerschmitt night-fighter and the bloody death of his flight engineer. He tried to recall how he had escaped from the burning bomber, but there was nothing other than the terror of his fall from the sky, the dark ground rising to meet him followed by the shattering sound of its impact and his standing here. Behind the turmoil of his mind's incomprehension, as strong as his animal instinct to survive, was the compulsion of his need to return to Laura. There was also the shadowy impression, no more than a thing of mist, that it had happened before, that there was in front of him an unending cycle of confused wandering he would be forced to suffer.

He shook it from him. "I'm coming, Laura!" he cried into the silence, turning away from the wreckage and starting to walk towards the unknown darkness.